"Suzanne Hudson in her raucous new novel, *The Fall of the Nixon Administration*, has conjured a girl-cousin for Ignatius Reily and rendered her obscene and outrageous. CeCe is a comedic queen, consorting with a covey of femme fatales, while confessing to one sane and saintly housekeeper, Lindia. Oh, and the man-in-the-middle? That too-good-looking Will Luckie, well, he loves on pet chickens named after Nixon's cabinet, and some there are who think they gotta go! LOL! This book is at once hilarious and salvific."

Sonny Brewer, author of *The Poet of Tolstoy Park*, the current *Syllables Go By: Six Hundred Eighty-Three Lines at a Time,* and the forthcoming *Other Ideas—A Brief Novel on the Illusion of Meaning and Purpose*

"Thank you, Suzanne … for understanding and voicing all these whackadoodle people and giving us a rollicking yarn. With a bite."

John M. Williams, prize-winning author of fiction, nonfiction, and the musical play (with Rheta Grimsley Johnson) *Hiram: Becoming Hank*.

The Fall of the Nixon Administration

Other works by Suzanne Hudson:

Novels
In a Temple of Trees
In the Dark of the Moon
Shoe Burnin' Season: A Womanifesto by R.P. Saffire

Short fiction
Opposable Thumbs
All the Way to Memphis

The Fall of the Nixon Administration

Suzanne Hudson

Cover art © J.D. Crowe

Interior art © Vicky Nix Cook

"I'm not a crook."

--Richard Milhous Nixon, November 17, 1973

"Have you no sense of decency, sir? At long last, have you left no sense of decency?"

--Army Counsel Joseph Welch, to Senator Joseph McCarthy, June 9, 1954

For Catherine Caffey Gardner
And
Eugene Hudson
In memory

Prologue

June 10, 1954

Dear Henry,

Grief is a thing made out of lead that sits on your heart and makes you feel a fierce and frail absence every single second. It makes you wore out from toting it around all the time, but it mocks the tiredness by keeping you awake in the night. It settles up top of your stomach so strong that even the notion of food gives you nausea, because the thought of eating brings up guilt like a dry heave. How can I eat when you aren't here to enjoy a meal with me? How can I sleep without feeling your presence, the weight of your spirit on the mattress, next to me? How will I go on with my walk through this life now that you won't be alongside?

Worst of all, grief takes over your soul and makes you curse God and Jesus and all the faith you been nourishing for a lifetime. And, Henry, I know that would kill you all over again, go off like a bomb, like that H-bomb those militaries exploded out in the Pacific, that bomb you promised would make Armageddon come upon us right quick. It would take you again just like that heart of yours did, as sudden as a murder, as cruel as a crucifixion.

It hasn't even been a month. I been going my moods from numb to down in the floor pain to fury to crazy, when the sounds coming out of my own mouth go back and forth, wailing howls into the laughter of a crazy person. I see little glimpses of you in things like a hummingbird or a butterfly or the way a branch bends in the wind. I feel the force of you when I hear the call of an owl or a whippoorwill. I love to think of these as signs of your spirit, as postcards from Heaven. They always make me smile, if only for that little minute.

I tried to watch the rest of those Army-McCarthy hearings on the TV set, because it was a thing we were doing right when it happened, your heart attack. Plus, you putting such an interest in the hearings and in politics and current events is one of the best things I love about you. But I couldn't care about that witch hunting ranter and raver, much as I know you wish that I would. Just yesterday, *yesterday*, the high court ruled for Brown in that case from Arkansas, and it was like a hot poker to my gut because of our married life's work for education. You didn't get to behold that victory, so it multiplied my pain even though I know you wish I would enjoy the ruling. I know exactly what *you* wish I would do, but I didn't know what to do *myself* until now. My Cousin Brenda told me to just sit myself at the kitchen table where you and me took our coffee every day of the last dozen years and write you a letter. And I think I might have done found me a way to make a path for myself, through the loss of the only man I could ever love and cleave unto. It's a way to honor you, to honor us, and to keep my mind away from the darkness. It's a way to talk over the current events and news stories the way we always have. It's a way to keep hold, to be together

Brenda wants to me go back to Florida with her, back where she stays, and she even got me a job as a domestic. I been dithering over it right smart, because it's a far fall from the work you and I did over the years, with the church and the NAACP. But Brenda's right when she says there's no other way, not here in east Mississippi, with no blood family, nothing but cotton to pick, and the klans in their hoods just beyond the next bend in any road.

The Calhouns is a rich white family, Henry, and Brenda heard about the job from the Calhouns' yard man, Cletus Robbins. Cletus is a good friend to Brenda, takes care of her own yard for free, and she reckons he's set on wooing her, but she ain't having it. Anyway, Cletus allowed that these Calhoun folks are even crazier than your regular crazy white folks—and that the woman of the house runs off maids right regular. Plus, there's a little girl that's run off her own share of the help, what with her spoiled ways and tantrums. Brenda says I have the temperament to put up with all them shenanigans, though, but that is a thing I can't know until I try it on for size. Everything is uncertain now, behind your passing, and I been trying to talk to Jesus about it all, while I wonder how He could take you like he did, out of the blue, weighting me, now, with our times past.

They say the grief gets better as the months and years go on, but that gives me fear, thinking that if the heaviness in my body and soul is ever truly lifted, it will leave me hollow, like a cored apple—skin, meat, and nothing. What was once a vessel for the Holy Spirit, for the hallelujah and the joy, would just be an absence. A profound absence. A nothing. Not even a space for the Lord to dwell in. And much, much more worrying is that I might not even care.

But I will try, Henry, because I know you want it that way. Just like I know you want me to keep my faith. Just like I know you want me to take pride in hard work, even if it *is* for crazy white folks. It's easy to know what you want for me, Henry, because you know me, through and through, like the best friend and spirit twin and beloved mate you are. Were. *Are.*

I love you always, Henry, even through the numbing weight of this sadness that is certain to become the essence of me.

Yours Forever,

Lindia

August 9, 1974

1
Cecelia

In light of my current situation with the law, I suppose it's a good thing I did not shoot Will Luckie in the back of the head when I had the chance. And anything else that happened today was strictly a crime of passion, as you will see with crystal clarity, once you have all the facts. The only thing that even came close to resembling premeditation was my momentary lapse, a fleeting intention to blow Will Luckie's brains out, and I obviously did not do that. Just imagine how I would have been looked down upon if I had ironically done this world a favor, become a murderess, and purged that freeloading miscreant from our midst. After all, if folks are going to get all tore up over the demise of a few pulletts, then there surely would have been a mighty hew and cry over Will's departure from this life—even though he is no better than any of the yard fowl I exploded with my DD's---that's the family abbreviation for "Dead Daddy's"---Remington Model 1100 12 gauge automatic. And I refuse to say otherwise, even if they put hot lights in my face, withhold food and water, interrogate me for days on end, or attempt to beat any endearing words out of me. Will Luckie has single-handedly brought down the Calhouns and I will never forgive him. He has burrowed his way into my decrepit old MiMi's—that's Mother, by the way--he has burrowed like a boll weevil into her heart. And he has augmented that crazy part of her brittle-arteried brain to the extent that she has allowed him to populate the back lawn with egg-laying fowl, one straw among the many he has lain across my symbolically bent and battered back.

Straw by straw, that's how he drove me to do what I finally did, and the straws got bigger and fatter and longer as the months wore on. The largest straw, until Mimi's birthday luncheon just yesterday, was this past Independence Day, when he awakened a heretofore dormant lust in the pit of my gut---not for him, mind you. God, that thought is the epitome of revulsion and leprous disgust. Rather, it was a realization that devoured me, forced me to reconsider the nature of my relationship with my husband. Which brings us to the very last straw—Lord, that one is still too unbearable to even contemplate, beyond anything I could have ever envisioned, the bile of Satan. And the cause? The root of all evil? Will Luckie, of course.

Now, I admit that Mother has always lived in a mental solar system that is a few light years from the rest of us, and she has done some outrageous things over the calendar years. But the only times she failed to step up to her role as hostess and grand dame extraordinaire were when she was hospitalized for some mental, physical, or psychosomatic malady—or when she was in one of her "moods." Then, about four months ago, out of the blue, or rather out of the blue of her consort Sir Luckie's eyes, she suddenly refused to participate, aside from intimate little gatherings with our very most dear inner circle, in the social doings of the community that is our home, where we are the primary community leaders. And it has everything to do with that hard-bodied, no-brained sex factory of hers.

First of all, you have to know that Will Luckie is a descendant of the mouth breathers who live out the Pipeline Road, where they pass their beer-ridden days hauling pulpwood, diddling one another's wives, and having an occasional trailer burning to collect enough insurance money to buy more beer and pulpwood trucks. He grew up in *East* Pollard, which is the socially polar opposite of just plain Pollard. And outside the city limits, even, of East Pollard. He is through and through Florida Panhandle white trash—pure cairn---and I have been subjected to his low-class ways ever since he entered our once picture-perfect lives.

For one example among the myriad, he keeps a pouch of Beechnut in the front pocket of his double knit shorts, which makes for a rather unnerving bulge that is, at best, in bad taste, and, at worst, just plain lewd. And he knows it. To be thoroughly honest, he rarely, if ever, wears underwear. I can safely say this because of the revealing nature of sand-colored double knit; it just does not afford the barrier as does, say, denim, or heavy cotton. And when the heightened level of sexual arousal that has settled upon my mother's abode is thrown into the mix---well, let me just say that I am quite certain---and I apologize for being so graphic---but it is more than obvious that the smarmy little gigolo is not even circumcised. Besides that, I have had occasion, which I don't know if I dare tell you about, to surmise that his steely member has a life and a will of its own.

Plus, he spits. He spits that stinking concoction between his index and third finger, pulling his lips taut and skeeting that mess out in high, arching streaks of darkening amber. His presence, ergo his spittle, here at MiMi's house, which has always been the showplace home in Pollard, has cheapened the entire property right along with the Calhoun name. At present there are tobacco juice stains dotted across Mother's patios, in puddles next to the ornamental urns, down the stone walkway that once wound so pleasantly among the pines, and all around the swimming pool, where he passes the days sunning and sipping fruity drinks of gin bearing paper umbrellas. Lord knows, at this precise second three of mother's Waterford Crystal tumblers hold a few ounces of that nauseating looking, tobacco-infused saliva; I have even regularly found one of Grandma Lucie's sterling silver goblets perched on the toilet tank, floating those little black flecks across a phlegm-glazed surface of bubbly brown spit. I have told Will Luckie repeatedly how repugnant it looks. He laughs every time. "Tell it to Bob Haldeman," he says, laughing.

He has been laughing ever since he moved into mother's antebellum-style home on the farthest edge of town, where it is framed by the horse pastures, piney woods, and, beyond the trees, our farm land. My DD loved the planting of the crops, the overseeing of the fields, where migrant shacks lined the rows of potatoes, and, in summer, corn. It was a hobby for him, one that the family did not share, so we've not had crops since he went to be with God. We do have a Mexican, Jesus, who comes each day to tend the horses, cut back the growth, and generally maintain the property, but I rarely see him. MiMi lets him plant crops over by the shack where he stays quite alone, beyond the woods, and he brings us corn and butterbeans and all kinds of seasonal vegetables and fruits that he grows, leaves them by the pasture fence without a word. Will, of course, laughs and calls him "the phantom yard man" and makes fun of the fact that I often refer to Jesus as "my Mexican." Which he is.

"Want to set on the porch, sip a mint julep, and watch your Mexican work?" he'll say before he doubles over laughing.

Will's sense of humor mystifies me, and his laugh is like nails on a chalk board to me.

He has been laughing all the way to the bank, I would guess. After their first date, I tried to warn her about what an obvious gold digger he was.

"Don't be silly, CeCe. If I choose to spend money it's because I am having a good time."

"But what about your position? What about people talking? You know they're already chattering their simple little pea heads off."

Mother giggled. "Isn't it fun?" she said.

I was stunned. Not a week earlier Mother had been planning the Yard of the Month luncheon for the Garden Club, but, once sucked into the orbit of Will Luckie, she abruptly turned it over to Bitsy

Burgess Swafford, the mayor's daughter and my social nemesis. "I shall have you declared incompetent," I said. "I swear to God I will."

"Oh, don't be such a sour-puss. If you could grab on to some fun for yourself, you might not be so set on preventing me from having my own good time."

This is the kind of thing she says to me all the time now, as if she does not believe I am perfectly satisfied with my community service, my club functions, and my husband. "CeCe, I cannot bear the thought of dying without seeing you living your life," she will say. "Run off to Nepal, for God's sake! Go to a goddamn nude beach in Europe. Have an affair in Lisbon and breakfast in Madrid. Do not fester and stagnate as I once did." Or: "Cecelia LaRue, you have no hunger for life. Where is the passion you should have inherited from me? Jumping Jesus, if you would just come alive you would begin to claw at this provincial little coffin of a town." Which is just a pure-D lie, you see. She was perfectly content with her life BWL (Before Will Luckie), when we worked together planning parties, judging at rose shows, and organizing fundraisers. True, she was always domineering and downright bossy, but it usually had to do with what color napkins or which set of good china to use at some function or other—never an attempt to encourage me to have an illicit love affair!

"She overshadows you," my DD used to say. "You've got to learn to talk faster, act meaner, and cuss louder than she does." Easy for him to say, with his bourbons and baseball. With his hunting camp whores and wooded weekends. That man had a switch in his brain that he could usually flip to the "off" position whenever mother was acting crazy. Or he would just pack her off to a rest home if she got too out of hand. But it simply is not in my nature to be passive-aggressive, like Daddy, or overbearing, like Mother. And I do my best not to curse—certainly would never take the Lord's name in vain. I feel that I, as a community leader, role model, and Christian, should project an image of calm competence and ladylike strength. It is merely the glorious burden that comes with my position and all. Heaven knows, I have even been called a saint by some who have observed my devotion to Mother.

Our maid Lindia only calls me a fool and makes comments she never used to make, as if Will Luckie's presence gives her permission to express strong opinions. I swear, that woman has worked for us for going on fifteen years with her mouth shut, verbally non-committal, even when her thoughts were *solicited*. But here lately she has gone so far as to tell me she thinks I should get a new husband, "one that don't swish," she says, leave Pollard, and let the chips fall, insisting that mother would be just fine. She even thinks Mother should be allowed to have her way with this-- character of hers. "She deserves it," Lindia will say. "She went long years not getting none from your running around daddy. Well, she's damn sure getting plenty now." You can see from that how the awareness of raw sex has seeped into the minds of everyone in MiMi's vicinity, from top to bottom, right down to the lowly servants. Our yard man, Cletus, has even taken to flirting with Lindia under everybody's noses, and Mother finds it delightful. Nobody seems to know their place anymore, let alone *care* that this—love-in seems to be affecting everyone.

"Don't be a prude, CeCe," she will say. "Live and let live. Love and let love. Make love, not war, as the young folks say."

But I cannot let it go. Not when the whole town is watching and talking and looking at me with the false pity of peons who just eat up a good, high-society scandal with the same sticky spoon. Not when Mother and Will Luckie go on trips to India and Morocco, come back loaded down with expensive trinkets, ivory, rich fur pillows, hand-woven rugs—my God, her home decor has become a bohemian ode to the Kama Sutra. And her bedroom—oh, my word, it only took about a month of courtship for him to replace her canopied queen sized bed with a king sized waterbed. Ran the hose pipe up to her second story bedroom window, which faces the county highway, mind you, so that passersby could gawk at the rubbery, redecorative foreplay going on at Miss Maureen's mini-mansion.

"That pornographic puddle is going to come crashing down through the living room," I warned. "This old house was not meant for a hippie-fied waterbed."

"Don't be a Silly Billy, CeCe. This old house was built solid," Mother retorted. "And Will checked the beams. He knows construction."

Apparently he also knows home décor, as he further spruced up Mother's boudoir with incense burners, lava lamps, black lights and the attendant posters, plus an eight-track stereo and turntable with ginormous speakers in every corner of the room. He dragged in box upon crate of LP albums and tapes, much of which is that drug-addled psychedelic nonsense, along with Motown R&B with its thumping bass and sex-siren saxophones, good for nothing but coital accompaniment. Next thing, I am sure, will be a whorehouse mirror on the ceiling.

And of course you know who is paying for these trips, trinkets, and decorative flairs. Yours truly. I am not only paying with my birth-right, I am paying with my once impeccable reputation. My mother, pillar of the church and society matriarch, has traded my dignified DD for a Hugh Hefner bosom devotee. He even subscribes to the infernal magazine, and I blush every single time I see Mr. Gorman, our mail carrier. He knows exactly what's in the package and it might as well be stamped with that ridiculous bunny-eared, cuff-linked, wasp-waisted, fluffy-tailed logo. And that's only the iceberg's tip. Just listen to a few of the other things that piece of filth has done to cause an avalanche of shame to come cascading down on the Calhoun family:

First of all, he moved in with her after just one dinner date to Rosie O'Grady's in Pensacola. Swept her right off her chubby little size five feet (mine are size nine; she refers to them as "Jesus-Christ-walk-on-water skis"). I believe the off-color line he wooed her with was, "Baby, you sure do make my rat crawl," or something equally disturbing. At least, that's how she tells it, delighting at the gag reflex-inducing reaction she gets from me and any other listener of character. No marriage has ever been discussed (as if I could ever allow that!)—just a craven union of depraved lust and musked-up sin, which in and of itself is all the town ever needed to justify looking down on me.

Second of all, he buys lubricating jelly and female hygiene spray at Mr. Cleo Williams' pharmacy, and I don't have to tell you the lurid tales that swarm around Billy's Barber Shop and Mr. DeFrancisco's House of Hair in the wake of that. Don't even ask me about the hand-held muscle massager.

Thirdly, I think I already mentioned he laughs at me and runs me down to both my face and my back. He calls me a "social-climbing, flippy-tailed prissite," as if I have to do any climbing, being as I am—or was—at the top of the social heap. It is just that I care what certain people think. I care, and he ridicules my caring nature, knowing how it wounds me. He says I have a "crazy twitch-eye," which, yes, my left eyeball *does* jump around sometimes, but that is a testament to my intense and passionate nature. I simply believe in doing the right thing, plus, I am near about always right, although Will Luckie mocks that quality in me. "Take cover, everybody," he drawls, "it's the charge of the Right Brigade." He says other things to me—crude things, obviously intended to provoke, but I usually mange to hold in, just as I have always tried to do with Mother. "You need to loosen up, girl," he will say. "You got the biggest bug up your butt I ever seen. Must be one of them dung beetles. You need a dose of Uncle Luckie's Root Treatment." Or he leans in close and flirtatious and whispers, "So who's cutting your stove wood? Cause I know your fruity old man ain't got the ax for it."

Winston has even witnessed him toying with me, insulting me, yet my own husband refuses to take up for me. All he will do is bring me samples of Valium to settle my nerves and knockout pills to put me to sleep at night, then turn around and give Will Luckie all the free medical attention he needs, and then some. Knowing that "Uncle Luckie" doesn't think Winston has any testosterone, all the time asking why Winston and me don't have any babies after six years of marriage. Then, when I try to tell him something like I guess Jesus isn't ready, he says, right in front of Winston, "More like Winston ain't ready. And Winnie won't be ready unless you get yourself a dildo. Maybe that would turn him on." Then he laughs while Winston blushes. Of course. "Bet I could take care of Winnie's retreads if he made a little pit stop on my turn." The gall. My mother's boyfriend flirting with my husband! "Hey, Doc," he says. "My dick stays harder than Chinese arithmetic. I need to come in and get it de-pressurized, alright? Just drain off a little fluid."

I swear I am not exaggerating. He continues his slimy talk and his questioning of Winston's virility and man-nature just because he knows crude behavior is one of my Achilles' heels and my husband's effete demeanor is the other. I already told you Winston is a touch feminine, but that is just the way of some folks with superior breeding. Plus, I always used to say that there's more to a successful marriage than wallowing around in bed linens. But don't try telling that to MiMi or Will Luckie. Their sordid little soiree goes on in front of all of Pollard. Here's what I mean:

In recent years Mother has taken to routinely calling the police department, fire department, or ambulance company when she needs little errands done. Once, at the conclusion of one of her extended hospitalization-slash-vacations, she even phoned up Cheatham Jackson at the colored funeral parlor to drive her the four blocks home, just because the medical clinic's sole ambulance was out on a call and she simply *had* to get home right that very minute to set up for *mah jongg*. Yet this town's three bored cops---plus it's merry band of assorted paramedics and firemen---seem to get a kick out of it, driving up to the big house, sirens blaring and lights ablaze, to see what the eccentric socialite wants this time. This behavior never used to bother me too much BWL, as it was quite harmless then; Lord knows, I used to sometimes be there to enjoy the company, when Mother would wave the back of her hand at Grady Fortner, a big fat semi-winded paramedic. "No, darling," she would chirp from her multi-pillowed perch beneath the yellow dotted Swiss canopy. "I'm just fine. Really. All I need you to do is run to the kitchen and pour a little Tab over ice."

And he would.

"Run to the liquor store for me, sweetie pie, and pick me up a fifth of Canadian. I'm all out and I'm parched as a goddamn nun's drawers."

After a two a.m. call the honeyed command might go something like, "Be a sugar-doll, won't you, and run downstairs to the garage. I woke up with this feeling of dread that I forgot to extinguish the lights on my automobile. Oh—and if it's necessary, be my precious and check the battery. It might need you to put some new juice in it with those cable thingys."

But after the arrival of Will Luckie the visitors became more like salivating voyeurs at a peep show in a Bourbon Street sex salon. Lord, they can't get to Mother's fast enough to gather fodder for the next tale they will share at the barber shop, and she never lets them down. Just a few weeks ago, when Mother's hairdresser accidentally fried the hair he was supposed to be touching up with henna highlights, it turned into yet another show for the P.C.P.D.

When I laid eyes on Mother, all done up to perfection except for the frizzled tufts of hair zigging and zagging from her scalp, I briefly hoped it would be the death knell for Will Luckie, scare him off, maybe. After all, she looked like Bozo the Clown with a singed afro. And mother's looks, which I did not inherit, by the way (I only inherited my place in the pecking order of Pollard), are known to be strikingly beautiful, even at her age and poundage. She has flawless skin, too smooth for wrinkles to wreak havoc, and the greenest eyes this side of Vivien Leigh. I, of course, had acne and kept several Pensacola dermatologists in business throughout high school, and I have these washed-out brown eyes. Where Mother is petite, albeit a hair chubby by now, I am a ski-footed amazon, stout, with a thick waist and saddle-bag hips. But I have nice hair, a dazzling smile, and a moral character, which is really all that counts. Not to mention that I have Jesus on my side.

Anyway, the evening of Mimi's hair frying incident, I sat with her in the study, in the dark, waiting for her Man, struck by the strobe of firelight hitting her face, playing upon the burned out barbs of frazzed hair. She held a cigarette in her left hand, a scotch rocks in her right, smoking and sipping in the slow silence. She wore a red and purple paisley djellaba with black slippers decorated with sparkles, and swung a crossed leg nervously at the night. Her pearl handled Derringer lay in her lap.

When the doorknob rattled to his touch, Mother simply sat, smoked, sipped, inhaled. When the slat of light from the porch fell across the room and caught a glint of sparkly slipper, she exhaled.

He flipped on the study light, jumped, and uttered, "Sheee-it."

Mother drew on her Virginia Slim, blew a cool plume of smoke. "Will, darling." Pause. "This is the new me." Pause. "Like it?" Such comic timing would be a thing of beauty if not for the circumstances.

That man regrouped quicker than any man I have ever encountered. "Mmmm, baby," he said, all the while unsnapping that hideous pink cowboy shirt with the embroidered yellow lassoes he is so fond of. "That is hot. You kind of look like a soul sister. Like Foxy Brown."

"Good," Mother said. "Because if you didn't like it I was reconciled to the idea of putting a bullet into my feeble brain." She picked up the pistol with a dainty little flourish. "Here, sexy. Do something with this instrument of death."

He took the gun, steady slurping at her neck while my lunch wanted to be upchucked. Of course, I might as well have been invisible, and he kept on lapping at her like a horny mutt, talking about how he always wanted a taste of dark meat.

"Ooooh, darling," MiMi squealed. "You know that makes me want to give in to wild abandon. It's absolutely criminal!"

He grunted. He still had not acknowledged me, you will note, intent as he was upon whipping my elderly mother into a hedonistic frenzy. Well, she went into a frenzy all right, and she shared it with the town of Pollard. While that skanky man licked her neck like it was the last lollipop on the planet, she called the police. As was the routine, an officer—this night it was Paul Baggett—let himself in with the spare key Mother had given the department to keep in their one and only squad car. Baggett just stood there, smirking; I was overcome by a paralysis of shame.

Mother stood and swept an accusing arm at Will Luckie, who was mixing himself a fruity gin drink at the bar. "Officer," she panted, "arrest this man!"

Will laughed. I felt denuded.

"Arrest this man on the grounds that he's too goddamned sexy!"

Paul Baggett, too, began to chuckle, licking his chops, I am certain, at the prospect of playing barbershop troubadour the next day.

"Oh, you think I am funning with you?" Ice cubes clinked reiteration in mother's favorite gold-rimmed scotch glass. "Well, if you don't arrest this man immediately, I am going to have to tear off my clothes and make love to him with the ardent fervor of a sixteen year-old. And God help your conscience if I have a stroke from it."

Paul Baggett ended up having a beer with them. In uniform. It seems all decorum and rule-following goes right out the window with that horny pair of humpsters. I went home to Winston.

The thing that absolutely stuns me is that people—even well-bred ones—seem to like him, up to a point, contrary to all personal moral codes, as they surely must object to his gene pool and his flimflamming of my mother. Maybe it is because he drags out that cheap guitar and sings country songs and folk songs and Old English ballads for goodness sake. The shameless blasphemer even sings hymns with a disturbingly rich voice basted in irony. Then there are those "humorous anecdotes" that always eventually descend into the blue depths of hard core porn. Maybe it is that not-so-subtle, satyr-like sexuality that seems to intrigue both genders in spite of themselves. Maybe it is the Newman-blue eyes, the semi-dimply smile set in high cheekbones above a square jaw, or the George Hamilton lacquered-in-a-tan physique of one who has spent the past ever-how-many years in the Marine Corps. No matter. *I* consider him an idiot savant of a Svengali who tapped into Mother's sense of herself as a poet who should have lived the life of an artistic expatriate rather than "atrophying" here in Pollard. She never did appreciate her status.

Status. The state of us. There is the crux of it, as far as I am concerned. Mother has called me shallow, but preservation of superior blood lines and civic responsibility should never, in my opinion, be taken for granted. You cannot fully appreciate this whole fiasco unless you understand that the Calhouns are the single most prominent of the three most prominent families in Pollard, which is prominent in itself as the original county seat, stolen away to Cantonment during the Great Depression. "We occupy the penultimate position of prominence," Mother used to like to say, given her penchant for alliteration. And because of this family duty, I am always willing to take on causes and fundraisers and charity work. I was even chosen Citizen of the Year in '71—the youngest *ever* Citizen of the Year in Pollard's history—behind my successful raising of funds for the addition of a wing onto our tiny town's teeny-tiny library. And that resulted in my joining Mayor Burgess as grand marshal of the annual homecoming parade. How many people can say they were honored in a parade? Although I should make it abundantly clear that my motives are pure, that I do not seek out public recognition, not at all. It is because of a complete sense of civic duty that I am president of the Ladies' Club, parliamentarian of the DAR, brownie scout troop leader at the Methodist Church, Sunday School class coordinator at the Baptist Church, and I would have beat out Bitsy Burgess Swafford, the mayor's evil daughter, as president of the Daughters of the Confederacy, just last month, if not for the shame of Will Luckie. As it is, I feel that my genetic destiny as a community leader has slipped; if I had chosen to do nothing it could have taken years to rebuild the family name. So I did something about it, albeit apparently too much to ever hope to repair the Calhoun name now. And mother? Mother simply fails to care one whit about the shambled legacy she has foisted upon me.

You see, my DD's DD was a circuit judge who survived the Crash and three bouts of cancer before he died of age, and naturally he knew everybody and their legal business. My DD was a banker with the foresight to buy all the timber land and mineral rights he could get his hands on, so naturally he knew everybody's financial business. He was a philanderer and died of gallstones, or, rather, a cascade of complications thereof. My husband, Winston Dozier (though try as I might, I can only contextualize myself as a Calhoun) is a physician—the only one in town besides Dr. Dave, who is ancient—and Winston knows everybody's personal business, so it does not matter that he is a tad prissy for a man. And my mother is from an extremely well regarded political family in Birmingham, Alabama. So she could know everybody's political business if she had the inclination. Did you know that right this second her brother is some Big Ike in the Nixon administration? Hell, she and Daddy went to the first inauguration—and the main ball, not any of the little rinky-dink ones. And she acts like it is no big deal that the Nixon administration is falling into a mangled heap, running around like a bunch of decapitated biddies.

And all because of a bumbling band of burgling stooges playing political spy games. Oh, I didn't take it seriously at all, not at first. But then came the press with their not-so-hidden agenda, to take down a decent, red-blooded American president, to frame him, of course. I do admit that when those hearings were televised last year, I was given pause—serious pause—but I didn't allow myself to give up on him. I voted for the man, after all, and loyalty is another of my more admirable traits. Not to mention my being probably the most patriotic female in this town.

"You can't let your Republican bias excuse a law-breaking megalomaniac who defies the sanctity of the constitution of the United States of America," is what my mother says. "In addition, I have found that blind patriotism is a mighty masquerade for a traitorous nature. One might even go the extreme and enable a despot."

Yes, those are direct quotes from my traitor of a mother, who, aside from being personally powerful on most fronts, is likely the wealthiest woman in three counties, thanks to her DD and my DD. But what does my traitor of a mother do, after not even two years of mourning my daddy? She takes herself a boyfriend twenty-four years her junior—making him four years younger than *me*—and sets all the town's tongues to wagging about my own family's familial business. Are you beginning to fathom why Will Luckie might be so intrigued with my withering up old mama? And why I have so much to lose?

That rat turncoat John Dean claimed he warned one R.M. Nixon that there was a "cancer growing on the presidency." And the lying politicians on the Sunday news shows are saying that Dean will be remembered as one of the good ones, a patriot, who tried to sound the call, take a Paul Revere-style gallop through the hallowed halls of the house on Pennsylvania Avenue. That's the kind of glowing praise a rat gets from the three TV networks these days.

So be it. To borrow from the rat, I say there is a cancer upon this family in the form of a homunculus with a rat-crawling member down below that poses as his brain. And even as I shout my most heartfelt, honest, and righteous warnings, I am met with denial, disbelief, and even ridicule. But I know, deep in my Christian soul, that ultimately I shall be vindicated as the teller of truth, the fighter for right, and the savior of the Calhoun name, as I excise this wretched, classless cancer from the body of my blue bloodlines.

Amen.

2
Mimi

I have often wondered over the years if Cecelia LaRue Calhoun were not fathered by some stranger who drugged me unconscious then had his way with my pliant flesh—flesh that momentarily encased a rare, ripened ovary, as CeCe was the product of my only pregnancy. This stranger could have been anyone--a rapaciously randy Fuller Brush salesman, for example, or an errant milkman who harbored milky lust among the clattering bottles. Perhaps a love struck elevator man had me between floors or carried me down to the underground world abandoned by the Phantom of the Opera. Maybe it was the Maytag repairman, who hypnotized me with the rhythm of the wash cycle before he gave me a spin, spilling his seed into my delicates. He could have been any of the men who have fringed my life with their necessary presence, men with whom I would never have willingly carried on, but who might have harbored some kind of furtive desire for me. I don't mean to sound conceited, but it is the only way I can explain Cece's being born of my body, in the same bed where my own mother birthed me. We bear no physical resemblance to one another, neither height, breadth nor hue, and I feel like a munchkin standing beside her. Furthermore, she does not physically resemble my departed husband,

Wickham, certainly does not have his quiet recklessness. And, although Wickham was a trifle overly concerned with the impression we made as a family, CeCe's prudish temperament goes to another level and is an utter mystery, which is why I often speculate upon her parentage, in a hypothetical way. The result of our tenure together has become a cacophonous back and forth between two who have chosen, with a deafening resonance, completely different paths in life and are determined to grab the other by the arm and drag her, kicking and screaming, down that chosen path. It is beyond absurd. Oh, I love her, of course. She is my child, after all—mine and some mystery man's. But it should be apparent to any fool that we are poised on opposite ends of the artistic and emotional spectrum, and ne'er the twain shall meet, I suppose.

I am a poet. CeCe is a priss-pot. The Poet and the Priss-Pot. It sounds like the title of something, and I do appreciate the alliterative nature of our roles in this life, the complementary angles we share, biologically, but God help us if we try to understand one another. That child is living the life I have finally, with an uncharacteristic clarity of mind, decided to wrest free of. I am speaking, of course, of the muted gray, small town decadence of rural redundance, banal chitchat, and social ass kissing. The lame land of the lumpen proletariat. After decades of carrying an unconventional core of creative ecstasy in my bosom, muzzled and harnessed by the life I chose at the weakest of moments, I am finally freeing my pent up spirit to taste all the pleasures of the flesh in my waning years. And it was Will Luckie who tapped into that gusher of a wellspring.

You see, just as my daughter bears no resemblance to me, Will bears no resemblance whatsoever to my late husband, Wickham Calhoun, who passed away in June of '72, on the heels of the Watergate burglary. Not that the break-in at any way caused my husband's demise, although I do see a certain symbolism at work, looking back on it. I mean, those little gall stones that eventually were his undoing masqueraded for the longest time as gas, ulcers, and general malaise, so there you are. His gall bladder was burglarized, I like to think, by those galling stones that caused his liver and pancreas to go into full revolt against his health.

Anyway, Wickham was wealthy, refined, disloyal, avaricious, subtly controlling. He cyclically tolerated and tormented me, in his own quiet way, growing more and more ashamed of my antics over the years. Will, on the other hand, delights in my flashes of insanity, is pure and kind-hearted, with an accepting devotion—not to be confused with sexual fidelity—and a rare generosity born of poverty. He is an innocent in so many ways. He is lustful, yes. He is bawdy. He is even quite raw, knows no inhibition. He is the essence of *id*. He is like unto a mythological wood creature who unabashedly feeds his desires. But vulnerable in so very many secret ways. A true diamond in the rough.

I do not call what Will and I have love. Certainly not romantic love, true love, the idealized love of the poets and of youth. I am not some silly old pre-menopausal woman grasping at someone to marry, make me whole, give my life meaning, be my knight with the armor and all. That would be truly naïve and pathetic. All I am doing is eating the proverbial peach, living in the moment, exercising a lust for life, and joining in the sexual revolution, which was tailor made for me, what with my repressed bohemian spirit and all. Not to mention the big o.

I had always known I had incomplete physical love with Wickham. Yes, it was tolerable with him in bed, in the beginning, but it was never anywhere near fulfilling. If I had not been such a wanton woman before our marriage, perhaps I would have been content with the kind of one-two-three loving my husband gave me, but, unfortunately, I knew better. I knew because, unbeknownst to Wickham, I was not a virgin when we married, and my only other experience with love was so complete that I suppose no one who followed would have passed muster.

When I was a girl, the soldiers were going off to Europe to chase the Nazis back into the maw of Hades, and short-lived love affairs were the affairs *du jour*. So it was that, in Memphis Tennessee, over a period of nine days in August of 1942, I had my own affair *du jour*, which became the *piece de resistance*. I met a pilot whose name I cannot utter without crying, a handsome young idealist minted in California-golden hair and skin, who made love to me at the Peabody Hotel for the entire nine days before he was to report down to Pensacola to get his orders. It was nothing short of magical, my handsome pilot, the Scott to my Zelda. His lips traveled the entire terrain of my flesh and the muscles deep inside me swallowed themselves in shudders of profound ecstasy. I am not ashamed to say that I cried out, breathless shrieks of delicious satisfaction. It was in the throes of this fevered, pink, and dampened desire that I wrote poems to our love, to divine desire, and to his duty. Over the following months, letters dense with passion flew back and forth across the Atlantic between us. And, later still, more poems to his death over France, lines that pulled me down into the heart of darkness and loss of will. I was so tightly bound up in that true, true love that I even contemplated suicide, thinking to join him on the other side. Of course I lacked the nerve, so, true to the coward I was, I quickly married Wickham, he who offered emotional insulation and financial security, he who pleased my mother and father's ambition for me. It was the one thing that did me in as an artist, casting myself in a role that only caused frustration and fits of nervous exhaustion over the years.

I tried, and valiantly I believe, to be the wife I was expected to be. I joined his Methodist church, organized rummage sales and cakewalks for dried up little old ladies. I charmed my husband's cronies and the wives of the cronies, walking a delicate line between flirtation and camaraderie. I did volunteer work, offering myself up as a Pink Lady at the hospital, cheerfully bestowing *The Reader's Digest* and *The Pensacola News Journal* upon my bedridden charges, thinking it ironic that I, a Scarlet

Woman, should presume to pose as a Pink Lady. I gradually joined the clubs, commiserated with other ladies about the tragedy of fallen cakes, dry rump roasts, and poor help. Pre-Lindia, I went through the requisite number of maids, and then some, directing them to serve from the left, directing them to commence cutting the crusts off bread for dainty little cream cheese sandwiches, directing them to make certain the celery is well strung, directing them to polish my DM's extensive collection of silver for teas and such—events that were written up every week in *The Pollard Gazette*.

But, alas, I was always a few beats out of step. In the Piggly Wiggly, I was always pushing my cart against traffic, a disoriented goldfish swimming upstream against the minnows. I did not care if my whites weren't white, if my husband had ring around the collar, if my floors did not shine and sparkle and mirror my reflection. I did not want to be rescued by the Jolly Green Giant or Mr. Clean. Still, I blundered my way through the grocery shopping and compared notes about purchased products with the other hausfraus at the next Bridge Club meeting. And I would always, invariably, do something that Wickham found distasteful, whether it was taking CeCe skinny dipping in the pool with me, or dancing a whimsical, seductive tango with Mayor Burgess, or siding with those two or three Pollard souls who favored desegregation, and a stifled resentment grew inside me. How dare he find me, the cosmopolitan free spirit who could be the toast of New York or Paris, distasteful?

I tried to be a good mother to Cecelia, but I was miscast in that role as well. I wanted to be dancing barefoot on the beach at Rio de Janeiro or reading my poems in some smoky coffeehouse in Greenwich Village. I wanted to retrace Hemingway's footfalls and scrawl heady lines at some Parisian *café*, relive my affair *du jour*. Instead, I was schlepping baby food, sterilizing glass bottles, and rinsing green shit out of diapers dipped downward into the toilet, before pitching them into pails of ammonia. I was locked into a desperate mind set, a bid to prove my fitness as a mother, heed all the Dr. Spock-isms, keep my little doll dressed in bows and embroidery to show off at the park at the biweekly gathering of breeders. And my doll, my little play pretty, grew into an individual, a person, a real, human child who frightened me with her dependence upon me, who looked up at me at times like a stranger. I knew I was no glowing and serene Madonna, that I would not do well this job of motherhood, and, sure enough, CeCe seemed to be always sizing me up, measuring me against the other mothers in the neighborhood, quizzing me, trying to trip me up.

"Who invented the hot dog?" she asked when she was five.

"Phineas T. Hot Dog," I replied matter-of-factly. And she believed me.

"Who invented the hamburger?"

"Baron Strom von Burgermeister of Hamburg, Germany."

"What is that rubber bag for?" she asked at six, of my douche regalia.

"It's a strawberry washer," I said. "You just fill it with water and spray down the fruit." Which, I suppose, is true in its way.

"What does daddy do at the bank?"

"Oh, he has such fun! He sits on a huge pile of Oriental pillows inside a giant, elegant safe and counts his money."

"Where does the bank get the money?"

"Well, darling, they steal it. But only a little at a time, you see, so no one will notice. For example, they stole ninety-seven cents from me last month, which doesn't seem like much, I know. But when you multiply that by the hundreds and hundreds of customers, well, there you are."

"Why do we go trick or treating on Halloween?"

"Don't tell a soul, but it's a dark chocolate conspiracy by Mr. Brach and Mr. Hershey to make money by bribing little devils not to roll our yards with Scott Tissue or light paper bags of dog feces afire on our front porches."

"Why don't you put your hair in pink rollers and watch *The Secret Storm* like Janet's mother?"

"Because, Sugar, hair rolling is for hairdressers and my life in and of itself is a magnificent soap opera that I am living out just to see what will happen next."

"But why aren't you like the other mothers?"

Here I would give her one small dose of truth. "Because, Precious, the war did things to me."

The poor child. Sometimes I think it is no wonder she is so rigid, with a maniac like me for a mother. She was seventeen years old when I finally got a diagnosis and became a legitimate looney, a card-carrying manic-depressive, but she would fuss like a blue jay if I mentioned it. Because of the humiliation, she said. The shame. I found it quasi-amusing, though. A bit of a status symbol, a conversation piece. And it certainly explained a lot. It explained why the thoughts bounced around in my head at times like the popcorn in that popping machine down at the Ritz Theater, and my mouth manufactured stories and lies as fast as my fevered brain could think them up. It explained why I sometimes stayed up for days and nights with stacks of magazines, cutting out Betsy McCall paper dolls and their wardrobes for the ladies at the nursing home or writing silly lyrics to standard tunes or refusing to talk in anything besides heroic couplets, thinking in iambic pentameter. It explained the hyperkinetic frenzy of vivacity I felt when I regaled my friends with stories about the characters I have met around the world, or spoke French just because I longed to hear it again. "*Bon jour*," I would say to CeCe. "*Comment allez-vous aujourd'hui?*" Then I would burst into "*Le Marseilles*" while she rolled her eyes at her father.

Then, too, it explained the days of cloistered darkness in my room, the dimness weeping along with me like a thick, sticky molasses, a wall of steel mesh topped by barbed wire surrounding me, an impenetrable barrier for everyone who existed on the outside of that room. It was after one of these episodes that I made the mistake of mentioning suicide, in an offhand way that Wickham seized upon to temporarily banish me, I am certain, from our home. A piece of advice: if you ever seriously intend to kill yourself, which I did not, say nothing. Once you bring that sordid little word out into the light of day, well, folks are on you like white on rice, as the country folk say.

I had been to many a "restful retreat," where I was given facials and massages and earnest psychiatrists, but on this occasion I was thrown into the snake pit, the state hospital in Chattahootchie. It was as if Wickham were trying to teach me a lesson, get me to behave myself, as if I could actually control the way my mind moved.

"You don't understand. I don't belong here," I said to the intake nurse. "I am here under false pretenses."

She gave me a little nod and a smirky smile, as though she had heard it all before.

"I do not want you people plundering through my brain," I told a very young, very green, very self-admiring psychiatrist, puffed up like a pouter pigeon with his *carte blanche* to get inside my head.

"How long have you had the belief that people are plundering through your brain?" he asked.

"You obviously are not a reader of poetry or fiction. If you were, you would recognize hyperbole rather than try to make me out to be suffering from paranoid delusions. I wonder how many others you have misdiagnosed because of your lack of a liberal arts education." I had hoped that my foray into hell would at least be an opportunity to engage in intelligent conversation with a bright young man, but even that was not to be. This pimply-faced boy was a dullard, and wired for sound besides. He wore some kind of device that kept chirping away like a manic Jiminy Cricket---phone messages from Insanity Central Control or some such phone bank that keeps tabs on the world's madness. There must have been a plethora of mental emergencies that night, for he chirped incessantly. Perhaps the moon was full. At any rate, we could not even make bland conversation for the clicking of his electronic system

"Jiminy, you are not real," I said to him. "You are a robot and will most likely blow a fuse any minute now."

His little computer brain punched in "nod and smile patiently" before his next attempt at navigating the winding labyrinth of my brain. "So you find me to be like a robot."

It was an attempt which I cut short. "You are wasting my time and your batteries. I prefer a good book to this robotic conversation, so kindly disappear." Which he did.

The nurse tried to coax me into the day room the next morning for group therapy, which consisted of sitting in a circle with a bunch of women in various stages of drug-induced drooling, ranting if necessary, then listening to someone playing the piano very badly, with everyone singing off key.

"No thank you," I told her after only one session. "Count Basie is the only piano player I've ever really enjoyed. Besides, I do not care to spend time with that cornucopia of vegetables you have circled up in there, covered wagon style, soaking in a sea of saliva."

I was heavily sedated and put on a ward with bars on the windows—the snake pit—full of women who were literally stark, raving mad. They rambled and screamed and moaned in the night. Some peed on the floor. One tried to fondle my breasts. At one point I wondered how many women were here because they were miscast in roles of wife/mother/lover when they should have been writer/Nobel prize winner/architect, but the medication did not allow me to concentrate very well, wrapping a little cat-footed fog about me like my mother's mink stole. When the fog cleared in a week or so, I got my diagnosis, which, to my utter amazement, seemed to be correct, and went home with some little pink "happiness" pills.

"How could you humiliate us like that?" CeCe said of my stay at the nut house.

"Well, goddamn, CeCe. It's not as if I went roaming the streets naked like Debra Bracken did that time. All I did was mention a word in passing that your daddy did not approve of. A word that never signified anything I would do. Ever."

"You blame him for everything you do that embarrasses us," she whined.

I simply proceeded to take one of my "happiness" pills, living by the Grace of God and Parke-Davis and Company.

"No one else's mother has to take pills just so they can have a personality," CeCe whined. "And then you have to go bragging about it like it's something to be proud of."

"Oh, CeCe, it's quite chic to have some sort of mild mental disorder these days. And to have one's own head shrinker is all the rage."

"My God, Mother, this isn't New York. I swear, nothing you do is appropriate for Pollard."

Thus it was that I constantly disappointed my daughter with my mental illness and my inept interpretation of motherhood, a motherhood which only added to the discombobulation of my womanhood, and, over time, my physical desire. I reached a point when I was glad for Wickham to go to the woods with his prostitutes and floozies, just so I would not have to service him as his "lady of the evenings at home." My sex drive simply vanished. Gone with the Wind. Poof. Until I happened upon Will Luckie.

I had a sexual encounter with Will Luckie on the very day we met, two strangers who dared to eat a peach together. Afterward, lying there in the mangled sheets, I remember thinking that my bridge club, along with the Ladies' Circle and others, would undoubtedly be appalled when they learned of my shift in life-living, but I was standing right at Robert Frost's veritable fork in the road. It was a pivotal moment and I knew at once that it would take me back to myself, the girl who lived, breathed, and loved at the Peabody Hotel. The genuine me was an artist, after all, a marginal thinker looking for a country. The decades of wheel-spinning in this little panhandle town had come close to doing me in until Will Luckie kissed me out of that Cinderella slumber. I literally came to. I was the girl who had studied painting and poetry writing at Judson College, who had traveled extensively in Europe and the Orient throughout my growing up. My world was the one outside the realm of Pollard, Florida. I had attended private schools in Pensacola, was reared in the Catholic Church, worlds away from the basic Baptist-Methodist-Pentecostal mentality of Pollard, and my deep affection for the Pope was thoroughly ingrained and sincere in spite of my belief that religion was, as a noted communist once opined, "the opiate of the people." Pius XII, John XXIII, and Paul VI—these are the patriarchs of my lifetime, the greatest hits on my spiritual Billboard. Naturally, I felt like a traitor to the Holy See all the while I became Methodized during my engagement to my husband, as his family had been influential members for eons. I even tried to work like a little Trojan in the Methodist Church throughout our marriage, just as my mother would have done if dropped into that circumstance, Christian martyr and *grand dame* that she was. But I never could live up to my mother, as I was not cut out for martyrdom. And my unlikely pairing with Will Luckie brought everything into such perspective that it chills me to think that none of it would have happened if not for those two perfectly hideous bumper stickers.

You see, on the day I met Will, I arose at 7:00 a.m., as usual. Lindia came in at 7:30 to start breakfast and to complain, yet again, that the screen door was just about off its hinges and was bound to fall off soon and knock her half silly. As usual, I let her histrionics roll off my back and by

7:35 I was, as usual, having my cup of Maxwell House and my daily devotional, my routine clutching at the zeitgeist of Pollard, out on the patio, absolutely swathed in that luscious scent of sweet olive and the dew of dawn in the garden, my dear little poodle dogs, Rosencrantz and Guildenstern, at my feet. Psalms! Such poetry! Such a lush preponderance of beauty in which to bathe the spirit.

I next tended my prize roses, courtesy of Cletus (my yard man). After a Lindia-made plate of grits, eggs, sausage, and sliced tomatoes, I adjourned to my upstairs dressing table to put on my face. The Psalms kept my spirit impeccably serene right up until the very instant I laid my eyes on those dreadful, hideously tasteless bumper stickers on my way to the Piggly Wiggly.

Before I go any further, I must make it abundantly clear that I, who in my youth considered no conversation taboo, had come to find certain topics truly offensive. I was just brought up that way and my raising kicked in just a bit after I surrendered to Wickham in marriage, often helped along in my uncharacteristic conformity by medication. One's income, I thought, was not a topic fit for polite conversation, as it is extremely personal in nature. One should not make a show, I believed, unless one is tragically *nouveau*, of one's wealth, nor should one reveal what lever one has pulled in the voting booth or proclaim one's party affiliation on the chrome of one's automobile. And one certainly should never, ever, in this world, publicly advertise one's religious faith in any way, shape, or form.   One should simply go, without fail, to Sunday school and church (always stylishly yet tastefully clothed), tithe the appropriate percentage of one's income, and belong to the socially correct Ladies' Circle. And to plaster one's vehicle with words praising the Lord is still, to this day, beyond the peripheral limits taste allows.

I know it all sounds so stereotypically prudish, but I assure you that at my core I was most assuredly not a prude. I read D.H. Lawrence. I devoured *The Second Sex* and Masters and Johnson and *The Feminine Mystique*. I hungered for interesting conversation all the while I tried to follow my mother's admonitions and rules. Ultimately and tragically, as happens to so many southern women, I had *become*, in one of my many incarnations, my martyred mother. And when my martyred mother, via yours truly, saw the bumper stickers on the truck in front of me she/I was beyond appalled, having refined a false air of indignation to a high art form. Fortunately, while I still believe that those poor, pathetic, bicycle-riding Jehovah's Witnesses and Mormons and other such creatures who roam the streets witnessing to their faith reach boundless heights of rude behavior, I have become much less judgmental since my delicious tryst with Will began. These days no topic seems to be out of bounds and all is right with the world.

I was on my way, as I said, to the Piggly Wiggly for sweet milk and Puss 'n Boots cat food for Mr. Monsieur, my devoted tabby, when I saw the words in front of me, adhered to the bumper of one of those abominable eyesores of a red Ford pickup, all covered in lumber, a ladder, and heaven knows what all else. I noticed it at an interminably long red light. "Honk if you love Jesus!" Then the other, and it was perhaps the juxtaposition of the two that set me off: "America: Love it or Leave It!" My serenity dissolved and I was livid.

You can imagine the extent of my chagrin when what I at first considered to be a pickup-driving cretin turned his truck into the Piggly Wiggly parking lot and, as if manipulated by the hand of God, into the parking space right beside my own powder-blue Lincoln Town Car. Yet it was in that precise millisecond when a powerful urge swept over my spirit, a resolve to confront him regarding such unforgivably poor taste, not to mention bad politics. Momentarily I found myself full of searing, passionate outrage and face to face with a rather scruffy, late twenty-ish, self-described carpenter's helper. The irony was certainly not lost on me.

As noted, my semi-beloved husband, Wickham, had passed away less than two years earlier, and I had only been touched by one other man in my entire life, the man who was my soul mate, the pilot about whom I have told no one, save you and Will Luckie. I did, however, always acknowledge the urges one has from time to time, although I had become reticent about self-gratification over the years. So you can imagine how mortified I was to find my eyes on this—*person's*—nude chest and shoulders. The heat had apparently rendered him shirtless, and trickles of perspiration were literally racing down his body, patched with sawdust here and there, the brown and gold hair of his chest all moist and curled, sweat coursing down to his unbelted jeans.

Years of what I assumed had been manual labor had been kind to this man's body, and the muscles in his chest and arms were solid and practically shimmering like morning dew in the sun's first light. Poor Wickham was a sedentary banker and became quite rotund over the years. I sometimes had full-blown fits of panic and claustrophobia, lying there beneath Wickham, who, sexual gentleman that he was, always did the honorable thing and graciously rolled off so that I could collect myself. This perspiring man, however, struck me as one who would never, ever, roll off—would, in fact, push harder, finding depths of pleasure, untapped reservoirs of glorious exhilaration, driving, driving—well, let us simply say that my spiritual center had shifted, along with my entire world view, which was never truly mine, anyway.

I was breathless, all hot in the face, but I managed to explain that I needed some work done and thought it fortuitous that I would find my vehicle beside that of a carpenter's helper or some such in the parking lot of the Piggly Wiggly. He was my *savior*, I told him, and I would be devastated, absolutely prostrate, if he did not come to my home immediately, this very instant, to look at a door that was bound to knock my maid silly. "And heaven knows," I told him, "my very life would be in dire peril without my maid. I would simply cease to function."

He seemed quite understanding for a working man and was most agreeable about doing this job for me with all due speed. He smiled at me, one of those undressing-you-with-the-eyes kinds of smiles that held out a damp promise of warm kisses, and my lost desire was back in a rush. When he told me he was a year out of the Marine Corps, I felt that my affair with my golden Air Force pilot had come full circle, that this was some kind of divine destiny. When I learned that the truck, and therefore the bumper stickers, did not even belong to him, the cake commenced to be iced. Then he smiled more broadly, dimples deepening, and brushed his fingers across the taut muscles of his sweat-slick stomach. "You know what?" he said, and his voice was rich with layers of meanings. "You're one good looking lady. You kind of make my rat crawl."

Well. I confess I forgot all about Mr. Monsieur's Puss 'n Boots cat food. I confess I went straight home with his truck close behind and gave Lindia the remainder of the day off. I quickly retrieved the K-Y from the medicine cabinet, as I knew the long-rusted Tin Man that was my randy rosebud was going to need its oil can until the "joints" adequately, well, *loosened*. I had been a very celibate widow, after all. I then took a long, anticipatory soak in a hot bathtub full of English Lavender bubbles and Estee Lauder bath beads as Rosencrantz and Guildenstern looked on quizzically. I confess that, as I drowsed in the steamy vapors and the candlelit glow of the master bath, sipping a vodka tonic and counting my blessings, I could not help visualizing certain sensual renderings upon the canvas of that ex-soldier's physique.

I contemplated my allegiance to the Methodist Church, and I still somewhat believe that the Methodist union and intimacy I had with Wickham was blessed by God, in spite of my ambivalence about religion. I do confess that as I waited there, perspiring in the rising steam from the bath water, I found my surface faith leaning once more in the direction of Catholicism now, almost fifty. Actually, I was quite certain that I could be a most satisfactory member of the appropriate Catholic Church—one in a nice little neighborhood in Pensacola where my late mother's garnet and pearl rosary would be appreciated, as opposed to being coveted by my rather greed-ridden daughter.

I do confess that, when Will came into my bedroom to mingle his pungent, earthy sweat with the perfumed confection of my own pores, I felt the layers of my oppressive foray into small town life peeling away like the walls that surrounded my once asphyxiated libido. It was perfection of an orgasmic spirituality such as I had never known.

Oh, yes, Father. I do confess.

3
Marlayna

I was brought up to love the Lord, love God and country, and take no shit off of nobody. I don't suffer no fools and the long hairs can kiss my lily white ass, putting the American flag on the butts of their jeans, smoking their wacky weed, and spitting on our military men. I'm proud to be an Okie from Muskogee, if you get my drift.

Jesus. God. Country. Take no shit. That's how my mama lived her life and that's how I planned to live mine, and then all this stuff started happening on account of Will Luckie coming back and all. I never would have thought it would get me all wadded up with a bunch of rich folks in Pollard, but it looks like that's just what it done, and I still ain't real sure what to make of it all. And on top of, things I was so sure of for all my life—like the Lord's will, my true love, and even the long hairs—have all of a damn sudden reared up and bit me in the behind. Like GooGoo says, it's "fuckin' with my shit." Literally. I'll tell you about GooGoo in a minute.

See, besides not taking no shit from nobody, I've always had these certain ways of doing things, and I don't change my ways of doing for nobody. That's something that started with my mama, too, because she was the same way. Like when I was growing up, there was a different routine for every day of the week and no other day would do. It's just the way it was. Like every Wednesday, just to pick one day. On Wednesday I was supposed to do these things in just this order, rain or shine: clean out the bird cages after school, go to the mailbox and get the mail, but only if there was more than three pieces of it, dust the living room, call my Aunt Freida in Ocala just to say hello for three minutes, then set the table for supper. And all four of my sisters had certain jobs to do on certain days and a phone call to make to some relative or another down in Ocala. But my main day was Wednesday, and Mama would say "Wednesday's child is full of woe." If it was Wednesday, Mama was going to fix fish sticks and English peas for supper, so I knew to set the table with the white dishes instead of the flowerdy ones she got out of boxes of detergent. We used the detergent dishes on Saturday nights when she fixed meat loaf and smashed potatoes. She always matched the meals to the dishes, she had the same bunch of meals for every night of the week, and if I didn't set out the right dishes she'd say there was demons in me and go to beating my butt with a metal spatula.

On Tuesday evening we would go to church and eat pot luck, which I liked because I didn't have to worry about setting out no dishes, and mama would dance around and roll in the floor and try to pray the demons out of me and my sisters. On Wednesday night, after the fish stick supper, was prayer meeting, and mama would holler and roll around some more. We was raised up in the Pentecostal services and I reckon it took, cause I do love the Lord. And I had done came to find out He's the only man that can be counted on for anything. Which brings me to my daddy.

On Saturday day, I went with Daddy wherever he was going, whether it was to the fish market to sit around and drink beer with his friends, or to the pool hall, or riding in the game reserve, or dove hunting, or fishing off the railroad trestle above Burnt Corn Creek. I would ride in the back of the truck, sitting on Daddy's big cooler of beer with our dog Stupid Marvin laying by my feet. Whenever Daddy tapped on the back window I'd reach around to the driver's window, take his empty, throw the can in the bed of the truck, then pass him another beer out of the cooler. I saved up his empties to hurl at signs on the road and I got to be a dead aim. Them Saturdays was boring a lot of the time, but I did get to learn to shoot Daddy's guns, he let me pick up the dead doves he killed, and he bought me Circus Peanuts and Honeybuns and Dr. Peppers with salted peanuts dumped in the bottles. I reckon Mama figured having me ride around with him would keep him away from other women of a Saturday, and I reckon it did, at least up until he dumped me back at the house around dark and eased on off to the bars.

See, my daddy was a county laborer who cut the grass on the side of the highway, drank too much, and tried to mess around with other women from time to time. My mama used to say, "You think cause you're a grass cutter you can cut all the stuff you want, but I'll be done cut you." She talked like that a lot, in spite of being a church lady, but she loved my daddy's sorry self for some reason. So she would carry me and my four little sisters to whatever bar he was at and kick whoever's ass was in the way. Then she would use a knife or an umbrella or a big old rock or whatever to get Daddy in the car while me and Sara Jane and Melinda and the twins, Janay and Renee, would hunch together in the back seat, giggling. Wasn't nothing scary about it. Mama won every time. Hell, girls would scatter like hens before a neck-wringing when Mama drove up to the parking lot of any bar, so I reckon I come by my mean streak honest.

Like I said, Mama flat sure believed in demon possession. And she believed Daddy's drinking was on account of demons because that was one thing she couldn't get him to quit for more than a week or two at the time, no matter how mean she acted or how hard she prayed. One time, when daddy went on an extra-long drunk, Mama decided it was because this longleaf pine tree out back was possessed with demons. She said she heard it whispering to her one windy night when a hurricane was blowing around in the Gulf. She told us that tree whispered, "Saaa-tan. Saaa-tan" over and over again. When the weather broke, she made us gather around it and pray over it to cast out the demons. It got to be part of the weekly routine, praying over that tree and anointing it with Crisco oil every evening at eleven p.m. just so Daddy would quit drinking. She even got the preacher to come and lay hands on that tree to try and heal the demons away. I guess it worked, because Daddy did stop drinking after a while, for a couple of weeks, but I was always scared of that tree after that. In fact, I'm downright suspicious of most trees, but mainly longleafs.

It wasn't just house chores on certain days and pine trees to be prayed over, and it wasn't just because of Mama that I had my own way of doing things. I began doing certain things my own certain way when I was real little and kept on adding more as I grew up. Like I always walked one certain way to school, even though it was longer and my sisters went another way. And I never stepped on a crack—still don't to this day—and Mama's back ain't broke yet, so I reckon I done some good. And there's a million other things. I don't go to bed at night until I check all the closets and under the beds for killers. I don't crank the car until I check under the seat for snakes cause a moccasin got up under our car seat one time at the creek. And I only pass other cars on the interstate when I can do it in threes, unless somebody's just poking along, and then I say a special prayer as a kind of a safeguard. So I'm like my mama in that way, and in loving the Lord, and one other way: I got her mean-ass temper, like I said. And the way I'm like my daddy is that I sure do like to fuck around, and I will take me a drink.

I guess it was them two things—drinking and fucking—that brought me and Will together in the first place. We went together through most of high school. And I always kept the pictures and stuffed animals he gave me, even had them laid out like a shrine on my bureau until I got married. I had his chinstrap and his football jersey—number 89—

hanging on the wall of my bedroom, too. Damn, we were the best couple in the whole high school— Escambia County High—we even got voted king and queen of the junior-senior prom when I was a junior and he was a senior. We were supposed to be together forever, and up until the other night I still thought we would be together, reunited.

See, Will went off to Vietnam because I thought I was knocked up, and I cried for a solid month after he left. Then I went straight to the Shining Love of the Lord Pentecostal Church and took to testifying. I had done got saved three times before, and I knew right where I belonged. Jesus forgives all sins, so even though I was a senior in high school and pregnant, I knew my soul was going to be high up in heaven someday, no matter what. I was kind of mad at myself, though, because it was right after another saving where I had swore off fucking when I let Will get me supposedly pregnant. See, I hadn't planned to let Will do it with me no more until we were married. When I told him that, he just laughed and said wasn't no way he'd ever be tricked into getting married like all the other pussy-whipped fools he played football with. Furthermore, wasn't no way he was about to give up fucking. It was something about how he said it that got me going just then. All of a damn sudden we went to kissing and grinding like there wasn't no tomorrow, and before I knew it he was tearing the foil off of that little Trojan package between his teeth like he always did when he wanted to get right to it. I always been a sucker for a good hard fucking. This time it was too hard, though. I reckoned that rubber had to have done leaked or busted or something, because I come up thinking I was pregnant not long after, making me an even bigger sucker for some good sex.

Then again, I'm a sucker for the Lord, too, if He's presented right, like at the Shining Love of the Lord Pentecostal Church, where I been going forever. To hell with them rich-ass churches where they sit all stiff and act like they're too good to hallelujah. Pentecostal is the only way to do it. Pentecostal is real. There ain't nothing like it—I mean nothing. You get that preachment a-cascading down from the pulpit, just a-throbbing with the pulse of the Holy Ghost.   You throw in a tambourine to beat out the rhythm of the preacher's anointed breaths while his voice rises, falls, rises, gets down in your soul and warms you with the sweet sweat of salvation, and when he goes to hollering and driving that rhythm right deep into your spirit— well, any woman that says it don't make her moist in the panties is a damn lie.

I was fourteen years old when I first accepted the Lord Jesus Christ as my personal Savior. It was at the New Hope Pentecostal Church of the Divine Advent, and old greasy-headed, borrowed-from-the-back-haired Brother Vastine Dupree, the regular preacher, had invited this guest preacher to give a talk who was some kind of fine. He was real young and sort of looked like Herman out of Herman's Hermits, and his name was Brother Rex.

Like I said, I was fourteen, and I hadn't never thought serious about getting saved, even though Mama swore by it. We'd been to every tent revival that ever passed through East Pollard but hadn't none of it took with me by then. Brother Rex was different, though. He had that crooked-toothed smile—the spit of Herman—and it was like he was looking right square at me, smiling at me in particular. It made me all tingly in the stomach, you know? My friend Rhonda was sitting next to me and she kept poking me in the arm with her elbow, whispering stuff like "He's hot for you" and "He wants your body," but I couldn't hardly notice her. All I could do was stare at Brother Rex's Herman-blue eyes and wait for the times his eyes would see mine, and that tingle in my stomach got bigger and bigger 'til I thought if that altar call didn't come on, I was gonna bust. Just the idea of his hands on my forehead, purifying the sin I was born in, had me all beside myself. I hadn't never felt thataway, that kind of craving—I was only fourteen, remember—and it was all wrapped up in that tingly feeling that had done by now took over my whole entire body.

Well, when I finally went up before God, the congregation, and Rhonda to accept Jesus Christ, Brother Rex gave me that Herman-like grin, looked deep down in my eyes, and put his hands on the willing flesh of my forehead while he prayed over me. I like to died, and finally my knees went all weak and liquidy and I fell out in the floor kind of like Mama does when she gets the Holy Ghost, only without all the twitching and moaning.

When it was over I had such a feeling of spiritual bliss all mixed in with some kind of carnal ache that it left me with the most satisfied and most uncomplete feeling I'd ever knew. That evening, laying in my bed, listening to "Mrs. Brown, You've Got a Lovely Daughter," I—well, I guess you could say that was when I begun to backslide into several years of lust and depravity.

By the time I was fifteen, I had done give the flower of my purity to three different boys: Johnny-Lee Dupree, the preacher's boy who picked his ear wax and who I went with right after my purification; Rhonda's stupid brother Claude Parker, my boyfriend till I was just past fifteen; and finally Will Luckie, the one that drove me back to the Lord with his two-timing, whore-hopping, blue-ball-bellyaching, bad-ass loving self.

It ain't no mystery why I put up with his cheating around. When you got a man who knows just how to please you, it comes clear that Jesus wants the two of you to be together forever, and you know that, through the Blood of Christ, you can turn him into a faithful partner. And I still thought I might could make him my husband someday, right up until and even after I went to carry him a stab in his heart strings to make my point, right up in the middle of a snooty pool party, which I figured would scare that rich bitch away from him. I ain't never shrunk from a fight, like I said before. And I had fought for Will Luckie before.

See, there was this one time in tenth grade when I caught him red-handed with this slut known as Bald Headed Sulley cause her hair and eyebriars had done fell out because of nerves. I guess if you ain't got no hair nor eyebriers, don't nothing make no sense but to become a slut. Anyway, they were in the back seat of a blue LTD in front of God and everybody in the parking lot of Pritchard's, this juke joint out highway 29.   So I rammed her rear bumper with the used Mustang daddy had give me for my birthday, I shot out all her tires with the pistol I took out of Mama's bureau drawer, and I would've shot her trashy white ass, too, but the cops come and throwed me up under the jail. I ended up with a juvenile record, but Mama said I had done the right thing and the girls at school gave me and Will a wide way to go after that.

It's just that Will did something to me and still does. When we would get alone he would look at me with them blue eyes, give me this hungry, growly smile, and my muscles would just go to water, just like they did with Brother Rex. Oh, I knew it was a sin to carry on like that. I knew I was wrong, and that once you step down the path of sexual sin it's mighty hard to get back right with the Lord.   I done it, though.   I stood before the congregation on my seventeenth birthday and confessed my sins to Mama, who fell out in the floor, and Brother Vastine, who always wants you to tell everything, and the whole, entire congregation, right on up to God. And I seen real clear right then that no matter how dark a stain my sins would ever get to be, the blood of Jesus could wash me clean. That was when I swore off fucking.

My mama was so proud she cried, and I taught Sunday school to the kindergarten class for four months.   But by the spring my feet were sticking out the side window of Will Luckie's pickup— again—only this time the Lord saw fit to supposably bless us with a young'un, which Will claimed wasn't his and then turned around and joined the Marine Corps right after graduation. In the middle of a war, even. That's how bad he wanted to get away from me and his baby. He didn't have no idea I wasn't going to give him up that easy. My mama and me take what's ours, and I figured Will was mine. I didn't care if I had to wait however many years it would take him to do his tour of duty. Of course, in the meantime, I had to get back right with God—again.

Turned out I wasn't pregnant after all, and that got me so depressed I went ass deep in the Holy Ghost for a long time, dry as a bone from lack of sex. Yeah, I went a right fair stretch without no sizzling hot sin. When I wasn't at church I was at Mama's, laid up in the bed, not caring about nothing but Will. What's the shame is I found myself getting old before my time. It's a awful thing but it's bound to happen when you give up loving, and it had done begun to happen to me. I had begun to wither on the vine. And once that thing starts to drawing up on you it's near impossible to get it juiced up without a whole lot of effort—and Will Luckie, the only man who could juice me proper, was over in some jungle somewhere. So I ran out to the Okay Lounge and got me some parking lot loving, kind of like my daddy used to do. Like I said, I'm a sucker for a good fucking. Problem is, can't nobody compare to Will. He's got this—attitude about it. It's like you know ain't nothing he won't do in the way of sex. It's the attitude by itself that gets you heated up. Parking lot men just want it quick. Hell, some of them go to jabbing without getting it ready, which don't do much for me. One time I even went to hollering because the thing felt chapped like all my innards was going in the wrong direction, which made the guy—I think it was Bill Ponder—cuss and stomp off round the back of the building and—you know, spit in his hand. That was one night when I missed Will like crazy and promised Jesus I would get him back once he came home from overseas, that I'd hold onto him no matter what it took. I didn't think nothing or nobody would ever come in the way of that, specially not no rich old lady that I figured was trying to buy his love anyhow. Shit, I reckoned I'd just as soon kick a rich woman's ass as a poor one's. It just goes to show you how many twists and turns your life can take.

I married Chip Henley after three years of parking lot sex, and the only reason I married him was because he worshipped me, made plenty of money, and I needed me a steady man who wouldn't try to boss me. Chip is blonde-headed and built real nice so I didn't mind him at all, but the best thing about him was he knew who the boss was, and that would be me. And he liked it that way cause that's the only way he ever knew it to be. Hell, everybody knows them Henley men'll lay right down in the dirt and let their women run all over them, and I ain't proud of it, but I had to have me a man that wouldn't interfere with my partying, a man I could run around on real easy, at least until Will came back. That's the day I was really living for at the time. Chip was only my "meantime" man, cause in the meantime I meant to have me some fun.

Chip called himself a turd wrestler because he was in the septic tank business with his daddy and his three brothers. When we were courting I'd go out on calls with him because he was so fired up to show me all about his job. Gag a maggot. It didn't never occur to him that he had a pure and plain grody, nasty job, that he spent the days plunging his hands down in shit holes, busting up sewer lines and vacuuming out septic tanks. He called himself a turd wrestler like he was some kind of superhero doing this bad-ass job wouldn't nobody else do because they were scared to do it. Well, it didn't take me long to get a bate of watching him wrestle them turds, so I carried my happy ass, more and more, back and forth between the church and the beer joints. All I had to do was stop from time to time and give Chip just a little so he'd be easy for another couple of weeks.

I didn't have no babies because I was waiting for Will to get back. Kept true to The Pill. I knew Will would realize what kind of life he needed to have with me, once he got all that traveling and Chink-fucking out of his system. When I got wind that he was headed home, well, that was when I moved out of Chip Henley's house. I stayed with every one of my sisters and their husbands, taking turns and moving whenever Chip would figure out where I was and come begging me back. He begged right up until the divorce was final, around Christmas. I took custody of our half of a duplex and his pickup truck, slapped some bumper stickers on it to make it mine, and, come January, here come Will Luckie, sniffing his way back in betwixt my legs, lighting the teenage flame of our high school romance.

"Hey, you got any place this old rat of mine can crawl?" he said, when he came up in my front door, just like it was a regular day, as if he hadn't never been gone a minute.

I wasn't going to let on that I had waited, just for this very second to happen. "I guess you don't think I should care that you left me high and dry, thinking I was with your child."

"You know me, Lainie."

"I reckon you know there ain't no baby. The rabbit died."

"I heard." He grinned "Or else I wouldn't be here. And that rabbit died a long time before you quit being preggo. You kind of freaked out." And he went to gnawing on my neck, which makes me turn into Silly Putty.

"Well, you treated me like dirt," I tried.

"Oh come on, Baby," and he licked and tickled behind my ear with that magic tongue of his. "I didn't mean nothing by it. I was just young and dumb and full of cum."

The goosebumps commenced to popping, and I was his once again.

It was good like that for a while—through the spring and into June, all the while that them Watergate hearings was going on. Didn't nobody give much of a shit about them, but Will Luckie did. "It's a clusterfuck," he would say. "Keystone cops meet Katzenjammer kids. No wonder Viet fucking

Nam was a no-win. 'Peace with honor'? The words of a double talking, double dealing crook."

I didn't argue, even though it took every bit of energy in my whole body to keep from popping off about his ragging on the U S of A. It was hard to tell him not to talk shit about Vietnam when he'd done been there, got wounded and scarred up even, but I didn't like it one bit. And I didn't like the way folks were doing the president, either, talking crap about him. Ain't nothing lower than a lying snitch, like them cabinets people that stabbed that Nixon in the back. But I didn't aim to let a stupid thing like politics come in between Will and me. What did some dumbass Watergate silliness have to do with us anyway? I kept on hanging on. Or, like The Supremes said, before them Vanilla Fudge people psychedelic-fied and hippie-fied it all up to hell, he kept me hanging on.

He did odd jobs on construction sites, and I let him use the former truck of my former husband, to tote materials and such. I thought it would be smooth sailing, right on into marriage and several children. But . . .

They say war will change a man. And Viet Nam is a doozy, what all I hear about it. But when Will took to singing the praises of that John Dean, that one that big time turned on President Nixon, I admit I lost what little cool I had.

"A cancer," Will said. "Dean said there was a cancer growing on the presidency. Way back. And you know how they do a cancer, don't you? They cut it out. Old Malignant Millhouse needs to be impeached, radiated, sliced out of the white house, by god."

Like I said, love of country runs through my veins, so I kinda snapped. "That's the president and he was elected. You can't say things like those words about the president."

"He ain't above the law. And he's crooked as hell."

"Will, I'm serious as a heart attack. He's the president, so God bless him and God bless America."

"Fuck America."

"What the hell did you just say?"

"America sent me to a shit hole to lay down my life for folks that didn't want me nowhere near their country and fight an enemy that was in-fucking-visible. And when I came back home didn't nobody want to see me, making *me* invisible. So yeah, fuck America."

"To quote my bumper sticker," I hollered at him, "love it or leave it."

"Show me in the goddamned constitution where it says anybody has to love this place," he snapped. "And I'll show you where it talks about impeachment in the constitution. That's some ignorant shit you're talking."

"You calling me ignorant?"

"If the mortarboard don't fit."

"Have you gone and turned hippie or something?"

He just laughed. That was when the storm clouds began to swirl, just like a hurricane. But even still, I held on. Through sure-enough hurricane season, dog days, full moons, and holidays. We fell into the kinds of routines like most couples do, which I thought was a good sign for a marriage, no matter about a president. I begun to wonder if I ought to let myself go ahead, plot and plan and get knocked up, but something—maybe the elbow-nudging of the Lord—told me to hold off on that.

He carried me to Pensacola in the winter to see *The Exorcist*, and oh my loving Lord in heaven, that was the scariest movie of all times. It had all kinds of puking and floating in the air and all them Catholic preachers talking all that foreign language shit and flinging their holy water all over the place. And that poor girl's head swiveled all the way around and I can't for the life of me figure out how those movie people did that!

But that movie really got me going, because you know I've seen demons cast out. Not like in that movie, but the point is that demons are real. In real life, demons ain't no special effect. So *that* got me worrying was Will maybe possessed by some kind of demon that made him hate his country and be so mad at Richard Nixon and so set against having babies. I prayed about it as often as I could. I begged the Lord to cast them demons out of him.

I reckon the Lord didn't see fit to hear my prayers, though, because by the time spring rolled around I could tell—a woman just knows in her intuition—Will was getting restless. He'd taken up smoking dope around Christmas, and his love-making had lost its edge over the months after that, or at least that's how I read it. I tried not to bitch about it, the dope, but I told you I ain't got much for no hippies and their wacky weed. I tried to coax him to church, to cast out the urges that was pulling us apart. He downright cackled at that. "Only thing worse than a crooked politician is a preacher, any preacher. They're all weasels and hypocrites."

"You better tell Satan to get thee behind you!"

"Come on, Lainey, I know you've been boiled, baked and basted in that voodoo since you were an arm baby, but you ain't going to put it on me. That's your trip."

"I don't understand how anybody can go against the Lord."

"The Lord's cool." He lit up a joint nub with one of them doctor tools clipped to it. "I'm cool with JC. It's all the loonies that make themselves out an authority, all the while they're plundering in little girls' drawers."

"Billy Graham ain't done that!"

"Selling their snake oil, pulling in cash hand over fist."

"That don't hardly never happen."

"Let's see . . . Billy James Hargis, Marjoe Gortner. You know I saw that documentary about old Marjoe when I was out West."

"Who the hell is that?"

"Just a child prodigy evangelist who was trained like a dancing monkey by some greedy-ass parents on how to fleece all you Bible believing sheep. And you never even heard of him because that movie was too scary to even be shown in vicinity of the Bible Belt. Goddamn con men."

"Shit, Will! You make everything out to be exaggerated. There's bad apples in all the bunches."

"Man, you give people a little authority, a little power. They come to believe they're powerful, above it all. Them snake oiled, snake handling preachers think they're the gods of their little universes. Same with corrupt politicians. Think they're untouchable. Just look at Nixon."

But I didn't want to look at Nixon, so I just clammed up and went my ass to prayer meeting. Which, I don't generally go to Wednesday night prayer meeting since I been grown, but I needed Jesus to work on my temper, right then.

It wasn't long after, on a Wednesday morning, that my old friend Paul Baggett, who is an officer in the P.C.P.D., called to let me know he saw Chip's—I mean, *my*—truck parked over at that rich lady Calhoun's house. The cops around here do gossip something fierce, but it came in handy for me.

"She wanted me to fix her screen door," Will said, laughing, church-keying a bottle of Blue Ribbon when I asked him about it that afternoon.

"That and what else?"

He squinted those pretty blue eyes. "Well, let's just say the old thing needed dusting off—and a little WD 40."

"That door or the old lady? Hell, she must be at least—fifty! She ain't even marriage material. Her eggs and equipment have long been dried up."

"Pretty nifty fifty," he said and winked at me. "And that K-Y is a miracle salve. But, truth be told, she don't turn fifty till August. What kind of birthday present do you give a woman who has everything?"

That sent me off the edge. "Give her a damn wheelchair!" This wasn't no politics that he felt strong opinions about. He was officially trying to fuck with my head.

He just chuckled. "I know. Maybe I'll just . . . sock it to her. Again. She seemed to really appreciate it."

"I'll show you how to do that," and I went to pummeling on him with my fists, him laughing the whole time, saying he told me all along and ever since high school that he wouldn't be pussy whipped into marriage, didn't want no kids. "You're okay, Lainey," he said, "but I just don't fit your bill. You'd be a lot happier with another kind of guy."

And he flat fell right out of my life and into that wrinkled up old lady's bed.

After that, I was so sad and weak I went home to Mama. She carried me to church and prayed over me and let me lay up in her trailer because I wasn't even close to being able to take care of myself. All I could do was go from the bed to the sofa to the toilet and think about Will and what to do to get him back. I looked at the TV but I couldn't tell you what I watched. It's just a blur of game shows and soaps. I did read some—the Bible mostly. Well, I *tried* to read the Bible, but that thing gets boring pretty fast, and whether you're a Christian or not you have to admit that. I tried to read *The Exorcist*, since Will and I had done seen the movie, but I felt like I was in Satan's neighborhood, and it gave me the chills. So I stuck with the *Enquirer* and some movie star gossip magazines, like that Rona Barrett one. Every now and then a romance or a mystery book.

Then, right out of the blue sky, Mama told me I could just *have* that trailer because she was moving to Ocala with her new boyfriend. See, she and daddy got a divorce a few years back after Daddy run off with this woman from Mama's church. It was a big goddamn mess, but the point is I ended up with a house trailer, no way to pay the rent on the lot where it was parked, and in no state of mind to hold down a job. Which made me even more miserable, because I've always been a worker bee. I ain't afraid of no kind of job. Hell, I worked in the Judy Bond blouse factory at Cantonment in the summers when I was in high school. A cuff clipper. Try doing one repeating set of motions on an assembly line all day long and you'll know what a hard day's work is. I worked my ass off until the other ladies on the line—older ladies that had been there forever—told me to slow it down, that all we had to do was make production and I was making them look bad. I slowed it down, but it ain't like me to be a slacker.

Anyway, about my misery, the good news is I had done had enough of laying around being like warmed-over death on account of my man. I had business to settle with Will Luckie.

Lord-a-mighty, I've done said a lot. I don't think I've ever told this much about myself at one time, even to Jesus. But I know you won't say nothing. I know you can't say, on account of that doctor and patient thing where it has to be secret.

You know what I think, bottom line? I think some things just don't change. Like a low-down man. Like a woman's desires. Like that funky, monkey, Pentecostal love thing. I just can't get enough of it. I still take my spiritual hungerings to those services and soothe my soul in the blessed anointment of the Holy Ghost. I reckon it's true about your first time—you just can't leave it go and you're forever going back for more.

Even still, GooGoo got me to thinking maybe I been reading the wrong road map where men are concerned. And that maid that was so nice to me, she's got me thinking maybe there's more to the Lord than just what Mama and them Pentecostals told me. It's got me all confused and turned inside out. But, no matter. Because even when I fall from grace, I know Jesus is one man who will take me back. He forgives, no matter how many times you go to cheating on Him. And even after all these years, when I think about sublime salvation in the blood of Christ, I still get moist in the drawers.

4
Lindia

Mr. Will keeps on telling me I need me some loving. That's just how he talks to everybody. Thinks loving is the answer to all the ills of the world. And I reckon he's right, only it's been so long since I studied about it---a man's loving, I mean. It's been so long because I ain't missed it too bad until here lately.

See, I already had what precious few women get. I had the love of, not just a man, but a good man. A man of God. Can't nobody give a woman the kind of loving a preacher man can, and can't nobody take my man's place. That's why I ain't studying getting me no man now. What I'm going to do with a man? Old as I am? Shoot. But I can do one thing. I can tell when a man's done caught the scent. I can tell when can't nobody else. Once you had a preacher man you can see them kinds of things in folks.

I met Pastor Henry Johnson, Jr., back in 1942, when I was seventeen and he was thirty-three. I was visiting my cousin Eula near Warm Springs, and she took me to her church. The Mount of Olives Free Will Baptist Church. Child, it was packed like sardines full of soldiers, like those Triple Nickels from over to Fort Benning and some of the plane pilots that trained at Moton Field, and I ain't going to lie. After the service we had dinner on the ground—fried chicken, greens, cobbler, and gallons of sweet, sweet tea with lemon. Them boys was looking fine in their uniforms, cutting the fool and trying to get us girls to go to the clubs over by Phenix City. But they were boys, and Pastor Johnson was a man. He was a man with a gift of The Word and a pretty face. He had Chicago polish and confidence from being raised up north, the son of a Pullman porter. I'd be grouped in amongst them soldiers but all the time giving a look, sideways like, at Pastor Johnson, and I'm here to tell you I opened up that man's nose. Then here I go home to Acree, down in South Georgia.

Two weeks and three days later that man—the Most Right Reverend Henry Thomas Johnson, Jr.— took a bus from Columbus to Albany, Georgia, got drove by a friend to a crossroads, and walked—I mean to tell you he *walked*—four miles out to where we cropped, nose wide open the whole way. I spent the next twelve years with him as his wife and helpmate, and he kept me satisfied the way a real man can. So I'm here to tell you I know when a man's done caught the scent and I can take one look at a woman and know has she been satisfied.

The Lord didn't bless us with no children, but Henry and me had the church and our mission work over the years, so we were blessed. We had a natural partnership, what with the Gregg shorthand I learned from my Aunt Clary who was a real secretary to my own pastor growing up. Henry would dictate letters, sermon notes, and such to me, then I'd copy it over in long hand for him. We read books and talk about them. Henry had a library of the classics, and even though I wasn't too good of a reader at first, I got to where it was a real appetite, those books. We would have our book talks and all kinds of other talks—funny, serious, even silly—in the early mornings over cups of coffee and drop biscuits. No cross words, ever. I praised Jesus every day for bringing that man to me. And I still praise Him for the dozen years I had with my man. Then he was gone, and when Henry went to Glory back in 1954 I had to make me a decision. Oh, I prayed about it and prayed about it because I ain't too crazy about no white folks. But my daddy was a sharecropper and my mama took in laundry, so I know hard work ain't a shameful thing at all. Living off the government is the shame, and Henry Johnson, Jr., would turn over five times in his grave if I was to do that. So I took me a big old deep breath, went to live with my cousin Brenda in Pollard, Florida, and went to work for some high-class white folks.

I bought a stack of diaries, dedicated to purging out any of the harborings that might not get completely prayed away. Prayers and written unburdenings have flat sure got me through it all, from the hollowed-out, physically tiresome feeling of the deceased's absence to silly tales of the ridiculous pettiness of those rich folks I fell in with. In the beginning years of my grief, I wrote lots letters directly to my Henry, messages to heaven, kind of like having a real talk with him, like we used to do at the kitchen table of a pre-dawn. Sometimes the letters were lovey-dovey; sometimes I just told him what all was in the news—like when Miss Rosa got arrested and when those assassinations happened a while back, Dr. King and all. Here lately, though, it's not so much letters to Henry, but wonderings about who I am— who I was and who I've come—am coming—to be. There's a rumbling in my spirit; I can feel it, and all of my meditations—at the church, unto Jesus, in my writings—give me comfort and peace, help me hold in when I might give over to meanness or ill will. Or when I struggle, unnaturally so, with the becoming. These pages, these ones right here, hold the very essence of me.

Now, it's a fact that white folks ain't right in the head, but the family I ended up with for the next up on twenty years was crazier even than most. I spent me a lot of time talking to the Lord behind them people—still do. I do a lot of scribbling in these journals. When you work around folks that ain't got no sense about how the Lord means for his children to live, all the time worrying over what kind of a show they be putting on and thinking up ways to spend up a bunch of money, well—it could make your heart harden up with bitterness and eat your soul up like a cancer. So I just think about what my man said when we met our trials over the years.   Henry said forget everything—even everything wrote down in the Bible—everything except what come out of Jesus' mouth, and that bitterness ain't going to happen.   And it's the Gospel truth, because I've tested it and tested it.

Until this past spring, Miss Maureen was always a club woman—bridge club, Garden Club, Art Club, Ladies' Club, you name it—and she had more silver for me to polish and more gatherings in a year than Henry and me went to all the time we were married. If things didn't go full tilt her way, she'd go to throwing china and screaming that she's just trying to be a *grand dame* like her mama and ought to be appreciated for it instead of getting all the time criticized by her family. Then she'd take to the bed for days on end and I'd have to be toting her meals up to her. She'd say I was the only one who understood her because I was from the old school. I'd just smile and say yes ma'am and go to thinking she nothing but a crazy old Scarlett O'Hara big-eye bitch. It beat the snot out of a wart hog what all went on in that house.

Her husband was rich for a living---I think he sat up in an office at the bank sometimes---so he stayed half drunk most of the time. Then she'd get a bate of it and go to dog-cussing him, accuse him of having girlfriends up to his hunting camp in Lowndes County, up there in Alabama. Next thing you know he'd buy her some jewelry, and things would settle down again.

From time to time that woman tried to have some interest in what her husband liked to do for hobbies. Things like watching football and going in the outdoors to hunt down the wildlife. But I don't reckon he really wanted her up in his doings, because he never encouraged her like you'd expect a good husband to do. Like my Henry would do.

Miss Maureen would take her an odd notion sometimes, like when she got it in her head that she was going to collect up roadkill to make herself a raccoon coat. And I never would've known about that plan if I hadn't been looking for some more salt meat, which you can't cook a mess of collard greens without.

I went to look in the deep freeze in the garage. I hadn't cracked the thing for a couple of months, but I knew she had a mess of salt meat in there because she always bought up all the meat when it was on sale at the Piggly Wiggly. And the salt meat had been on sale a while back. I liked to peed my drawers when I saw all them eyeballs staring up at me from them raccoon faces, with their little black masks. Three rigid raccoons laid out on a plastic trash bag. Six eyeballs. I must've screamed because Miss Maureen come running.

"It's perfectly all right, Lindia. I've simply been scooping them up off the highway whenever I come upon their poor little car-smacked corpses. Once I get another, oh, four or five, I'll skin them and make them into a lovely coat."

"But, why would you do that yourself, Miss Maureen, when you can hire somebody?"

She sighed. "I'd just like Wick to see how self-sufficient I can be. And how handy in the wild. I might should have been a pioneer woman."

I knew not to say nothing. She would get an odd thing in that head of hers and clamp onto it with the jaws of a bulldog. Didn't matter that it flew in the face of any kind of reasonableness. Didn't matter that your regular human would see it as crazy. It would only get bigger and bigger in her mind.

She never did make that coat. She tried, though. And I never would've know *that* if I hadn't found the trash cans full of rotting raccoons and crawling maggots. A wiggling mass of white worms amongst a stink of death and rot. It gave me the heaves, and I must've hollered that time, too, because here she came.

"Please don't tell Wick, Lindia. You *can't* tell Wick."

Turns out, she had consulted with Bo Barton down at Bo's Taxidermy Emporium on how to go about skinning the things. Then she thawed and toted them corpses down a dirt lane in the pines. And she had herself a caper knife with the idea of going to carving on the things.

"I just didn't have it in me," and she was even crying a little bit. "Those little hands look so *human*, I just wanted to wish them back to life. And what with their sweet little faces looking right at me, I absolutely crumbled. I was not about to thrust a knife into those poor little creatures. Now promise me you'll never tell Wick."

Of course I nodded yes. I didn't ask why she didn't get Jesus the Mexican to bury those critters out in the pasture or the woods somewhere and prevent the stink and the maggots.

Every year or two she'd have herself a breakdown and go away for a month or so to rest and I'd tend her young 'un. That girl child, Cecelia. I reckon I tended that child over the years ten times what her mama done. I told you the Lord didn't see fit to bless Henry and me with no children, so I took me some time and care with Miss CeCe. I tried to teach her how to live right and love the Lord behind all the Catholic voodoo her mama was giving her behind her daddy's back. I tried to show her how to be blessed with a happy heart, but she was already eight years old when I went to molding her. Her ways were set.

"Does not play well with others," is what just about every teacher she ever had wrote on the "conduct" section of that child's report card. And everybody knows that's just a polite way of saying the young 'un was a bossy, loudmouthed bully. She never kept a friend for very long—except for a teeny-tiny dedicated group that did as they were told. And she and her own mama fought just like trailer park trash looking for a tornado.

Nope, the nut doesn't fall far from the tree, because Miss Cecelia is every bit as crazy and a large measure more ill-tempered than her mama. She grew up to be queen bee of the Pollard muckety mucks, found herself a rich doctor to marry, and you would've thought the Queen of England herself was getting married for all the carrying on her mama did.   Threw the biggest wedding this town ever seen, with more dressed up white folks, black ladies in aprons, and black men in bow ties than you could shake a stick at. There were two big tents, one with a sit-down dinner in it and the other with a band and dancing. There was Oriental rugs and antique furniture set out on the grass and more presents than the Taj Mahal. And do you know what that crazy woman give her daughter for a wedding present? A fancy cottage next to her big old house and the use of her maid. Me.

I know you must think: Slave times is over. That's what my cousin Brenda said. All I could say was, I need to have a talk with the Lord. So I went to services and clapped my hands and stomped my feet and called out to Glory and swayed and sang and gave my meanness to Jesus. Then I went to work for Miss Maureen *and* Miss Cecelia. I watched Miss Cecelia get eat up with clubs, just like her mama used to be, and boss that prissy husband of hers right and left. And I can tell you this: that woman, Miss CeCe, don't only be crazy; she ain't never been satisfied by no man to boot.

Funny thing is, some folks can change. Because, one day just this past spring, here comes Miss Maureen with a young man from across the creek. One of them flat-bellied limber-backs. Good looking. Pretty. She went straight up to her bathroom and got some bubbles to going as soon as she gave me the rest of the day off. That man was Mr. Will.

I was just standing there in the kitchen, looking at that pretty white man, knowing Miss Maureen was fixing to get her some real good stuff. I didn't know exactly what to say, so I asked him, "Do you love the Lord?"

"Damn straight," he said. And he grinned. "Where's the bar?"

It's been about four months since that day, and Miss Maureen has come to be right human. She talks more *with* me than *at* me. Seems like she's trying to let go of that "old school" talking. She even tries to show an interest in current events when it comes to black issues, which is pretty ridiculous, but I do appreciate the effort. She's taken up a new kindness and honesty that most folks don't ever figure out. It's something real; you can't fake it at all.

Brenda says white folks are poison and maybe she's right. But if Miss Maureen can turn human then maybe there's hope for the rest. Looks like all it takes for some is the loving of a good man, because I see Mr. Will as a good one. Oh, he's odd. He'll talk crazy and nasty sometimes, and he thinks the sun rises and sets on his chickens. But he makes me laugh, when I used to would get in a Christian tizzy. He's taken a good bit of the judgement out of me, and that softens the spirit, is what I've come to know. Plus, he made a human out of Miss Maureen, and that goes a long way in my book. It's got to where I even enjoy working up in Miss Maureen's house, mainly because of Mr. Will.

Miss Cecelia is another story, though. I ain't much on going to her house, but she's all the time having me do for her. "Wipe down the baseboards, Lindia." "Run me a bath, Lindia." "Cook up a mess of fried chicken, Lindia." That fool woman can't do nothing for her ownself. On top of that, the good Lord knows she ain't never opened up no man's nose, and that one she got—Mr. Winston—well, I don't think his nose been opened up by a woman. That man ain't right. Cletus says he's a fairy and can't even think about satisfying no female. So Miss Cecelia's walking around with some kind of poisonous spiritual boil festering up in her womanhood that ain't never been lanced, and it makes her just as crazy and mean as a car-struck dog.

Here's just how mean she is: Back in May, I think it was, I noticed her out the kitchen window, creeping across the lawn toting Miss Maureen's cat, Mr. Monsieur. Nobody was on the property but me, and Miss CeCe ain't never showed no interest in none of her mama's pets, so I knew right quick she was up to something. She eased open the gate to the chicken yard, looked around, then went for the one chicken that Mr. Will had put a crucifix on, round its neck. That was the chicken he called "Chuck," the one he liked to pet the most, the one he talked to. It was an odd thing, to be sure, talking to chickens, but I figured anybody that came through Vietnam could be as odd as need be.

Anyway, that no good CeCe walked up on Chuck and throwed that cat right at him, kind of underhand tossed the thing. It hit me right then that the spiritually starved bully-woman was trying to commit a chicken killing. Murder by cat. Death by natural enemy. And the whole time knowing how fond Mr. Will was of that particular chicken. That just shows you how deep the veins of meanness run in that child. Going to take the life of the beloved pet of a shell shocked war veteran. And she's all the time bragging up her love of country.

Well, Mr. Monsieur wasn't having none of it, especially when the chickens scattered and a couple of them ran at him, wings flapping and claws splayed. Miss CeCe tried to intercept him, but Mr. Monsieur spat at her, bolted, climbed right over the gate, and spent the rest of the day hiding under the house. So even the animals can sense the off-kiltered soul that lives in the earthly vessel of Miss Cecelia Calhoun Dozier.

It ain't none of my business, I know. But I couldn't let it stand, not an attempted murder on Mr. Will's odd choice of a pet. I promised myself that very day to let him in on such shenanigans and downright sins. I'd spent my employment with them crazy people keeping my mouth shut when it came to giving an opinion or describing an observation, unless I was asked. But there's something about Mr. Will, like I told you. It would feel like a betrayal not to let that kind man know the forces set on getting him gone—not to mention getting his chickens gone. I can't have that on my conscience.

I can't do nothing about them other folks I got to be amongst. But that's all right. Because as long as I got my conscience, the Lord, my memories of Henry Johnson, Jr., and a church home to go to twice a week for satisfaction of the spirit, then that poison ain't going to do me in. I can look Miss Cecelia in the eye and keep a straight face when she goes to gushing about how I be one of the family and how much she loves me like a mama. I can laugh on the inside when Miss Cecelia and Mr. Winston going on about the Civil Rights, saying "nigrah" this or "nigrah" that, and then get all hushed up when I come up in the room. I can watch Miss Cecelia bring them rich club women that call themselves Christian up in her house and know their faith in God is just an excuse to have a club meeting.   If I'm right with Jesus, I can just shake my head and say ain't it a shame. But you know what the biggest shame is?   Don't neither one of them—Miss Cecelia nor that girlish husband of hers—be satisfied in the bedroom, that's what.

I told you I know when a man's done took the scent. Well, when I left out of Miss Maureen's house that day Will Luckie followed her home to supposably fix the screen door, I stopped to talk to Cletus while he was working on Miss CeCe's flower beds. He's stooped and bent over from working in the white folks' yards, don't you know, but he sure can cut the fool for me. He said, "Let me give you just a little sweet stuff, Miss Lindia."

I just be laughing because, like I say, I ain't studying no man.

He said, "The Ladies call me SweetSweet, 'cause I got me some sweet, sweet love."

I said, "Go on, niggah, you crazy."   And we janked and carried on like that for a spell.

"That knot of yours is a mite tight," he said, talking about how I've always worn my hair, in a bun. "You trying to be a school marm?"

"Somebody ought to school you on more proper manners," I said, and I surprised myself just then by thinking the opposite—the *not* proper side, and how fun it could maybe be.

"You wrong to chastise me. You do me wrong, like a sad, sad song."

Sometimes Cletus makes up silly rhymes like that, kind of like Muhammad Ali.

We laughed for a while about how much money them crazy white folks throw out on their sets of dishes and their parties, and about how Miss Maureen sure does need a man, and Miss CeCe, too, only her mama about to get one for sure. The funny thing is, I felt touched by some kind of wall-eyed electricity, kind of like I was coming back to life again, as a woman. It was like Will Luckie had done begun to breathe the life back in all of us, and the pores of our skins were humming like a swarm of hornets with the energy of it all. And him only been there just a little bitty minute in time. Before I knew it, I was cutting my eyes and cutting the fool back at Cletus, just a little.

You know the Reverend Johnson could make me scream with his loving and the Good Lord can still make me scream with jubilation. I know I've been satisfied. That day, when Will Luckie come his pretty self up in that kitchen, I figured Miss Maureen was fixing to be satisfied, too. One thing for real sure: I knew all I would have to do was take one good look at her the next morning, and I'd be done know the answer.

Sure enough, I took one look. And sure enough, she was satisfied. And she's been getting satisfied from then on, and right smart, too.

5
Cecelia

In old movie westerns, when the Indians sneak up on the cowboys, creeping on their bellies, all covered up in wolf skins, to the place where the white man's scalps are abundant, there is always the requisite bunch of corralled horses that immediately begin to dance and whinny in skittish anticipation. They snort and blow and tap their hooves in a little ballet of fear. There is danger afoot, and the animals know it by instinct as they make to avoid it. Such is the case since Will Luckie arrived. Just like the infernal smog from the paper mills down the highway, a coarse blanket of lust hangs thick in the humid air that blows inland from the Gulf of Mexico, mingling with the ether that washes over all living creatures in its ethereal realm, and even the animals have gone insane. Here is what I mean:

Only a month or so after that no-count redneck officially moved in with Mother, I was alone in the cottage Winston and I occupy on Mother's property, next door to her big, white-columned three-story. And here I must interject that I am in the process of naming both properties, as that is expected of landowners of a certain class. Mother is resistant, of course, calling it "showy" and "pretentious." But one only has to look into the homes of the wealthy to see that I am, as always, in the right. I've thought of keeping it simple, understated, almost wry by naming them what they are: The Big House and The Cottage. But that thought always gives way to something much more aristocratic for mother's house, like Longleaf or Stables of Calhoun and perhaps La Petite Maison or the more pastoral The Meadows for my own home.

Anyway, I was already sleeping fitfully, worried as I was over Mother's flagrant indiscretion, when I was awakened at one a.m. by a shuffling, grunting sound outside my bedroom window. Naturally I was seized up with fear, as Winston was off at a medical convention, leaving me to fall victim to God knows what. I lay quite still, cataloguing all the assaults, robberies, and murders I had read about over the past year. That poor rich girl, that Patty Hearst, was among the latest, having been snatched right out of her apartment, right under her boyfriend's nose, by a bunch of radical revolutionaries, negroes among them. I certainly did not want to be abducted by communists or negroes and forced into a life of crime, robbing banks and such, so I held my breath and listened all the harder.

The noise did not abate, yet it did not seem to be coming closer. Taking courage in the fact that this sound seemed relatively stationary, I lifted the satin comforter, slid my size nine Jesus-Christ-Walk on-Water-Skis into my slippers, and crept to the window that looks out over the back lawn. I brought the curtain back just a crack, slow motion style, to peer out, immediately dropping to my knees when the movement of what I thought to be a very large, shadowy man caught my eye. He was huge, kneeling there on the lawn, and was certain to overpower me, even though I am, as noted, an Amazon.

I must have cowered there on the floor for a full five minutes, thinking what to do. I had no gun, baseball bat, or brickbat. I thought to make my way to the living room fireplace for a poker or to the kitchen for some cutlery. I thought to call MiMi or the police but knew the man, right outside my window, could hear and would quite probably break through the window to cut me off from help, would quite certainly rape me till I bled, would possibly slice my throat with a jagged knife.

I was afraid to breathe, scream or run. I could still hear muffled grunts and baffling little snuffling sounds from the dim lawn, then louder grunts and a strange, barrel-like echo of metal. Finally, I gathered the courage to bring my eyes to the windowsill again and made another slit in the curtain. What I saw there in the moonlight confirmed for me the extent of the pox Will Luckie had cast upon fish, fowl, flora and fauna.

A few feet from the window was an ancient propane tank that Mother insisted we use for our gas water heater, as she claimed it was cheaper. I always argued that it was an eyesore and planned to have it enclosed in lattice. If I had already done so, I would not have been witnessing what I saw there through the window. Nudging up against the propane tank, emitting throaty grunts and staccatoing breaths was, not a man, not a member of the Symbionese Liberation Army, but a wild pig.

In fact, it was a two-tusked, hairy bodied, wild boar hog, nuzzling and snuffling and becoming more amorous with the passive gray tank with each moment ticking by.

I was absolutely dumbfounded at the aberration.   The boar hog sidled up to, rubbed against, and boar-hog romanced the dirigible-like structure, which gave no response save an empty echo of metal every now and then. It was wholly disgusting and I let out a disgusted sigh, long of breath. I reached for my Floral Empress telephone, no longer paralyzed by fright. Naturally, Will Luckie answered.

"You must come over here at once. And bring a gun."

"Is it a prowler?" He sounded groggy with orgasmic exhaustion.

"It's worse. It's a wild boar."

"Up in your house?"

"Of course not. It's outside my window. It is trying to mate with my propane tank."

"The hell you say." He laughed, that awful sound I have grown to despise. "It's humping the goddamn tank? No shit?"

Of course he would find it amusing, would use a vocabulary full of crude admiration. Any attempted copulation in existence, however freakish, would be held in his esteem. "I hardly see the humor in it," I said. "It is aberrant animal behavior and it is not ten feet from my bed."

"Probably the most action your bed has seen in a while, huh?"

"How dare you make inferences about my love life? I'll have you know my love life is magnificent."

"Who you seeing? Cause I know old Winnie ain't got nothing magnificent to lay on you."

"This is beyond belief," I said. "Just do as I say and bring my DD's shotgun over and kill that wayward pig."

"Oh, let the damn thing alone," he said. "Go back to sleep. He ain't bothering you."

"You don't understand what a fuss it is making. It is nauseating."

"Shit, what you got against a animal having a little fun?"

"It's unnatural. It's disgusting. I won't have it."

"Hell, girl," he said. "Get yourself a gun and shoot it, then. I'll carry it to the sausage house tomorrow and we'll be broke out in bacon."

"All the guns are over there. That is what I am trying to get you to understand. Winston does not like guns in the house. And besides, a wild boar would be too gamey to eat."

"Fact is, wild boar is fine eating.

"Winston would never touch such a thing. And how did we fall so far off the immediate subject?"

"Damn, girl. You got yourself a first class sissy."

"That is enough of your insults about me and my husband. I must have a gun over here at once."

"Come and get one, then," he said. "I'm fixing to get me some rest."

"Naturally you would say that. You ought to come over and shoot it yourself. You would if you had any gentlemanly qualities whatsoever."

"Hell," he said. "I'm gentleman enough for your mama. She's done wrung me out. I'm tired."

I almost slammed the receiver down that minute. The nerve of him, referring to sexual relations with that old woman. "I can't sleep with all this noise," I said.

"Shit, there's four other bedrooms in that what you call 'cottage.' Just move. That pig'll leave once he realizes there ain't no pussy to be had over yonder." He chuckled. "Ain't been no pussy to be had over yonder in a long time, is it?"

That is when I *did* slam the phone down, seething at his insults and at the insult that smitten pig was perpetrating on my propane tank. I threw back the satin comforter, reached for a Valium, and resolved to tune it all out. Of course, that was impossible, and I was drawn back to the window throughout the night, to gaze at that oval of a propane tank being seduced by that misguided wild hog, its corkscrewed little penis erupting through its sheath there in the porch light, the animal making unsuccessful attempts at mounting the object of its affection. It seemed that the whole world had caved in to carnal amorality and perversion, and I could not sleep for thinking about it. When I finally did doze, I half-dreamed of little propane piglets, and when I was wide awake I counted two-tusked boars instead of sheep. It was only after another Valium and a tall glass of low shelf wine—Boone's Farm Strawberry Hill—that I slumbered.

The next morning the pig was still there, lying beside the tank in a posture of spent passion. I banged on the window, cross from the cheap wine headache and still groggy from the pills. It did not budge. I gathered some caffeine-induced energy from a cup of Folger's, then stepped out onto the porch and beat on a pot with a meat mallet. "Go away!" I screamed. "Go!" Sluggishly, it lifted its massive head and stared at me with its deep-set little boar eyes, and a shudder of revulsion ripped clean through me. The ether had been infected. Aberrant re-occurrences were now de rigueur.

Finally, I had the game warden come and tranquilize the boar and haul it away while Will Luckie and MiMi looked on.

"Poor somebitch just wanted to get laid," Will said, and nuzzled Mother's neck while I cringed inside. At that moment I resolved to get the best of him, though I did not know how until a bit later.

Of course I must stress that, throughout this whole episode of mother's second sexhood, I have attempted to be fair where Will Luckie is concerned. It simply would not be Christ-like to do otherwise. I am the first to concede that Mother is not—well, "ordinary" is the adjective that comes to mind. She is a bit of an eccentric, as so many of the wealthy are, and she has always been fond of drama. She is not above pressing a palm to her chest or the back of a hand to her forehead and uttering plaintive little bleats of suffering peppered with curses. Mother can swear with the fluency of a wounded sailor, although certain words, such as the "f" word, are absolutely off limits. Naturally, her dramas and her imminent death are all in her head; Dr. Dave has been giving her sugar pills for years.

There were times throughout my childhood when her oddities became too much for us, such as the time she refused to speak anything but French for days on end, even though no one else could understand her. That was one of several times she went off to a sanitarium for a cure. Whenever she disappeared for a couple of weeks or a month to take a cure, she would come back very calm and compliant, and Daddy would seem almost bubbly in his happiness. But, of the two extremes, I could never truly decide which mother I preferred. I only wished for one that was normal, falling somewhere in the middle, on the highest point of the bell curve.

But whichever mother I am handed at any given moment, I am determined to be the devoted daughter. This is made easier by my childlessness, my own lack of rival siblings, my only encumbrance being a limp wristed Baptist husband who is not much use for helping with my mother and her shiftless little slut of a boyfriend. Now don't get me wrong—I heartily embrace my daughterly duties. Heaven knows, I have never failed to be at her side when she was mid-crisis, even throughout the hypochondriacal frenzy of her early forties, on the cusp of her golden years, having cheerily taken up residence in the white Creole—my wedding gift— next door to her. Many are the times I have delivered satin bed jackets and Merle Norman cosmetics to her hospital rooms, spoon fed her while that popping jaw of hers nearly sent me over the precipice and into a ranting, maniacal conniption fit, and taken all the verbal abuse I should have to stomach in five lifetimes.

"CeCe, have you ever had the worship of a lover?" she slurred one time through a haze of hospital medication. "Could you ever relax and let a man ravage you till you screamed? Or are you carved of moonstone? Tell me. I want to know who you are."

Of course, she doesn't remember such conversations, when she has made vague references to someone in her past, not my daddy, I think, who fulfilled her on some base level. These are things I do not wish to know about her.

Sometimes it occurs to me that my daddy died of gall stones and Will Luckie is full of gall. My daddy smoked expensive Cuban cigars and Will Luckie spits. They are day and night. My daddy was a gentleman even if he wasn't faithful and got drunk a lot. He took care of us. And you know, my DD always told me I would never have to work, that the money would take me into old age, a plush casket, and a choice plot overlooking the Conecuh River, with plenty left over for a dozen children. But here I am, childless, because Winston has such difficulty with The Act that we've taken to separate bedrooms over the years, making blundering attempts only when he's had enough merlot, which is difficult for a teetotaler. And Daddy certainly never figured on mother having a geriatric sex-fest with a redneck cowboy swinger who is as low-down as gulley dirt, talks to chickens, and has his eye and his fist on my inheritance.

Oh, Lord, the chickens. I *must* tell you about the chickens. They were the deserving objects of my rage after Will placed the absolute last straw across my load-weary back. He brought three hens and a rooster when he moved in with Mother, which was just about immediately. Then he had the nerve to convert Cletus' gardener's shed—which sits near my own yard—into a chicken coop. It sends that fecal chicken yard odor across both our back lawns, not to mention the pre-dawn rooster wails and nonstop clucking and flapping. The half-assed fence he put up routinely fails to contain them at all times, so they end up wandering over to the pool and even into Mother's kitchen just last month. Of course you know what Will Luckie did, and Mother and Lindia, for that matter. They laughed. Here you have a yard hen, filthy, full of parasites and histoplasmosis, meandering about the place where food is prepared, and those fools thought it was just about the most humorous occurrence of the decade. I spent the evening Cloroxing Mother's kitchen floor, an already festering incubus of resentment building toward those damned birds, whose numbers have grown considerably.

You see, he has kept on adding more of the feathered beasts throughout the weeks and months of his cohabitation with Mother. A few more pulletts, a couple of Dominekkers, all slick-feathered in rust and green, even though I tried to tell him you shouldn't put different breeds together. Witness Will Luckie and my mother, the inbred and the well-bred.

"There'll be no segregation in my chicken yard," he said.

"You mean *my mother's* chicken yard, don't you? This is *her* property, not yours."

He responded by cranking up the volume of his portable radio. "Mock, yeah, ing, yeah, bird," blasting James Taylor and Carly Simon across the expanse of chicken yard.

Next he bought those hideous, plundering guineas that got into my summer garden and landed us all in court. Judge Watson, of course, who has always been one of Mother's male sycophants, and who was utterly taken in by Will's charm, would allow me to sue neither Will nor the guineas. "Sue a guinea? Why, Cecelia LaRue Calhoun Dozier, you can't sue a guinea," Judge Watson drawled. "Why, a guinea is just a bird. A bird in the world." And he swept a robed arm at an imagined horizon. As if I did not know a guinea was a bird!

To celebrate his victory over me in court, Will Luckie bought Mother a peacock, which she adores because it is so flamboyant, like her. It is even named for her—Maureen. Will Luckie named it, of course. He said he could justify using her name because it fit in with the whole Watergate setting of the chicken yard, no matter that the Maureen peacock is a male. Oh, did I forget to mention that he put a sign on the chicken coop that said "Watergate Hotel" and named each chicken after that whole Nixon bunch? And with no regard whatsoever to gender. Well that is precisely what the no-count fool did.

It started out as a cynical joke, as Will Luckie makes no secret of the fact that he believes he fought in a great big con job (i.e., Vietnam) and spends a great deal of time belittling Republican politicians (of course, my DD is turning in the grave in a whirlwind of cremated ashes at the prospect of Mother copulating with anything resembling a Democrat). He regularly bemoans the fact that, after he did two tours of duty in Vietnam. "The longer tours," he likes to say. "Jungles for thirteen months and then anywhere in the world for r and r."

He was bitter that he had come home just as the Watergate hearings were cranking up. "That's just exactly what you want to hear about after you spend a couple of years in the damn jungle. You want to hear that your commander in chief is a goddamn lying crook. But I always knew he was slimy."

I did not point out that it takes one to know one.

"And just as slimy over there. Cambodia. We all knew it. Didn't need no Pentagon Papers."

I did not point out that we were fighting the Red Menace and that we'd likely be speaking Russian any day now, what with the withdrawal of troops. I had read my DD's John Birch materials over the years, and I knew it was going to be either us or them, DC or Moscow, in the bitter end. I held my tongue, which just goes to show you that I do know how to keep my cards close, anytime I have to.

The chicken project took on yet a deeper meaning for him when he began keeping a daily log, entitled "The Chicken Sheet," in which he records each bird's name, egg production, idiosyncrasies and infirmities. The shell-shocked buffoon began to see the ornithological specimens in a new light; they took on the personality traits characteristics of *homos sapiens* in his deranged mind.

"Martha Mitchell looks peaked today," he writes in the log, or "G. Gordon has been spurring Haldeman all afternoon. Haldeman won't even look him in the eye," or "Erlichman is starting to realize he don't carry no weight in this chicken yard—he has been trying to show out but everybody else ignores him," or "McGruder—three eggs but not a lot of enthusiasm—maybe constipated?" and on and on. It is the only thing near a job I ever witnessed him doing, so you can see right there how useless and sorry that man is. And I am here to tell you he takes that job seriously. J. Dean, Erlichman, J. Mitchell, Secord, E.H. Hunt—these are their names. There is even an Egil Krogh, which he spells E-a-g-l-e C-r-o-w. And the fastidious detail that goes into the recording of the daily lives of the yard fowl is quite disturbing. He acts as if they are evolved even beyond pet-dom, as if they are his bosom buddies, chatting with them as he inventories the nests, caressing that nasty, slimy-looking plumage. Chuck Colson grew so tame from the attention that he let Will Luckie loop a chain dangling a diminutive gold crucifix about his gullet, which he has been wearing ever since mid-May. But it gets even more insane. Right after Memorial Day, Staff Sergeant Luckie added a bit of green cloth to the chain. He then pinned to the cloth some kind of ridiculous war medal he supposedly earned, making that absurd chicken look like the military dictator of the Watergate Hen House. Then he said something that I did not understand until later. "This medal, Cecelia, is mine," he said. "And it is the medal Chuck gets for surviving you. That is his victory. And mine."

"Just what in the name of Frank Sinatra does that mean?"

"The trees have eyes." And he gave me the strangest stare, one that set off a shudder in me.

I swear, it is obvious that his tours of duty in the jungles of Southeast Asia effectively booby-trapped his little birdbrain. Still, I did not like his cryptic comment. It gave me a sharp but prickly chill down my spine that ultimately turned into the last straw.

Another, prior straw came only a week and a half ago, when a raccoon got into the shed and assassinated Tricky-D, the dominant rooster, of course. Mother and I were by the pool when that inbred idiot walked up, bearing the pulpy head of fowl, and announced, "Richard Milhous Nixon is dead." Then he actually teared up and began planning a funeral for the few feathers, that mangled head, and two-thirds of a wing he found stuck to a bloodied bit of a carcass. Then he insisted that the entire family attend the funeral, which was held beneath the scuppernong arbor. He strummed his guitar and sang "Amazing Grace," all weepy-like. Then he delivered an absurd little eulogy.

"Unlike the Doppleganger in the White House, Tricky-D was a good egg," he read from the spiral notebook where he keeps The Chicken Sheet, "misunderstood by some who couldn't appreciate his ways. According to The Chicken Sheet, he liked to scratch for grubs in the dirt, he took to pecking Erlichman upside the head for a period of four days, and he did tolerable at romancing the hens. He was particular about his posture. He always took care to keep a dignified strut. He didn't socialize much beyond what he had to do, kept to himself a lot of the time. At one point he seemed to want to be friends with Martha Mitchell but she snubbed him. But more than anything else, he liked Merle Haggard songs, 'Today I Started Loving You Again' in particular. I must have played that one for him a hundred times, so that's what I'm going to sing today at his burial service."

I was struck by his ability to write a coherent eulogy, in sharp contrast with his absolute verbal butchery of the King's English. But, even as he strummed his guitar, I wondered if I was the only one who found this whole scenario to be consummately insane. We were all there, Winston in his white coat, having left work only briefly, for this absurd tableau. He gazed at Will, seemingly enthralled by the twanging lyrics. Lindia and Cletus, too, were there, solemn, decorous, oddly captivated by the whole production. Mother wore black, with a black lace veil draped over her head, winding around her neck along with her DM's crucifix, which I mean to have one day, even though I am not Catholic. Everyone knows

Catholics are idol-worshipping, statue-loving fish eaters who place entirely too much spiritual worth on Mother Mary.

I had not known until that moment, there at Tricky-D's burial service, just how attached to the poultry Will had become, nor how attached to Will my family and my servants had become. It hit me hard that allegiances had shifted, that this con artist had scammed everyone, right down to my own husband, into believing he was somehow a worthwhile pastime for my brain dead MiMi. I had seen through him from the start, but at Tricky-D's funeral I saw clear to his blackened, criminal heart, and I appreciated at once what a liar he was.

It was his anguish over a fallen member of that herd of chickens that did it. He was not faking that anguish. His tears were genuine. Something about those animals filled a sick need of his, I knew not what. But this display of emotion, this chink in the armor was something far and away different from his randy romancing of my aged mother. His regard for the coop fowl made his regard for Mother, in my eyes, stand out for the fornicating fakery that it was. Ironically, this realization of mine undoubtedly saved Will Luckie's life, and forever altered mine.

6
Lindia

I didn't vote for none of Richard Nixon. And ain't I glad, now he's bound to be run out of office? Wouldn't that be a sight, if I had done voted for Richard Nixon, after all me and The Right Reverend Johnson went through—all the meetings, the organizing, the planning, the meanness we had to put up with. One night, real late, they even put a cross in our yard and set it afire. It was November of '51, and I can still remember smelling the gasoline and feeling the heat off that flaming cross all the way inside that cold little shotgun house where we lived near Panther Burn, Mississippi. I looked out the window and it was like a Christmas scene, the cotton fields across the highway all white like the snow I ain't never seen but in pictures, just pure white fields that must be something like real snow, behind that fiery cross in my front yard where I had combed the dirt into pretty swirls with a rake. I almost expected the cotton fields to go to melting, up against all that heat. Then, in a week or so, the cotton was picked and the fields were scrubby and ugly again, and there were little bits of cotton all along the roadside. But we left that nubby, black, stick and pieces of burnt-up cross in the yard just so they'd know we could pass it, day after day, and not be tormented by it.

It was still there on the day I moved away, just after Henry died. I carried his body back to Warm Springs and told him goodbye there. I gave all his papers and plans and letters to his brother Rodney. See, Henry aimed to work on changing the laws, for voting and all, and he had begun to make a mark when he died. That burning cross came behind him asking the town council for more money for the colored school. I figured Panther Burn didn't want to give off no money to the colored school, and I reckon they made their point. But Henry said it was more likely a reaction to all that Willie McGee mess earlier in the year, after more than one trial that brought communist Yankees down to Laurel to try to defend a colored man who beat and raped a white woman, or so they said. That Willie McGee was executed in May, and it was even put out on the radio, the broadcasting of the execution, which Henry said was barbaric and wrong. The white folks were in a state, to be sure, and Henry and me caught some of the brunt.

Anyway and in spite of, Henry kept on and on and on till he couldn't go no more. Finally, he up and died of a heart attack on a spring day, all of a sudden like. That's how fast a woman's life can change. When a man comes in or a man goes out. That's when a woman's life gets changed up. I ain't one for change, though. It's hard for me. Henry even called me a "creature of habit." Like I told you, I started keeping this diary and writing letters to Henry on the day he died. It's how I honor our time together.

Another way I honor my deceased is in my civic duties. Like I said, I voted for George McGovern, just like I knew Henry would have. I always vote like Henry would have if he had ever got the vote. It's kind of like a gift on top of honoring his memory. But Will Luckie says I ought to let go of the past, says a new man would breathe life back into me. He says I'm wasting away and that I have a dry puff. "You'll have a bumper sticker on your car," he laughed, "that reads 'Dry puff behind the wheel'."

Of course I couldn't be mad at him, even though it was more of his nasty talk. He said it with care, like he really wanted to see me have a better life in relationships. Another thing he said is that it was wrong to vote the way a dead man would vote, for that reason alone. "You ought to vote for your own personal convictions," he said. "Sure, you'd likely come to the same decision on a candidate, but it would be your independent choice. Ain't you heard of women's lib?"

Well I know some about the woman libbers. I know they're a bunch of rich white women that feel bound up in girdles and brassieres. And I understand the symbolism. I ain't ignorant. I just don't know what them woman libbers have to do with me, besides the fact that I work for one in Miss Maureen. She says she's a "free spirit," and wishes she was an original suffragette but was born too late. "But now there is liberation everywhere," she'll say. "And I am not about to miss this fresh wave of freedom! Thank you, Betty Friedan."

"Who's that?" I asked her one time. And she not only told me, she ran and got this book for me to take home. *The Feminine Mystique*.

"More like The Feminine Mistake," Miss CeCe said, all snotty like.

"It was a breath of fresh air," her mama said. "And now there are so many more air-fresh female voices in the world—Kate Millett, for example. And, oh—*Fear of Flying*!"

"That is nothing but pornography, encouraging women to have random sex with whomever."

"My Lord, it's a *novel*. And that is *not* the gist."

"I am aware. That it is fiction."

"Have you read it?"

"Of course not. I don't read pornography."

"You might learn a thing or two."

"Mother, I am not having this salacious conversation with you! It gives me the dry heaves."

"Them heaves ain't the only things that's dry," Will might throw in. And I can't help it. It makes me giggle inside.

Yep, that CeCe is another story. She'll get on her soap box derby about how America is going to hell in a handbasket on account of loose morals and the youth. "Our country was great once upon a time," she'll say, "but I don't see how we'll ever make America great again, what with all of the free love and the drugs and the vulgarity of the hippies and what not. There's even race mixing going on. No offense, Lindia, but it goes against my Christian sensibility to think of the mongrelization of any race—even the black race. I mean, the Tower of Babel told that tale, didn't it?"

I didn't bother to say how some plantation owner or overseer or random white rapist or another had done a little bit here and there to lighten up my own skin. There was no point. Some folks are thinking listeners and some folks never will be.

She'll blabber on and on and on about the woman libbers and what all they be up to. "They want birth control pills handed out to adolescents just like lollipops, even though abortion is running rampant ever since that despicable decision last year. Do you know there's even talk of an abortion clinic in Gainesville? Just right down the road? In a college town!"

"Well, they certainly don't need those clinics in retirement communities," Miss Maureen will say.

"And do you know they put those teeny-tiny fetuses out with the trash? I saw pictures of it. Their teeny-tiny feet and teeny-tiny hands!"

"Have you ever heard of a teeny-tiny hemorrhage? No? Oh, that's right—a hemorrhage is a big thing—and that's how your third cousin Gloria from Atlanta died. Just hours after she had one of those back alley things."

"But you told me Cousin Gloria died of pneumonia!"

"Well now you know the harsh truth. And I hope you won't be casting any stones, Miss Christian Methodist."

But nothing will shut that child up when she gets tuned up. "Lord help us if they get the ERA through and Uncle Sam starts drafting young ladies into combat," she has said many times. "There will be all kinds of fraternizing, you just know there will. And probably the military will offer its own abortions to the young ladies. Imagine!"

"The draft ain't used anymore," Will Luckie might answer. "And as long as there's unwanted pregnancies and coat hangers in the world there's going to be abortions."

"Well, the bottom line is, they hate men is what," she'll say. "And they're mannish, like that Billie Jean King."

"Athletic is more accurate," Miss Maureen will come back, "and a little exercise wouldn't do your frame any harm."

"Well, if that's not the pot calling the kettle then I don't know what!"

"Oh, CeCe, the point is that we could all use a little exercise, and it doesn't make us mannish."

"And they are just plain rude and shrill and too demanding. I could never be like that. If they were at all attractive or demure and ladylike, they'd simply use their feminine wiles to get their way. Everybody knows how easy it is to twirl a man around your little finger."

Although I ain't never seen *her* do that—use "feminine wiles." She just yaps out orders to that pansy husband of hers—and to anyone else, including me. And whatever you think you know, she knows more. She'll go to hollering things about how the country's done turned away from Jesus and about how socialists and communists have taken over where democrats used to be. And you *know* Will is going to poke at her and poke at her until she stomps out the house and across the yard to that prissy husband. And I'll just be shaking my head at the furor that can be flung up behind politics these days.

Here's a thing: Will Luckie voted for George McGovern, just like I did. He's the only white man—the only white person in Pollard, aside from Miss Maureen, I bet—to vote against Nixon. We talked about it in the kitchen one day. It all went back to his time in the war.

"If I hadn't seen what it was like over yonder, I probably wouldn't vote for no damn body." He was leaning against the counter, holding a stem of Miss Maureen's crystal for a spit cup.

"Over in them jungles?" I had seen that scar where some jagged metal had hit him in the thigh. It was a nasty looking thing.

"Damn straight."

"Did you lean on the Lord?" I'd heard Henry say there wasn't no atheists in foxholes, but Will shot that down.

"I leaned on my *brothers*. Jar heads. Never thought much of those who yell for the Lord in a pinch and forget about what all he said the rest of the time."

I had to bend. "That's what my Henry always said. Trusting in the words of Jesus is as far as you need to go."

"That's the damn truth."

"But Miss Maureen says religion is the opium of the people."

He sighed. "Folks quote that quote out of context all the time. And that damn woman is all the time bragging up context. I'm going to have to have a talk with her." He chuckled. "A 'come to Jesus'."

"Sir?"

"Stop with the 'sir'. It's just that I made it my business to read up on communism. Karl Marx. The goddamn history of Viet Nam. Before I even joined up. Hell, I was in high school."

"You don't strike me as one to be so serious in school," I said, before I could check myself.

This time he laughed real big. "I wasn't. But I *was* curious about things I wanted or needed to know. I've never been a great student, but I ain't stupid. Know what I mean?"

"I sure do." And I did. Like I said, I ain't ignorant.

"Here's the whole quote. I thought it was so pretty I memorized it. Ready?"

"Yes, sir."

He gave me a squinty-eyed angry look.

"Yes, Mr. Will."

"Here it is: 'Religion is the sigh of the oppressed creature, the heart of a heartless world, and the soul of soulless conditions. It is the opium of the people'."

"That *is* right pretty. It gets us through."

"If that's your inclination."

"Why you went into the marines to begin with?"

"Adventure. Belonging. Seeing the world. All the things that son of a bitch recruiter at the bowling alley in Pensacola talked about to me and Greg."

"Greg?"

"My high school buddy. Old Greg. A k a 'GooGoo.' We were desperate to get the hell away from Pollard just as soon as them diplomas were handed off, and that damn recruiter made it sound like paradise, the USMC."

"Y'all was just babies."

"Yep. Playing pinball and picking our snot noses at the bowling alley. Fresh out of high school. PFC Jacobson swooped down on us like a vulture, talking about how we could go in as buddies and glide all the way through. Made Vietnam sound like a little mud hole where you had a lot of down time." He spit in that pretty crystal.

"Doesn't seem right to go after babies."

"No shit. Thing is, I knew the history, about all the war over yonder. Soldiering is in their damn blood. But at the same time Greg and me felt fierce about fighting the commies, you know?"

"Godless folks."

"It's not the godlessness we was fighting. It was the ideology."

I gave him a look, but he just kept on going.

"Khe Sanh is all it took to really put it into perspective," and his voice kind of trailed off while his eyes looked out into some other way of knowing. It's hard to describe.

"Miss Maureen said, too, that war changes folks," is what I offered.

He startled, then, "Yeah, that's a fact. You see that kind of shit—war shit—and you're going to either do one of two things: live your life like a fart in a whirlwind or live it like a fart that's thick enough to track a chicken in. You know?"

He did like that sometimes—talked real serious and deep one minute, then went over to crude and rude town the next. He would talk all proper grammar for a little minute and then go to redneckin' it up the next. I don't know why that surprised me because I do the same thing. I speak one way at work and another with Brenda and them. And there was my truly official "Mrs. Rev. Johnson" way to speak, which was soft, refined and mostly unused since my husband's funeral. Mr. Will was looking at me real hard, behind the "living life like a fart" thing, and I believed he wanted me to understand, so I nodded. "You were robbed," I said.

"Hell, yeah. Robbed, duped, fucked over forty different ways." He spat in the glass. "Motherfuckers."

"Henry always said it takes hard times to get folks to take action." I wasn't used to seeing him get mad like he was.

"Well nobody has to kick me in the head. Wasn't no way I was going to vote for that slimy motherfucker. And come, bleed, or blister, something's got to give. His ass needs to go and go fast."

"It's a shame, alright."

"It's way past a shame. It's against the law. His ass belongs in a cell."

I think that was the day I finally decided Mr. Will was all right.

He especially likes to come up in the kitchen when I'm cooking. And we don't just talk about the weather or any old election or President Nixon. Lord, we talk about all kinds of things I never thought I'd be like to talk to a man about, especially not no white man.

"It's in my blood," he told me one day. I was getting ready to fry up a batch of chicken. "It's in my gene pool," he said.

"What's that?" I got up from the metal table where I had chicken parts soaking in bowls of milk.

"The Luckie men, that's what. The Luckie men are drove by the urge to put it someplace. Any place. Long as it's warm, wet, and fuzzy." He grinned them pretty dimples at me.

"Fuzzy?"

"If it ain't fuzzy it's like to be an asshole, which ain't an option for the Luckie men." He squinted his eyes. "Or a watermelon. Which *would* be an option," and he laughed.

"Law, you better shut your mouth."

"You think I'm lying, but I ain't. The Luckie men been drove by that urge for generations. No shit."

"Is that a fact?"

"Yeah, anyplace warm, wet, and fuzzy, don't matter where." He took a sip of his drink. "You know, I had a Great Uncle Gipson—ol' 'Gip'—who was nearly seventy years old when he up and grew himself a beard. A nice, thick grey thing. But he shaved it off just as sudden like. When I asked him why—and I was only about nine years old—he told me, 'Son, I had to let it go on account of I kept waking myself up with my finger in my mouth'."

And we pure cackled and guffawed. And I didn't even blush. That's how natural Mr. Will makes it seem.

"Ol' Gip had a famous saying, quoted far and wide in the Luckie family. He liked to say, 'The best three things the Good Lord made is George Jones music, Pabst Blue Ribbon beer, and pussy. And if he made anything else as good he kept it for his own self 'cause I ain't never heard of it'."

"Sweet Jesus!"

"Ain't he, though? It all just proves my point. So go ahead, Lindia. Go ahead and name some places don't nobody like to go that's warm and wet."

"Lord, Mr. Will!" I took down some flour from the cabinet. "What about a ugly woman?" I asked.

"How ugly?"

"Dog faced ugly. Make you hurt to look at her," I said.

"Well, that's kind of tricky. It's okay to fuck an ugly woman long as you keep your eyes shut. See, there's a real goddamn serious danger if you open up your eyes and behold her ugliness."

"What danger is that?" That man could sure enough come up with some crazy ideas.

"Hell, if you look at a ugly woman while you're fucking her, your pecker'll fold up in the middle like a goddamn Barlow knife."

"Mr. Will, you crazy." But I laughed and thought what would Henry think of me talking like this to a white man? To any man? Fact is, I couldn't ever talk to any man like this—not Cletus, not even Henry himself.

"Truth is," he said, "I think it's a mortal sin not to fuck any woman that wants it. It's like the beginning of *Zorba the Greek*, you know? When he confesses to the priest that he wouldn't fuck the fat lady in the village? He knew that wasn't right. We're supposed to see the world through Jesus' eyes."

I didn't want to put Jesus in the same thought as what he was talking about, but I just couldn't let it go. It was a head scratcher, alright, but Mr. Will would draw you in so it didn't even feel like nasty talk. Before you knew it, you'd be asking him to tell more, like I did just then. "So a big old fat woman is appealing?"

He climbed up on a stool across the table from me. "Well, she is if you're looking through Jesus' eyes. I know some men that prefer a fat woman because they say she can brace off better, claim they like getting lost in all that skin, but it don't do nothing for me." That man looked flat serious. "But my daddy used to say that fucking a fat woman was like opening up the front door and fucking the world. He said you need a two by four tied crossways behind your ass to keep from falling in. But I never knew him to turn one down. He had the curse of the Luckie men worse than me."

"You ever knew a woman with that kind of curse?"

"Just one that comes close. My ex-girlfriend Marlayna. Hell, she ain't no more scared of a peter than a blind mule is of a singletree."

"One of them pyromaniacs?" I asked.

Will laughed. "Something like that."

"Well if she liked it so good, why'd you cut her loose?" I couldn't imagine no woman with the drive of somebody like Mr. Will.

"Mainly because she's crazy as hell, wants to be all up in your business. Where you going, Will? Where was you at last night, Will? Tried to trick me into marrying her. Lied about being pregnant."

"That's low-down." I went to flinging spoonfuls of lard into a cast iron skillet.

"More like crazy. She went a whole year really thinking she was pregnant. It's called a 'hysterical pregnancy.' Wrote me letters telling how big her belly was getting, how she was fixing up a nursery in her mama's trailer, how she was going to marry me when I come back."

"Lord, did she get all right?" I lit the gas stove and that lard begun to skate around on the skillet.

"Well, she went to fucking just about every bar jockey in the county. Cheated like crazy on her poor old husband that wasn't no kind of a man. Hell, I figured her pussy probably got so big and blowed out after all that, if she was to long-step across two cotton rows at a time, her guts would fall on the ground. I had to check it out when I got back from 'Nam." He laughed. "It was still warm and wet, so I had myself a few helpings."

"Lord, you're bad. But I know there's men like that. Sure do. Thank the good Lord Henry wasn't one of them. Nor one of them fairy men."

"A pixie?"

"Well, you know."

"Here's a thing," he said, "and I know I give old Winnie a hard time, being a goober gobbler and all. But the truth is, if it's in your nature then it's in your nature."

"Say what?"

"Like, take them Navajo tribes. Hell a lot of the Indian tribes didn't never bat an eye at a homosexual. Called them 'two spirit' people. I read all about it."

"You don't say." I never knew what to think about homosexual people except that it must be some kind of pervert thing. But Mr. Will kept on.

"Like a man that acted all feminine or a woman that was a hunter like man. The tribe just let them be who they naturally were. No big deal. I keep rubbing Winston's nose in it because it's just plain dishonest of him. Unnatural, to deny his nature."

"That so?" It struck me right then. That was just one more reason for the misery in that marriage. And that poor woman not ever getting none on top of it all.

"See, the Indians believed that it was the natural state—the spirit—that counted. Were you a person of character and kindness? Did you contribute to the good of the tribe? Didn't matter beyond that."

"I'm going to have to think on that. Anyway, that's man and woman. You said you had to put it, well, *anywhere*. What's that called?" I skidded the lard around a little more, helping it along.

"Hell if I know. But it was in my own daddy's nature, that's for damn sure. He didn't hesitate to put it any place warm and wet. Hell, even up under a mule's tail."

"Mercy!"

"It's true."

"Ain't done it!"

"Damn sure did. I seen it. I was nine years old and I remember getting off the school bus one day and walking up to the house. I was hunting my daddy for some reason, so I walked to the back clearing where he had this little old piece of shit peckerwood sawmill set up, and I'll be damned if I didn't come up on my daddy fucking the sawmill mule."

"Law to Glory!" I was thinking that if anybody else told such a tale it would be downright filthy, but Mr. Will didn't care enough to make it nasty. He had me laughing so hard I couldn't get my breath.

"Hell, if I'm lying I'm dying. Had that mule tied to a sapling and backed up to a stump where he was standing up on it, just a-banging into the flanks of that thing."

"You ain't right."

"Hell, it's a fact. And you know the most amazing part of the story?"

"No, law. Don't make me laugh no more."

But he did. "The most amazing part of the story is that sawmill mule had it hiked up for him. Way up in the air. I mean it was lifted up on the side edges of its back hooves with its tail throwed up in the air, just a-straining for more."

I liked to fell over laughing. I'd done been flouring the chicken parts and a white puff of Gold Medal came up like a cloud.

"My daddy was known to be—you know, well-endowed." He held out his arm and indicated a point in the crook of his elbow. "The thing was that big, anyway. So that mule did enjoy it, I reckon."

"You know you ain't right," I said.

"I inherited my daddy's better physical characteristics," he said, and he grinned.

"Law, hush! Here comes Miss Maureen."

"Warm and wet," he said, right when Miss Maureen and that mean-spirited daughter of hers walked in the room. Mr. Will had been living there for a couple of months, and her daughter wasn't no kind of glad about it. That melted lard begun to pop a little.

"What a ruckus," Miss Maureen said. "Is he going on about that silly sawmill mule?"

"Good Lord," Miss CeCe said. "Don't ya'll know how the sound carries in this big old house? We could hear every word. Thank God we don't have company. I just don't understand how you can boast about something so sick as that."

"Well, CeCe, country farm boys have a whole different frame of reference for sexual escapades and experimentation, you know," Miss Maureen said.

"Good Lord," Miss CeCe said again. "So it comes to this. Bestiality." She had gone pale as a cotton ball.

"It's not as unusual as you might like to think, Miss Priss. I suppose the barnyard offers a menagerie of possibilities for little country boys. Men, too, apparently," Miss Maureen said. "No sense in letting Catherine the Great have all the fun." And she and Mr. Will went to laughing.

"There you go, Mother, repeating a vicious rumor about a monarch who was so unpopular they put out lies about her! And that's how it goes with me, all because of you and Will!"

"Heavens," Miss Maureen said, "I simply do not follow that reasoning. And are you comparing yourself to royalty? I mean, I know that's why you bought that silly Royal Empress phone."

"Floral Empress, not *royal,* although the Calhouns are not unlike royalty around here. If you wreck our reputation and we become grossly unpopular, well, the rumors can get out of control, just like with poor Catherine."

"You have my word that I will not spread tales of you copulating with an equine."

"Copulating with *anything*," Will murmured, then, "Hell, any kind of stud would help with that butt bug of yours—that crazy, twitchy eyeball, too. You'd be in a world of calm."

Miss CeCe was spitting venom by then, "How dare you advise me? And what has become of you, Mother? What kind of sleazy talk are you cozying up to? Are you insane yet again? All this nasty, nasty talk! And my eyeball is none of your business."

"Look here," Mr. Will said. "If a man's got a load needs letting, then it don't matter where he puts it. That shit'll go bad on you. And it don't do to have a load go bad on you. You could take a case of nut cancer after that, after all them poisons go noxious up in your goozle and your gonads."

"I am sick unto death," Miss CeCe yelled, "of your theories about how keeping seminal fluids and noxious gases in check causes diseases. I am sick of your fixation on the most disgusting of bodily functions. Winston is a doctor. Why don't you ask him if your perverse theories are anywhere near the truth?"

"Well, you know I did just that. Old Winnie got a kick out of the whole notion. I think it made his day." Will pulled the pouch of Beechnut out of his front pocket, some kind of slow.

I went to dropping that chicken in the skillet real fast and busy cause I knew Miss CeCe was just before throwing a screaming fit. But Miss Maureen jumped in right then. "Lindia, CeCe and I want to start planning our annual Fourth of July luncheon. It's only two weeks away, you know. I think we'll have the Burgesses over, so that's four more. And then Will's guest, of course."

"Will's guest?" Miss CeCe was going madder by the second.

Miss Maureen didn't bat an eyelash. "Yes, sugar, I have just about convinced Will to have an old friend over."

"Greg McGeehee," Will said. "Used to call him 'GooGoo' when we played on the football team together. But I don't think GooGoo's ready for this shit."

"Yes, Greg McGeehee," Miss Maureen repeated. "He's been out of the marines for a while and having a bad time, Will says. So I think we should take him in on such a patriotic day as the Fourth."

"Bad idea," Will said.

"But I want to meet some of your friends," Miss Maureen whined. "You aren't ashamed of us, are you?"

"My Lord and Savior, Mimi. Even Will doesn't want him here."

"Speaking of your Lord and Savior, don't you think it would be a Jesus-ish thing to do, CeCe? A charitable thing? To invite a wounded war veteran to Fourth of July luncheon?"

"It ain't that I don't want him here," Mr. Will said. "It's just that he don't know the way it works. He can be unpredictable. It's that East Pollard chip."

"East Pollard chip?" Miss CeCe was an echo.

"Something like class warfare," Will said. "He might not be comfortable with all the rules and refinery. And, like I said, he can be a loose cannon. He came away from that sorry jungle with a lot more—I just don't know if he'd want to come here."

"Of course he wouldn't," Miss CeCe said. "He would be as out of place as a nun in a brothel house, and you all know it. I mean, we're having the Burgesses! And he's a—what is his name again?"

"McGeehee," Mr. Will said, real slow. "GooGoo McGeehee." I declare that man's attitude took a turn when Miss CeCe pressed that snobbiness of hers.

"My God, is he one of those McGeehees that live all nested up like rats out the Pipeline Road?" Miss CeCe said.

"Well, I don't know," Miss Maureen said. "Does he live in a rat's nest, Will?"

"Only when there ain't no room in the sewer," Mr. Will kind of chuckled. He didn't like it when Miss CeCe went to knocking that GooGoo man. Not one bit, it was plain to me.

"I will not have it," Miss CeCe said.

"And you are not the head of this family yet. And I *will* have it."

"Good Lord, Mother. Why don't you just send out the city sanitation department to ride around the county and collect up all the trash they can find and dump it in the living room?"

"CeCe! I do not like that trash metaphor and you know very well I don't."

"Well it's true!" that child yelled. "And it's bad enough you have everyone talking about us because of Will. Haven't you done enough? No, of course not! Now you're inviting his friends to come for Independence Day!"

"Oh, don't exaggerate. It's just one friend. And just for Independence luncheon."

"It's America's birthday, ain't it?" Mr. Will said, but Miss CeCe had lost the last speck of her temper.

"Grandma Lucie was a *grand dame*," she hollered at Miss Maureen. "And you used to be one, too. And I want to be one, dammit! No, I am *going* to be one, whether you keep this hideous creature in your life or not. I will!" And she slammed the door so hard on her way out that one of the window panes shattered and glass hit that floor with a big old loud crash.

Miss Maureen shook her head. "Lord, sometimes I don't know whose child she is," she said.

That was around the time I come to know, in a deep down way, that Miss Maureen was sure enough different, not at all like her old self. Mr. Will had done changed her slant on things to where she was happy and laughing all the time. Used to, she would get in flat out mean fights with Miss

CeCe over the littlest things, and the big things would turn into all-out wars. Like when Mr. Wickham passed.

Being married to a minister, I seen many a funeral, and Henry and me learned a lot about folks from his years of preaching eulogies. And he always told me everybody should let it be known and put it on paper how you want your funeral to be, else the kin folks will go to flinging and flailing over it. And that's just what happened, 'cause Mr. Wickham didn't leave no instructions. So Miss Maureen and Miss CeCe had a Pensacola funeral director come to the house to talk over the arrangements. That was when Miss Maureen let it be known that she wanted to have that man burnt up like a Chinaman. I could hear them from out in the kitchen.

"But the cemetery plot!" Miss CeCe hollered. "We all own a cemetery plot. And nobody in this town gets cremated. Nobody!"

"And I say he *will* be cremated! And that is that!" Then she said to the funeral man, real sweet-like, "How much are the urns, precious?"

"An urn!" CeCe said. "It's barbaric! It's medieval! What will everyone say when there is no coffin?"

"Well, goddamn, CeCe, we can afford both. Let's buy one of each, only we'll bring Wickham back in a nice urn after we have a funeral for the coffin."

CeCe went to squalling then. "No! I want his body at the cemetery! I want to visit him at the cemetery," she booed and hooed. "I want to put flowers on his grave and pull the weeds and have an ornate headstone with cherubs."

"Show me your urns," Miss Maureen said to the funeral man, who drew a catalogue from his briefcase while CeCe went on moaning and sobbing.

When it was done and that man left, Miss Maureen had decided to find an urn someplace else, since she didn't like none of his and said they were overpriced anyway for what you got.

"What do you care if it's expensive?" Miss CeCe yelled. "You could buy urns for the populace of the entire state of Florida."

"Oh, sugar, I don't think they'd all want urns."

"But you could! And I shouldn't have to keep that propane tank in my yard, either, just because you think it heats water cheaper! You are rich! What do you care what it costs to heat water or how much you have to pay for my DD's urn?"

"That is enough, CeCe. You know it's in poor taste to talk about how rich I am."

Miss CeCe took on so bad then that her husband had to inject her with something to knock her out.

Still, when the day of Mr. Wickham's burial came, that young'un put on a big funeral for a two-thousand-dollar coffin—an empty coffin all covered up in a big old pile of flowers. She had finally got her mama to promise not to let on it was empty, and when them ashes was delivered in a week or two they were in what looked like a cloth flour sack packed in a cardboard box. Miss Maureen dumped them ashes in a Tupperware tub, put the lid on, burped it, and wrote "Wick" on the lid in black marker. Then she put that tub in the trunk of her car and rode it all over the place. Sometimes, I'd be in the car, too, right there in the back seat, and it give me the chills to think about her dead husband there in the trunk, right behind me. And every once in a while she'd go to talking to him, telling him the gossip or the latest news about that Richard Nixon.

"The feces have hit the fan, Wick," she said, not long after that Richard Nixon had done been inaugurated. "Your man is going to get pitched out on the curb. And the Good Lord knows what will happen to my brother. He just might be out of a job, thanks to your man."

One morning, when we were leaving out for the grocery store, Miss Maureen couldn't get the car to crank because she had left her lights on and the battery had gone dead. "Well goddammit, Wick," she said to the back seat, where I was sitting. "Couldn't you have turned off the goddamn lights?"

Finally, Miss CeCe wondered one evening what happened to her daddy's ashes. When it come to light that he had been in the trunk of the Lincoln for upwards of three months, Miss CeCe pitched another screaming fit. "All this time?" she shrieked. "He's been in the trunk with the tire iron, the spare, and the Rand McNally Road Atlas of the United States? Instead of at least in an expensive urn on the mantel?"

"Well, I have grown used to having him there," Miss Maureen said. "I'm comfortable keeping him there for the time being. Besides, I want to find the right urn for my living room mantel. Something exotic, I think."

"My DD's remnants are sliding around in a hot old car trunk in a Tupperware container while you smoke cigarettes and listen to the radio. Did you at least burp it for freshness?"

"Well you know I did, CeCe."

"But my God! You throw groceries—dog and cat food and fertilizer in the trunk of that car, right up on top of Daddy! Every time you career around a corner you send him end over end I'll bet. How do you think he is going to rest in any kind of peace? How? You don't have one iota of respect for him!"

"Goddammit, CeCe, he's *my* husband and if I want him riding around in *my* car with me, then that is how it shall be, and you just need to get that through your head right this minute. Some people put the Virgin Mary or Jesus on their dashboard or hang a St. Christopher from the rear view. Well, I keep your daddy in the trunk to look out for me."

"And, oh my dear Lord in heaven, everybody knows that you buy out all the sales at the Piggly Wiggly. Never mind that you're rich enough that you don't have to. Do you mean to tell me you threw those two dozen frozen chickens you bought at the poultry sale on top of my DD?"

"Well, goodness, CeCe, Wickham loved himself a fryer."

I thought that child was going to start steaming from her ear holes, like them cartoons. "What if you have a wreck? What if you get rear-ended?"

"I told you, your daddy is looking out for me."

"You're evil!" Miss CeCe shrieked out before she broke the same windowpane she usually does when she's slamming the door in the middle of a hissy fit. I think Mr. Winston probably had to inject her again.

The next day, Miss Maureen asked me to help her fill another Tupperware tub with ashes from the charcoal grill. Then she mixed in bits of hammered chicken bones. She put the lid on, burped it, and wrote "Wick" on the top with a black Magic Marker.

"If I know CeCe, she will go behind my back to get her daddy's ashes," Miss Maureen said. So we put the decoy ashes in the trunk and the real ones up under her bed. And did you know that woman was right? Her own daughter, her flesh and blood, flat went into the trunk of that Lincoln Town Car one evening, took that tub, had the grave dug up, the coffin opened, put that Tupperware tub full of fake ashes in it, and had it buried again, just that quick. I ain't lying.

Now, to my mind, that is low down. Anybody that'd steal a dead man from his widow is bound for hellfire and there ain't no more to it. But you know what Miss Maureen did? She didn't let on nothing about knowing Miss CeCe had done stole what she thought to be her daddy's ashes. She just put that box of the real Mr. Wickham back in the trunk and let her daughter think she never noticed he was gone. That was the first time I seen potential in that woman for a Holy nature. Somebody that can turn the other cheek in the way of Christ is a person with a good and Holy nature. After that, I felt a little bit different about working there. And when Mr. Will came, like I said, things got even better.

When I go to Glory, I plan to be buried next to Henry up in Warm Springs, Georgia, where we bought our plots. The coffin is paid for, too, a fine, steel box, embossed with angels, with blue satin lining. I want to be buried in the blue floral print shirtwaist dress that Henry liked so much. I have it packed away in mothballs, way in the back of my closet. I want my Bible with the gold lettering on the cover in my hands and my mama's gold cross round my neck. And I want that gold cross to shine fire at whoever looks at it, so they know I'm bound for Heaven's gates.

7
Cecelia

The Fourth of July luncheon was one of the really huge straws Will put across my back, and I know it will now and for all eternity be a classic standard, an oldie but goodie, in the repertoire of Pollard gossip. Of course, it was bound to be a disaster, what with that extra piece of trash Mother and Will had invited into our home. I was partially vindicated, however, because even Mother realized, if only for a short while, just how disgusting and Aboriginal that McGeehee person was. As I say, my vindication was short-lived, for, by the end of the evening Will had wormed his way into my own psyche in such a way that I was nauseated for days and unsettled for weeks thereafter.

I have to explain that the town of Pollard hovers above Pensacola, above Cantonment, the county seat, where an enclave of paper mills purges its rancid-smelling smog into the air that eventually finds its way to us. It is a town divided by Burnt Corn creek, which separates the classes and their respective blood lines quite effectively, before syringing into the Conecuh River. Those on the east side of the creek, in East Pollard, work in the paper mills, or closer to Pensacola, in the chemical plants, or in the oil fields north of us, or in pulpwood. They have their own mayor, city council, and schools (via the county school system). Their side of the creek is a dingy conglomeration of Pentecostal churches, a Bill's dollar store, a Little Quickie, two gas stations, and shotgun houses, some passably neat in their working class simplicity, others ramshackle, shedding boards and peeling paint.   But the Pipeline Road is the lowest of the low, winding out toward the oil fields above the most dramatic curves of the Conecuh River. The timber has been clear-cut in broad sections, leaving gaping wounds in the woods. And clinging like cockleburrs and festering scabs to those clear-cut swaths are scores of rusted out trailers and campers, clustered up by clans of kinfolk and others of an assortment of inbred populations who live by rules outside the realm of the civilized world. They are truly subhuman, guided only by Neanderthal urges and emotions. They collect junked cars and welfare checks. They spend a great deal of time in jail. They spend an inordinate amount of time looking at NASCAR races on the TV, watching souped up Chevys go round and round and round in circles, into perpetuity. They frequent the bowling alleys, bail bondsmen, and pawn shops in seedy areas of Pensacola. They spend many recreational hours in sleazy bars, gyrating into one another and beating one another about the head for no apparent reason. They have no appreciation or respect for esthetics or etiquette. And these are the people my mother wanted to sit down and have Fourth of July luncheon with Mayor Burgess, Kathryn Burgess, Bitsy Burgess Swafford, and her husband James Robinson Swafford, Jr., Esquire.

West Pollard, on the other hand, is simply known as Pollard, and the Burgesses founded the town, generations back. It is a solidly middle-class community, with clean streets, where folks edge and manicure their lawns in order to vie for awards each month. There are two cavernous churches with stained glass windows, the Methodists being a notch or two higher than the Baptists on the social scale. There is a small downtown, a new shopping center out toward the suburbs, and a country club that excludes those on the lower middle class fringes along with, of course, the coloreds. I should have mentioned that our coloreds, along with the East Pollard low classes, are bussed to the county schools in Cantonment, just twelve miles south. Integration. It's too bad about that, but we were smart enough to get around it when the hammer dropped in '69. We just started up our own all white private Christian school. Our former city school was made up of two classroom buildings, plus a cafeteria and a gym, all of which we shut down, just to re-open it as Burgess Christian Academy. It is supported quite adequately by the churches, the taxpayers, and the few truly wealthy families among us, including, of course, the Calhouns.

More subtly, because there are only a few very wealthy families at the tippy top of the social pyramid flanked by a scattering of the upper middle class, there is a great contest amongst the other citizens, the more middle of the middle class—and some of the lower middle, depending on pedigree—to be invited to our parties and teas and lunches and brunches. I know it sounds snooty, but it is a fact. I did not create the situation, mind you. I simply function within its boundaries.

Actually, there is also competition at the top, for even we are not immune to it. I already told you that, post Will Luckie, I was losing some of my prominence to Bitsy Burgess Swafford, who has been my best friend and rival since we were born. She has always held the fact that her blood is bluer than mine over my head, even though my family has tons more land and money than hers. She has always, ever since high school, made snide remarks about Catholics, "new money," and, of course, mother's odd behavior.

"I admire you so much," she said, tossing her long, black waves, when Mother had her grand breakdown, back when Bitsy and I were teenagers. "You are so strong to hold your head up when Miss Maureen puts on such a show of insanity. Not to mention that she was born Catholic. I just wish I could be more like you." The evil bitch. She was loving Mother's latest foray into madness because it gave her a way to feel superior to me.

"I don't think there has ever been any insanity in my family," she will say, even now. "Of course, James says I am crazy for him, but who wouldn't be? He is such a man's man, so athletic and outdoorsy." Well. I don't have to tell you that is a swipe at Winston's manhood. Lord, everything that comes out of that bitch's mouth is a dig at me. So you can just imagine how gleeful she was at Fourth of July luncheon, my own mother having handed her a double-barrel load of ammunition in the form of Will Luckie and GooGoo McGeehee.

The house was decorated beautifully, naturally, which mother has done up for the entire month of every major holiday. Just prior to July, the decorator came from Pensacola to hang bunting from the interior and exterior bannisters and railings, to place patriotic decorations in practically every room, as well as on the front balcony and around the gazebo that faces the swimming pool. There were red, white, and blue streamers and flags on the mantles, and ornate candelabras, and Grandma Lucie's silverware sparkled like treasure against the red linen tablecloth.

"GooGoo" had not arrived when the rest of the party was having cocktails in Mother's den, bathed in the glow of true blue American patriotism. The men, all save Will, were handsome in their requisite colors, the aforementioned red, white, and blue. Our family has always dressed this way for the Fourth, you see. This is just the way we do things. The ladies wore dressy dresses, Mother and Bitsy in blue sequins and silk, I in red and white satin with intricate blue beadwork, and Mrs. Burgess in red with blue piping. We were a picture of pure Lady Liberty love. Of course, Will, too, had dressed for dinner—cowboy boots, khakis, no belt, and a green plaid shirt that offset the blue of his eyes—in honor of our nation's birthday. And Will was, as usual, the center of attention, telling off color jokes, plucking that infernal guitar, slurping on my aged mother's neck while she cooed and giggled. In a while he began leading the group in singing patriotic songs.

That was when Bitsy took me aside and took a few slices at me regarding Will. "It must be grueling for you," she said, "watching that man with your mother. Imagine what your daddy would say." She sparkled in her size four blue-sequined dress, diamond earrings throwing more light against the backdrop of her black, black hair, dyed and sculpted by Mr. DeFrancisco at the House of Hair.

"It's quite alright, sugar. You see, I look at it as a chance to rise above and be a good Christian," I said, just as cucumber cool as you please. "And not many people get such a chance to grow in a spiritual way. Oh, but you wouldn't understand that, because everything is so perfect in your life that you don't have any tests from God." I let that sink in. "Of course, it won't be much longer now. He is bound to do something to alienate her."

"Probably," Bitsy said. "Then again, he gives one pause."

"Meaning?" She was being a bit unpredictable this night.

"Well, he does have a winning way that you just don't expect from those people. And I have to admit he's good looking."

I studied Will, who was strumming that fool guitar while they sang "God Bless America," which he bastardized by singing "brand that I love" rather than "land that I love." My God. His eyes were closed and the dimples played upon his tanned cheeks as he sang. "I guess so," I said, cringing inside, but determined to pick her brain. "In a rough kind of way."

"Oh, absolutely a rough way," Bitsy said, and cut her eyes at him. "And he's so attentive to her. And so affectionate."

I could take no more. "Good Lord, Bitsy, it is nauseating to watch."

"Well of course it is," she said, too quickly, "because he is so much younger and so—'East Pollard.' But if he were her age and from a good family it would be wonderful, don't you think? A perfect match?"

"But he isn't and never will be," I reminded her.

"I suppose," she sighed and watched him for a few seconds. "It just seems such a sad waste of a good man."

Of course, I was floored yet again at the way Will Luckie was able to infect those around me with his charm, appalled at the unseemly manner in which Bitsy was, in a word, drooling over him, yet I couldn't resist getting a dig at her while her guard was down. "I know it's hard for you, Sweetie. I mean James is so handsome and all. But he's so caught up in his law practice and his hunting trips— kind of like my daddy always was, you know?" I paused again, to let the silence emphasize the image of my womanizing DD and his drunken band of merry men. "James just doesn't *worship* you— isn't the type to worship any woman--the way somebody like Will would. Can you imagine?"

But I did not get a rise out of her. It was disturbing. All she did was stare at Will, nodding, and the air was thick with yet another layer of sexual tension that dripped like the wax on Mother's red, white and blue candles. Yet again, I wanted to scream that they were all insane, but at that moment my fortunes turned. Enter GooGoo McGeehee, already three sheets to the wind, loud-mouthed in the most grating of ways, and more disgusting than Will Luckie ever thought about being.

He was a big man who smelled of aged body odor, alcohol, and somewhere, as an under-smell, a hint of patchouli. His long hair was pulled back in a ponytail that hit between his shoulder blades, and he wore a t-shirt: "Grateful Dead San Francisco 69 Fillmore Auditorium 12/19/69." He made a stumbling entrance, carrying an empty plate and a roll of tin foil, shouting his greetings to Will, shaking hands too jovially with the mayor and company, making inappropriate comments about his foray into Pollard society. "My mama didn't believe me when I told her I was eating today at the big house," he said. "She liked to fell out. Course that could have been all them screwdrivers she's done drunk today. Anyway, she made me promise to bring her a plate. He held out the tin foil. "That okay? Mama's stove up bad with Old Arthur."

"Arthritis?" Winston said, politely engaging in talk of illness, asking questions, promising to look her over if she would come in to the clinic. Mother carried GooGoo's empty plate and aluminum foil out to the kitchen.

"What a lovely shirt," Bitsy cooed. "Did you attend such a concert?"

"Hell, no—I was in the jungle in '69, with Will. USMC. It's just a great t-shirt is all. Great band."

Will sat across the room and picked on the strings of the guitar, letting GooGoo drive the conversation, to everyone's—eventually even Mother's—chagrin. He had plopped down in my DD's leather recliner and took the Wild Turkey on the rocks that my hostess of a mother delivered unto him.

"Don't drink whiskey much," he said. "Turns me into a crazy man."

"That it does," Will said, smiling.

"Done told you I been drinking vodka with Mama all morning," he said. "She likes to bring in July Fourth with a shit load—s'cuse me—a bunch of screwdrivers. I felt like I ought to celebrate with her today, being as how I didn't get home till after last July Fourth, ain't been around for a few July Fourths before that. Vietnam. And then I had to spend some time in The Haight, see for myself what all the fuss was." His face was ruddy with booze, but he undertook his date with his companion bourbon in enthusiastic gulps. "Whoo! This is some fine shit. This here's the good stuff, I mean."

"The Haight," Bitsy mused. "Haight Ashbury is what you're referencing, correct? And what did you think?"

"Well," GooGoo reached a paw beneath his shirt, "I been wearing my love beads ever since." A disc of a peace symbol dangled from the multi-colored strand. "These ones have sure seen an orgy or two," he grinned. "I use the peace charm to draw 'em out, if you know what I mean."

Will guffawed. Bitsy looked puzzled. Mayor Burgess, patriotic to the nth degree, attempted to be respectful of GooGoo's status as a U.S. veteran and engage him in conversation about the death and glory of the front lines. "So you've just returned from Vietnam within the past year," he said.

"Well, I got sprung in '72, but, like I said, I decided to see America. Thumbed my way back across from Cali."

"You hitchhiked?" Bitsy said, as in awe.

"Sure. It's the only way to travel."

"I don't expect it's the way to travel to and from Vietnam," I said, challenging his ridiculous, sweeping statement about travel. But he did not miss a beat.

"Yeah, Vee-et-nam," the last syllable of which he said to rhyme with jam before waxing philosophical. "The Land of the Itty Bitty Tittie. Me and Will both. Will got busted in the thigh and I got burnt up pretty bad on my back, down to my knee-backs," he said, indicating the scar that emerged from his shirt collar and wrapped around his neck. "Damn gooks roasted me like a goddamn marshmeller. No shit—s'cuse me. That's why Will beat me back. He had a quicker recovery plus a earlier injury."

"*Plus*, you were busy frolicking with the love children in San Francisco for a spell," Bitsy said.

"I had to get me a look at the hippie world, and that was the place to do it. Then I decided to become one. A hippie. I bought me a love bug, plastered a bunch of flower power stickers on 'er, growed my hair, and gathered up some love beads. That was all she wrote."

"Not too many hippie freaks around here," Bitsy said.

"Yep. Rural idiocy," GooGoo said, and got a chuckle out of Will.

"Excuse me?" Bitsy's voice dripped with pure umbrage. "Are you calling someone an idiot?"

To which both men broke into unbridled laughter. It went all over me. "It's very rude to exchange private jokes in a social setting," I said, to even louder guffaws.

"Burns are a bitch to heal quickly," Winston offered, choosing a curse word and a change of subject, I am sure, to make our guest feel more at home *and* to quell some of the tension.

GooGoo took the cue. "No shit. And the government still owes me some more skin treatments. Ya'll wouldn't believe how bad those that's wounded get treated."

"That is a pure shame," Mrs. Burgess said, clucking her tongue as she "tisked."

"So how did you find the country? The people?" Mayor Burgess prodded.

"GooGoo and me had read up on the religion," Will said. "Mainly the Buddhism and all that. And a good deal of history."

"Oh, dear," Mrs. Burgess put in. "You boys read books?"

"And there it is," GooGoo said, with a sweep of his arm. "There's the classism. East Pollard boys are stupid, have a hard time walking and dipping snuff at the same time. Can't even jerk off and imagine a pussy at the same time."

"Easy, now, GooGoo," Will said. "Some folks don't know no better."

"I do apologize," Mrs. Burgess stammered. "I spoke without thinking."

"You damn sure did. I went and got myself marshmeller-roasted, just to come back and have folks think I'm a goddamn imbecile."

"What I found out," Will continued, in some kind of effort to soothe his friend, "is that the Frenchies brought Catholic doings to Vietnam, so the Catholics had the power. Of course the natives—the ones with no good conscience— sucked up to the French Catholics big time. And were the natives good Christians about it? Were they, GooGoo?"

"Hell no," GooGoo piped up, in call-and-response fashion. "They were ass holes, like they've always been. Like, listen at this." He was fidgety, excited to be imparting wisdom to the folks in the big house. "Remember that Buddhist monk that torched hisself back years ago? Remember seeing it on the TV? I was young—It made a harsh impression upon me."

"As self-immolation does," Bitsy murmured, and the others echoed a semi-respectful murmur.

"That somebitch was protesting the damn Catholics and what assholes they were to the other religious groups. Can you believe that? I didn't even know there was Catholics in country. Thanks to the Frogs. And that damn monk didn't even move a muscle, just burned hisself right the fuck up, cool as a refrigerator."

I was off-put to say the least. "Can we not talk about such disturbing topics on America's birthday?"

"Hell no, now ya'll, look at this: not only did he roast hisself—and I call *my*self roasted—hell, he ain't even budged, all meditated into the sky and all. And here's the kicker. When they went to do an official cremation on him, they found his heart intact, not damaged, not even swinged. Don't that give you some chills? How about that for salvation?"

"Nobody gets saved or goes to heaven after a suicide," I said. "That's Bible-clear."

"Fuck a Bible," GooGoo snapped, to a collective intake of breath, all save Will Luckie, who actually chuckled.

"How dare you?" I was on the verge of pulling the plug on his crude, offensive utterings. Thankfully, at the time I did not follow through.

"I'll tell what the asshole Bible reading Catholics said about that monk. What some government high-up Catholic Viet-cunt said—she said she'd be tickled to go to another monk barbecue. Yep, called it a damn BBQ."

"Buddhists are strange," Bitsy sighed, the "c-word" rolling right off her back.

"Were the people receptive to our being there?" James said, switching gears. He had an agenda after all. He was always fighting with his father-in-law about the wisdom of the war.

"I didn't talk much politics with them folks," GooGoo said. "But them Buddhists was fine, and they sang some real nice chants. Calming. And I'll tell you what: me and Will damn sure had some women, didn't we, boy?"

"Yep," Will said, focused on tuning his guitar.

"I mean I landed over there and wasn't nothing but some women. Then, whenever I'd get me a little R & R, I'd head for them Philippines straight out and lay up for days on end trying to get my money all spent up, didn't I, Will? Them Philippines had some flat sure fine whores."

"Normally I don't approve of such goings on," Mrs. Burgess said, sipping her vodka and tonic. "But soldiers at war have to keep their morale up, I say."

"Absolutely," her husband chimed in. "And the Philippines have always been hospitable to our servicemen. I was in the Pacific Theater in WW two, so I had occasion to tour the islands before the lid blew."

"But sweetie," Mrs. Burgess whined. "Surely *you* didn't visit *those* women."

The mayor blushed.

"Well if he did, he found some sure enough good looking women. And cheap? Hell, for twenty dollars a day you could get you a damn pretty one who would cook you a chicken, clean your room, wash your clothes and gear, press them trousers and shine them shoes. All of that, plus a—you know, a good honk on a root." And he winked at Mayor Burgess who laughed and winked back.

Kathryn Burgess gave Mother a quizzical look. Mother rolled her eyes dramatically. "Soldiers," she said as if to explain the, pardon the pun, thrust of the conversation.

"Will knows it's the truth," GooGoo said. "Don't you, boy?"

"Yep," Will said. "You was like a blind dog in a meat house. I'm surprised you ain't drawed back a nub the way you carried on." He began *strumming* the guitar, softly—"This Land is Your Land."

Mother went over and whispered something to Will, probably something about not encouraging GooGoo too much, the first sign that she was beginning to regret the invitation. Will looked back up at her and shrugged.

"Actually," Winston said. "You are quite lucky. I mean, what with venereal diseases and all."

Bitsy nudged me, nothing but tickled with our wayward guest. We sat shoulder to shoulder on the leather love seat. "Winston, my God," I said.

"No," GooGoo said. "The doc is right. Hey, doc. I bet you treat some sure enough eat up folks, huh?" He seemed genuinely interested in hearing what Winston might have to say concerning venereal diseases, and I cringed inside.

Will walked over to the bar and brought the bottle of Wild Turkey back to where GooGoo sat in my DD's chair. It was almost as if Will were saying to Mother, "I damn sure *will* encourage him and here's a bottle of whiskey for him, just to make my point." And it worked. Mother's face clouded over like I had not seen it do in a long while.

"Hell," Will said. "The doc there can tell you anything you want to know about VD or crabs or any of that army shit. You ever had crabs, Mayor?"

"You don't live like we did across the Pacific and not get the crabs. All manner of crawlers and jungle rot."

"What are crabs?" Mrs. Burgess asked. "You are not discussing the crustaceans, I presume?"

"Hey Doc," GooGoo said. "Ain't you worried about treating nobody with the crabs? I heard they's some that can jump six feet or better. You ever got any on you from a patient?"

"Well, no," Winston said in his doctorly voice. "They actually--"

"And what about this here? I got a question." GooGoo poured a generous amount of Wild Turkey into his glass.

"What is that?" Winston said.

"I know crabs can scutter like crazy sideways, but I never knew one to jump," Mrs. Burgess said.

Bitsy nudged me again and giggled.

"I always wanted to ask this to a doctor. It's about something they told us over yonder." GooGoo lit a cigarette, taking a little longer than necessary to line the lighter up with the end of the cigarette. "They told us there was some kind of clap over there that couldn't even be treated. Something penicillin can't even touch."

"I don't believe that is accurate," Winston said. "Who told you this?"

"Surely they don't clap their little pinchers together," Mrs. Burgess said. "And I am quite certain they don't jump or hop at all."

"Hell, the government, that's who. Showed us films, gave us pamphlets. Said there was some kind of souped-up dose of the clap would rot your pecker off. That true?"

"I honestly don't think—" Winston said

"Regardless, it's prudent to be careful about letting the mule out of the barn, I always say," Mayor Burgess opined.

"You hear that, Will? That's exactly what I thought. They lied just to try to keep us away from that stuff. Now, you know you ain't going to keep no troops away from none of that stuff."

"What stuff?" Mrs. Burgess said. "My, this a confusing--"

"The stuff that dreams are made of, Mother" Bitsy said.

"Since time immemorial," Mayor Burgess nodded.

"Perchance to eat?" Mother said, a little too brightly. "I do believe it is almost ready."

"Damn, Doc, I got a million questions for you," GooGoo said.

"And he's got the answers," Will said, encouraging him further. I thought what a fool he was being, risking Mother's wrath out of prideful male stubbornness.

"You know what, Doc?" GooGoo said. "There's one thing I would have asked you if I ain't never been over yonder and seen for myself."

"What's that?" Winston was thrilled with being the resident expert at the unfamiliar epicenter of the conversation, oblivious to where it was about to take him.

"It's this here," GooGoo said. "Will's daddy used to tell us—"

"I don't know, GooGoo," Will said. "That's a tough one for mixed company."

"Oh, do go on, Mr. GooGoo," Bitsy said. "Don't mind me. And you should know by now it'll go right over my mother's head, right James?"

Her husband, who was reading, or rather, hiding behind a *Newsweek* magazine, grunted. Nixon and Brezhnev, caricatured on the cover, shook hands as they held bunches of missiles behind their backs, "Testing Détente" in bold letters.

Mrs. Burgess rolled her eyes. "Ya'll stop," she said.

"Yeah," GooGoo said. "Will's daddy would tell us that them gals'—them ones over yonder—them gals' things run crossways. Because of their chinky eyes I reckon. Slanted, you know."

"Say what?" Winston said, while I was not quite sure what I was hearing.

"Yeah, crossways. Said the wider them legs would go the tighter it'd get. But I'm here to tell you they don't. Run crossways, that is. They run front to back, north to south, just like all the other pussies in the world."

Winston's grin went frozen and Bitsy let out a little whimper as the topic of conversation was revealed.

"Yep," GooGoo said. "Poontang is poontang in any language."

"Well I believe it should be clear by now that luncheon is damn well served," Mother said, herding us into the dining room, thinking, I am sure, to feed GooGoo and send him on his way. There is a limit to what even she will listen to, and, while Will Luckie has her bamboozled enough to listen to his own filthy mouth, she did not have the hots for, and therefore was not crazy about the way this GooGoo person was talking in front of her guests.

We all took our places around the beautifully decorated table. The centerpiece was a replica of the U.S. constitution flanked by more candles. GooGoo sat directly in front of it and set his drink and the bottle down on the imitation parchment. Mother flinched. He was unkempt looking, unshaven, wearing military boots and cammo trousers with his Grateful Dead t-shirt. He revealed that he was living in a camper shell behind his mama's trailer and hadn't been around many people since he came home. He slurred his words and threw spit as he spoke.

"I'm telling you, I just can't get used to my new skin." He waved a cigarette for emphasis, sprinkling ashes over Kathryn Burgess' empty plate to his left. Mother leaned over and blew them away, then cut her eyes at Will.

"Been raising hell about getting more operations," GooGoo continued, "but the government's gonna screw me all over again, looks like." He narrowed his eyes. "Somebitches."

"Son," Mayor Burgess said, "I certainly hope you are not bitter. Take pride—"

"Who's going to be proud of this?" GooGoo said in a violent tone, yanking back his shirt to reveal more of the scar that ridged his skin like wrinkled Glad Wrap.

"Oh, my," said Kathryn, while Bitsy wrinkled her nose to match his flesh.

Mayor Burgess and Winston tried to turn the conversation to Watergate.

"Richard motherfucking Nixon can kiss my left nut," GooGoo ranted. "But it got roasted, too."

"Roasted nuts," Will chuckled.

Kathryn dove into her salad. I could see Lindia peering through the kitchen doorway, eavesdropping.

"Speaking of Nixon," James said, "anyone think resignation looms?"

"Impeachment hearings settled that," Will said, absently.

I was beyond exhausted at the disrespectful talk, yet again, of our president. "I think it is rude to speak about politics at the table. You know what they say: sex, politics, reli—"

"And the tapes put the nail in his coffin," James interjected.

"Richard motherfucking Nixon," GooGoo muttered again.

I could take no more. "I will not listen to this utter disparagement of the leader of the free world. My goodness, it's all about a stupid burglary—one party snooping on another, from what I can tell, and they do that all the time. They all do it. It's not as if the Russian commies were in on it!"

"There, there, CeCe," Mother patted my hand. Such condescension! "Why don't you carve the

Boston butt, Will?" She collected the plates for him, and he set about the task of slicing the meat. "Now which brave soldier will change the subject?"

"That is one fine slab of barbeque," James attempted.

"And there's barbeque chicken, too," mother said, as Will offered another platter.

"Damn sure is," GooGoo said. "I bet that bird could sure enough strut."

"White or dark meat?" Will asked Mrs. Burgess.

"Dark."

"Yeah," GooGoo said. "Them is some big old breasts and legs for a yard bird. You know that thing could strut." He fist-grabbed the Wild Turkey by its bottle neck and poured some more into his glass, spilling as much on the tablecloth before setting down the bottle. "You know, a chicken makes a right good pet I hear."

"Is that so?" Mayor Burgess said, taking a plate from Will.

"I reckon it is so," GooGoo said. "I heard tell of a man, old Cleverdon Ellis, I think it was, over cross town there in East Pollard. They say he used to keep one like a pet. Like a dog or a cat, up in the house and all. Ain't that some shit?"

"Seems like that would be quite unsanitary," Mother said, absently.

"Goodness, Mother. It wouldn't be any more unsanitary than those two little pooping poodles of yours." And the dinner group laughed.

"Rosencrantz and Guildenstern are very low maintenance, for canines," Mother replied, and it cheered me to hear her use her crisp aristocratic clip. Not a good sign for poor GooGoo. Or Will.

"Well I heard," and GooGoo narrowed his eyes. "That is, they say old Cleverdon had it for more that a pet."

"Oh, dear, did he eat it?" Mrs. Burgess looked horrified.

"No," GooGoo said. "Ain't done that. But they say it was so tame it'd sleep up in the bed with him of a night. They say old Cleverdon took to making love to it, even."

This time the gasp of shock breathed in by the group sucked the air from the room, and the ceiling, I am sure, pooched downward.

"What do you say, Doc?" GooGoo went on. "Can a man do that?"

"Good Lord," Winston said. "I have never considered---"

"I figure it could be done," GooGoo said. "I mean, just look at a egg. If a egg can come out, don't it stand to reason that something else could go in? What about it, Doc?"

Will exploded in laughter, which infected the rest of the group, except for me, of course, and Mother, my unaccustomed ally. "You're a mess, GooGoo." He had distributed the plates of meat by now, and the serving dishes were being passed around the table. Mother was silent, speechless for once in her babbling life, and GooGoo showed no signs of letting up on his perverse line of interrogation of my husband.

"Goodness," Bitsy said. "I would have never thought to consider the egg. This is fascinating." I silently damned her. "The egg," she reiterated. And speaking of eggs, she was egging him on, being downright obvious about it, simply because she delighted in my embarrassment.

"Hell, yeah, to the egg," GooGoo said, lifting his glass. "Eat chicken. Drink Turkey. Merry Fourth of July." He fumbled at a bowl of butterbeans, but Bitsy jumped right in and helped him fix his plate. It inflamed my fury with all of the energy of a popped blood vessel.

"It is fascinating," Bitsy said, "what men will do in the absence of a woman."

"Shit," GooGoo said. "A woman ain't a necessary thing. That feeling can be reproduced without a lot of trouble."

"Oh, say no more, GooGoo," Mayor Burgess said, in an attempt to shut him up. "You cannot be divulging any of our masculine secrets."

"You can divulge Winston's, though," Will interjected, winking at me. Winston blushed.

"I'll vote with my astute father-in-law," James said. "I don't wish to be revealed."

"You, James?" Bitsy looked wide-eye at him. "What dark secrets are you harboring?"

Her husband's response was a sheepish look.

"What about calves' livers from the grocery store?" GooGoo was in his own one-sided, drunken world, still grilling Winston. "I tried it a few times. And they say octopus is pretty good, too, only you can't find no octopus in Pollard."

"Well," Winston said. "I suppose that bovine tissue is similar enough that, properly lubricated, it could---"

"My God in Heaven, Winston!" I exploded. "Have you forgotten where you are?"

Winston's cheeks were washed in one of his darker blushes. "Oh, I am sorry. Ladies, I completely forgot myself. Forgive me. I was taking a scientific--"

"Sorry?" GooGoo roared. "Sorry? You're apologizing to these ladies because you said something to me? Hell, we're talking about Mother Nature, the facts of life, Doc. Damn a mighty, there is some weak-ass men up in here."

"I beg your—" James said.

"Will?" Mother said.

"Damn good butter beans," Will said.

"Will!" Mother's voice was more stern and demanding. "I need to see you in the kitchen."

"Listen at how she's talking to you, boy. Look at how Doc there jumps to tell his woman he's sorry. Man, is this how the rich boys in Pollard act like men, Will?" GooGoo challenged.

"Pretty much," Will said.

"Damn, this kind of shit pisses me off," GooGoo said. The drunken meander of his voice had taken on a new tone, a very mean tone, and it was clear that his state of mind had shifted. Everyone at the table felt it. Eyes darted nervously to read between the lines. All eyes but Will's and Bitsy's.

"Whatever do you mean?" Bitsy asked, urging him on with renewed persistence, and, for once and at once, I was glad. The current of vibrations between Will and Mother was not good. An enormous fight was brewing between this couple who had done nothing but slobber over one another for four months. And a big scene with Mother over Will's friend could not bode well for the happy couple.

"Goddamn pussy-whipped, whiny-ass, suck-up shit. This right here is what comes of that women's lib shit. Why you got to apologize to some goddamn woman? You treat her bad? Huh? Tell me, Doc, you treat her bad?"

"Of course not." Winston looked baffled by the sudden turn of tone in the interrogation.

"Ever get drunk and put a knot on her head?"

"Don't be ridic—" I began, before I caught myself.

"Wait just a damn minute," James said.

"That is quite enough," Mayor Burgess said.

"Will!" Mother said, but he stubbornly ignored her.

"No, goddammit," GooGoo said. "You answer me. You ever beat this woman? Huh, Doc?"

"Well, of course not."

"Step out on her?"

"No," Winston said, blushing, and I thought his tone suddenly did not ring true. I had never considered that he might be unfaithful to me. Surely not. He would not dare.

"Then why the goddamn hell you going to apologize for having a conversation about the facts of life?"

"I'm going to get the butter," Mother said, motioning Will to follow. This time he responded and walked out to the kitchen with her.

"So what if you talk about shit. Hell, it don't hurt nobody. It's like a chicken fucking a basketball. Don't nobody get hurt," GooGoo said.

"Let's just forget it," Winston said, "and talk about something else."

GooGoo leaned forward and pounded his fist on the table for emphasis. "No, goddammit, I got me some more questions. Ain't every day I get to set down with a goddamn doctor, and I got plenty of questions."

"Perhaps you have some questions for our mayor?" Mrs. Burgess asked.

"Hell, no. I ain't got no use for a politician. They all crooks. Look at them Nixon folks, running around all cutthroat like. Flipping on one another like jailhouse snitches. Damn Nixon roasted my goddamn left nut. What kind of a woman is going to take up with a scarred up, nut-roasted fellow like me?"

"It's a badge of honor, son," Mayor Burgess said.

"Badge of honor my ass. Hell, maybe I ought to get my own damn self a pet chicken or a pig so I can get a little romance ever now and then."

"Heavens," said Mrs. Burgess.

"Would it be worse if it was a pile of calves' livers? Or a real live calf? Hey, Will!" he yelled to the kitchen door. "Remember that time, back when we was pups, maybe thirteen, fourteen, and we give you twenty dollars to do it with that calf?"

"Yeah," Will yelled back.

"Lord, Lord," I heard Lindia say.

I could also hear the sound of Mother's urgent voice, low and fast, and I knew she was telling Will to get rid of GooGoo. I began to celebrate the split that was sure to follow. It was bound to drive them apart, her disapproval of his friend. They probably grew up together, Will and GooGoo. They went to high school together anyway, played football together. They went to war together, for God's sake. Surely they were closer than brothers. And Will's twisted loyalty to one of his own kind would have to win out. I was also oddly fascinated by yet another discussion regarding bestiality behind the walls of Mother's house. Yes, of all the bizarre chitchat he had foisted upon us, the rantings of GooGoo McGeehee felt beyond bizarre, the genre of Will Luckie in which literal tales of the Wild Kingdom are rendered. This was quite a fluke—or a sign of some kind.

"We give him twenty dollars to do it with this calf, so Will dropped his pants, whipped out that big old pecker, and pulled its tail up. Only that calf had other ideas. Before Will could do anything, that baby cow took a shit that landed in Will's britches that was down around his ankles." He slapped the table, laughing. The entire group gazed at him in unbelieving, stony silence, but it did not deter him from continuing. "We held old Will down and pulled them britches up and sent him home with a pant load of calf shit. His poor old mama didn't know what to think, I bet. Did she?" he asked, as Will undertook the eating of his meal once again. Mother set down a slab of butter adorned with a tiny American flag attached to a toothpick.

"She thought I had done took some kind of intestinal sickness," Will said.

"Don't you know that boy's drawers was stinking?" GooGoo said.

"Good Lord," Kathryn said. "Would someone do something?"

"I think you better change the subject," Mayor Burgess said.

"Good God almighty, do the women run this here goddamn show? Is rich boys in Pollard nothing but pussies?"

"Has there been any more news on the TV about Watergate?" Winston tried, again.

"Hey, Luckie," GooGoo said, through clenched teeth, menacing. It was downright frightening. "You ever fucked a chicken?" GooGoo glared at Winston, daring him to protest, which he certainly did not, and my less than manly husband sank a little in his chair, of course.

"Who ain't?" Will winked at the group around the table, garnering a little more laughter, and it suddenly dawned on me that he was delighting in the whole show, even in Mother's disapproval. He was cutting off his nose to spite his face, and I was salivating at the idea of their impending breakup.

"Will has a whole chicken house full of pullets," Bitsy said. "It's called the Watergate Hotel. Isn't that clever?"

"Tell you what, if you go to fuck a chicken, the more he flaps them wings the better it is," GooGoo continued, seemingly fixed on getting the better of us.

"This is beyond belief," Kathryn said.

"Look here, now, Mr. McGeehee," Mayor Burgess tried again.

But GooGoo was determined to continue his description. "Tell you what else. You can slice off its head at just the right second, and it'll be the best nut you'll ever get, bar none."

"Hold it a goddamn minute," Will said, as if Bitsy's reminder about his own flock of fowl had reminded him that this GooGoo character was talking about defiling creatures that were, in fact, Will's pets. And then committing homicide upon them.

"No, I ain't shitting you. You slice its head off and it'll get to quaking with that dying quiver. My hand to God, it'll make you draw air in through your asshole."

It was as if Will were taking it personally, this talk of violating and murdering chickens, and he was up and out of his chair in a breath. "You don't need to be saying that shit, GooGoo."

"I'll say whatever the fuck—"

Will snatched him up out of his chair, which caught his foot, sending GooGoo into a heap on the floor. A glass of wine splashed across Bitsy's sequins and silk, and Kathryn got up to dab her daughter's frock with a wet napkin.

"You ain't saying shit," Will said. "Now get up."

"Mother, please," Bitsy said. "That will not work on red wine."

"I will have no fighting in my house," Mother commanded.

"There goes another order from a woman," GooGoo slurred as he stood. "You going to let a woman order you around, Luckie? You done turned into a pussy like all these other rich boys?" GooGoo punctuated his words with three shoves to Will's shoulder, which finally sent him into the table, spilling barbeque sauce, his plate clattering to the floor.

Will stood. "No, GooGoo, I ain't," he said, and threw a punch into GooGoo's left cheekbone, laying him out.

Mrs. Burgess screamed, "My God, you've killed him!"

"I am calling the police," Mother said.

"No!" I yelled, but I knew it was way too late to prevent this story from getting out, what with so many witnesses and all.

"Fuck you, Luckie," GooGoo said, standing again, swaying. "I'm going home. I don't want no pigs to show up and give a hassle."

"Then get the hell out," Will said.

GooGoo stumbled toward the foyer, where he staggered into the umbrella stand and fell to his knees. He let out a loud belch and uttered, "Motherfucker." Then he rose, swaying. Just as he reached the front door, he turned. "Hey," he said. "What about the plate for Mama?"

Mother had Lindia fix him up.

Before he turned to make his exit, GooGoo made this declaration: "I ought to apologize to y'all. I ain't a bad person, really. Ain't mean. I'm all about some peace and love, bottom line." And he flashed a peace sign at the group, to prove his point. "It's been real."

The remainder of the meal was subdued and marred further with a building tension that everyone was aware of. It was clear that Mother was furious even as she babbled with her trademark vivacity. It was also clear that the Burgesses were more than anxious to get out of the line of fire, declining dessert. Winston, too, went scampering back to the hospital, claiming he had to check on some patients. Lindia was long gone, having given up enough of her own holiday, full of stories to share, I am sure, in colored town. But I was not about to miss the death knell of this mismatched relationship. I took a place in my DD's big leather recliner in the den.

Mother was seething like a mini Vesuvius, smoking and swinging her leg as she sat at the bar, glaring at Will, who had taken up his guitar once more, that beat up old Martin D-28 he is so crazy about. "I ain't no Jimi Hendrix," he said, "but let's give it a try," and he began to pick "The Star Spangled Banner" while I quietly, contentedly, waited for Mother to spew lava.

She began with a low rumble. "I am going to choose my words carefully," she said, "because I know how sensitive you are about your origins."

"Before you start choosing them words, I had me a thought about old GooGoo," he said. This was going to be good.

"And what is that?" Mother said, in her aristocratic voice.

Will set down his guitar. "Just that old GooGoo and me grew up together, just two good ol' boys running the roads, hunting together, hitting the gridiron of a Friday night. He's a friend. A brother. He has a good heart, and I thought that mattered above all things, to you. So he carried that good heart right into the service, put six years into the Marine Corps, a good part of it fighting in a goddamn steaming, wet, bloody patch of swamp across the world. He gets his flesh singed off by some goddamn burning hut falling in on him, comes home deep fried, hides out in a camper shell behind his mama's skirts like a scared little shit because he's too afraid to hang out with his old friends. And the only reason he would even think about coming around me is 'cause I been there. Then he gets drunk as a goddamned boiled owl, comes up in this big-ass house, and he don't know how to hold out his pinky and discuss politics with the mayor. Who the hell would have thunk it?"

He was crazier than I ever imagined, to be going on the offense with Mother. And he continued. "I'll tell you who would have thunk it. Me. I knew he'd bring that East Pollard chip up in here, make a mess, and you can't say I didn't try to tell you. But you're a strong-willed woman, so I decided just to sit back and watch. And what I saw was a bunch of assholes who don't have the first idea how to treat somebody who's been through some sure enough fucked up shit. Don't know how to be kind to somebody that's done give the skin off his nut— hell, he's give a whole nut—for the big cheeses that sent him over there."

I was so engrossed in this absurd little speech of Will's that I literally jumped when Mother began to sob.

"You are right," she boo-hooed. "I feel just terrible. That poor man could not help it. And I was the one who insisted that he come. Oh, I am such a hypocrite."

I wanted to scream, jump in, and turn the tide back her way, stir her into a rage that would fall upon Will Luckie's head, but I had shut down in utter amazement.

"Just to think of the horrors that poor boy must have witnessed!" She put both hands over her face and howled.

"That is the goddamn truth," Will said.

"You have to forgive me," Mother sobbed, holding out her hand to Will, who rose and went over to her. This was too much. He let her cry tears and snot onto that green plaid shirt and grinned over at me until I wanted to spit. "You have to let me invite him back," she said, regaining some composure.

"No," Will said. "Well, maybe, if he can get that chip off his shoulder. That old East Pollard chip is as much of a scar as them burn scars. He was putting on a lot of that just for show, to get under some skins. Because of that chip. I think"

"No, we must make it right with him. I shall think of something. After all, he's a wounded veteran. Don't be a pooper." Mother slapped him on the shoulder in a playful way that made me heave, then she sniffled her face back into his shirt.

He tickled her ribs. "Come on, now, smile, Baby."

"You better stop," she squealed, then laughed. "It was a . . . GooGoo Clusterfuck!" and they both roared.

Surely this was not happening. She had uttered the "f" word. That was a new linguistic low for her. Surely she was not letting the whole thing go. I tried to open my mouth to speak but continued to be struck dumb. They wrestled around until Will went for the famous erogenous zone on her neck. "Goddamn," she moaned. "That is quite enough." She wrenched free. "I am going upstairs to soak in a bubble bath. That is where you shall join me in ten minutes, and later this evening we shall watch the fireworks on the TV. Cecelia LaRue, you should make yourself scarce momentarily. See you in the morning. Sleep tight. And God bless America." And she swept up the stairs that curved down into the marble foyer, a la Loretta Young.

That was when the magma began to rise in me as I sat there gazing at Will Luckie, who had just now manipulated my intractable Mother out of what had promised to be one of the major rages of her life. I certainly had never been able to do that. Ever. He stirred his drink and smiled at me. "Want anything?" he said.

I came up out of my DD's chair and crossed over to the bar. "You give me another glass of merlot," I said, low and mean, through gritted teeth, "and then you tell me when you're getting the goddamn hell away from my mother!"

He pulled the cork and poured a little wine for me while I glared with all the meanness I could muster. "Here goes your merlot," he said. "And about your mama, well, I reckon I'll at least be around till after that bubble bath she's fixing. And after that?" He squinted up at the ceiling. "I just can't say, you know? I got me some more low work to do for your mama right regular."

"Good God," I said, seething. "You are filthy. You know good and well you don't belong with her, and I for one have had enough of this sick charade."

He laughed in that slimy-soft way I cannot abide. "Well shit, Baby," he said. "I didn't know you felt so strong about it. Maybe we can do something about that."

"And what would that be?" Perhaps he wanted cash. I decided, in that moment, that I would get him all the cash he needed in order to disappear him from my life. But surely it was not going to be that easy. And, of course, it wasn't.

"Well, I ain't really booked for tomorrow afternoon," he said, winking at me. "You got some chores for me? Grass need cutting? Hell, I know Winnie ain't up for all them chores." He grinned.

I knew right then he was talking in double meanings to me, which only fed my rage. "You are perverted."

He outright laughed then. "I hope the hell I am. But, hey, you can have some, too. How about I come stay with you a while after your mama and me bust up? Like I said, ain't no telling when that might be, but I'll take care of that bug you got up your ass."

I was literally shaking I was so mad. I knew he was trying to push me to the edge of sanity and I would be damned if I'd let him. So I took another tack, tried a rational approach. "If you really care about my mama, you'll get out of her life," I said. "She has a lot at stake—her position in this town and her friends. Goodness, we all have appearances to keep up."

"Yeah. I know just what appearances your friends are keeping up," he said in a sarcastic voice. "And I know what they're keeping down, too."

"And what is that supposed to mean?" At once I was sorry, though, for letting him pull at my curiosity.

"Oh, can't say. Wouldn't be the gentlemanly thing to do, kiss and tell."

"What in God's name are you insinuating?"

"I ain't insinuating shit. I'm saying outright you got some mighty hot friends. You take that Bitsy. Man, she can go like the piston on a locomotive, and makes near bout as much a racket." He laughed.

"You are not only a pervert. You are a bald-faced liar." This was too much even for Will Luckie, to be manufacturing tales just so he could get my goat.

"Hell, I know what I know. And I know what I seen. Man, you talk about a sweet little ass. Petite. She's built way smaller than you. I can perch her right up on that thing like a canary on a swing."

"How dare you lie about my friend and insult me." I took a long sip of wine, trying to collect my thoughts and keep a lid on my rage.

"I'll tell you what else I know. More wine?"

I nodded and he poured, still wearing that disgusting grin.

"Here's what I know for a fact. I know just why you want to be so mean all the damn time. I know just why you tote that edge around with you."

"What edge?"

"That edge that's got you shaking right now. That mean-ass edge that needs to be honed down where you're like to relax a little."

"There is not a mean bone in—"

"That goddamn edge needs to be honed down, and we both know old Winnie ain't got the time nor the tool to do the job."

He was squinting those blue, blue eyes at me like he was studying some specimen in a laboratory, making me feel naked and humiliated, effectively deflating my offensive and putting me on the defensive at once. I leaned my back against the bar, steadying myself with my palm on the stool beside me while he went on. "Yeah, we both know what you need, don't we? And you need a big-ass dose of it, too."

"I don't like what you are implying," I managed.

"Ain't implying nothing. I'm outright saying you need a big old healthy dose of Uncle Luckie's Root Oil to cure what ails you. We'll grease that big old bug up and slide it right out of your mean ass."

"So this is how you think my mama's boyfriend should behave," I said, suddenly recognizing that he was handing me a trump card. If my mother knew what he was up to she would kick his behind to Timbuktu.

He laughed again. "Baby, for all that meanness you are one naïve little girl. You need to let me fill you in. Come on. I'll give you the special treatment, something old Winnie would fold up in a heap before he would do."

"This is unbelievable," I said, reaching inside myself to revive my now rage, finding only a fraction of it, confused. "Winston and I are happy as the rich clams we are."

"And I'm a monk in a no-woman monastery," he chuckled. "Come on and stop denying what you know you can't. Ain't none of that shit you do going to make it get no better."

"Whatever are you talking about?" Shut up, I yelled inside my own head. Stop letting him pull questions out of you. My rage was beginning to build again, all right. But at myself.

"Hell, the goddamn parties. The big time social events. The frills and the write- ups in *The Pollard Gazette*. Ain't none of that going to make it no better. Ain't none of it going to take that big old knot out of your crotch and you know it."

This was going too far and I knew he was winning. My hand tightened on the wine glass and I thought of all those movie scenes where the beautiful starlet throws her drink in the leading man's face, demeaning him, perhaps even spitting for emphasis. "You don't have any idea what you are talking about."

"I reckon I do. I reckon it's the one thing in my life that it's for damn certain I do know. I know that if you got an itch you need to scratch it or let your man scratch it. And Winnie ain't going to scratch it cause he ain't got the fingernails for it. Not no nail file, neither. But me, I know right where to scratch it, how long to scratch it, and just what to scratch it with." He leaned his elbow on the bar and grinned those dimples at me.

I wanted to hurl that wine. I wanted to slap him. I wanted to run. But my body was at odds with me, refusing to move, leaving me stammering and frustrated. "You are—you—you have to be so full of yourself to be –"

Then he stepped over yet another line. He set down his drink, leaned over, and put his lips close to my ear. I could feel them move in my hair as he whispered, blowing hot gin breaths against my neck, sending chills rippling down to my shoulders. Here is what he said: "I'm trying to help you out, Baby. Doing you a pure favor cause we're practically kin. I know I could help you out. Come on and let me."

It was repulsive and eerily intriguing at the same time. And I was engaged in a battle not only against Will Luckie but also with my own being, which would not respond to the will of my intellect. It was as if some foreign invader had gained control when my guard was down, some foreign instinct that was at this moment tap dancing inside my stomach, sending reverberations down to the base of my pelvis, my upper thighs. I was struck dumb and Will Luckie moved to take advantage of this. He leaned even closer so that his lips moved harder against my hair, his low voice vibrating into my ear, muffled into the web of my hair. "Come on, Baby," he said. "Let's get that burr out of your drawers, okay? Okay?" And he moaned, drew back and looked me full in the face, a look which gave me the sudden force of will to hurl the contents of that wine glass I held, sending merlot splashing across his left cheek.

Do you know that man did not bat an eye? No, he did not. Instead, he scooped a few napkins emblazoned with popping firecrackers from the bar, took a swipe at his face, then rubbed his cheek on the top of his left shoulder, all the while laughing and stepping around in front of me while I stared, arms limp at my sides, deep in a shock and confusion I have never experienced in my whole entire life. He put both hands on the bar, effectively cornering me so that, even if my body had been cooperating, movement would have been difficult. And what he did next was tantamount to assault.

That man looked straight into my eyes, leaned the crotch of his khakis into my left thigh and said, "Come on. Let's be friends. You know you want to be my friend." He gave me the smile he offers Mother when he wants to take her upstairs, but I managed to keep my face expressionless, utterly betraying the chaos that was unfolding deep inside me.

He leaned in a little more, steady staring into my eyes, searching, I am certain, for a crack in my will. I was so caught up in the stare-down that seconds passed before it dawned upon me what he was mashing into my thigh. My eyes must have widened a bit, because he smiled even more broadly. "Come on and let's undo that knot in your crotch, okay?"

It felt as solid as a tire iron or a jack handle, only much larger, angled sideways toward his pants pocket, and it sent my mind racing unchecked. I attempted to run through the possibilities of its physical properties but came up empty handed. I knew that it would surely burn its impression into the flesh of my thigh so I leaned back harder into the bar, drawing back from it. I tried to speak, but my voice was taken by the shock that infests nightmares with mute screams, and Will Luckie was smiling and shaking his head slowly as if to reiterate the coarse words he had put between us. And the girth and length of that appendage was signaling the *coup d'etat* inside me to keep rising up, take me to some terrifying place where pain and pleasure mixed in a way I could not imagine.

And then---you will not believe this, I know---it moved. I swear before God, it moved. It nodded a little nod into my thigh and I drew in a sharp, sharp breath, poised on the edge of a sudden verge. I was liquid. I would have surrendered, even as my mother's voice came singing down the stairs, from up in the master bath.

"Will? Yoo-hooo. Are you coming up?" she yelled. "The bubbles are staring to pop!"

For a fleeting second I feared my hands would clutch at him, desperate to satisfy my sick curiosity, but, thankfully, they did not. They did not have to. He leaned in so very hard then, speaking into my neck this time.

"You know what, Baby?" And his lips moved on the skin of my neck. His tongue touched my neck.

"What?" I whispered.

"I got to go take care of your mama. That woman has one hefty appetite." And that monster, Will Luckie, stepped back, laughing. At me. At my weakness. At the story I could never share with my mother, not now. And even then—God help me, even then, my eyes were drawn to the area below his unbelted khakis to where the thing aimed like an ICBM into the fabric, leaving a circle of wetness on the cloth, turning the tan color to brown.

He laughed harder. "I'll try to save you a little," he said, as I pushed him aside.

"Go and burn in hell where you belong." And I ran into the hanging humidity of the July air, past those infernal chickens of his, into the kitchen door of my warm, cozy Creole. I collapsed into a chair at the kitchen table, just inside the back door, cursing myself, cursing Will Luckie, resenting Winston anew. Michaelangelo's David was a lie, his shriveled little manhood nestled there like a withering maypop. All the great works of art were lies, misrepresentations of the potential that apparently lay between a man's legs. Winston, who, even with his lack of desire and effete behavior, had at one time seemed more than abundant to accommodate my frame, was now and forever relegated to subjugation, in the shadow of the living, independent creature that resided below the belly of my aging mother's gigolo. My mind would not let it go, this discovery, this uncharted ground. It shamed me no end to be wondering what it might look like in the light of day.

I poured another glass of wine and went into the living room. I turned on an oscillating fan and let it buffet my hair and cool my cheeks. My eyes caught the July Fourth gift basket Winston had brought home, a Hickory Farms basket stuffed with cheeses and rolls of sausages and pepperoni and other logs of meat and I wondered. I studied the bottle of merlot I was diminishing and I wondered. And I wondered, in spite of my best intentions, over the next couple of weeks until, just last night, when I did finally get a look at it. I got a look at it bathed in moon glow and under the very worst of circumstances. And that, I am afraid, was my undoing

8
MiMi

It's amazing how quickly Will managed to set the tone around here, since way back in March, when he first brought unto me a most delicious post-winter thaw. We frolicked through April, loving Paris in the springtime for five days before spending another five in Rome. In May our foray was to Spain and Morocco, for another ten days, taking the express from Casablanca to Marrakesh. We wandered the Majorelle botanical garden, fancying ourselves the original pair in God's creation, in that Edenesque setting. I had not trotted the globe since those years prior to Wickham, back in my freedom days of passengering aboard ocean liners, prior to the affair with my flyboy. But that spirit of adventure and wonder re-arose in me like the charmed head of a cobra from out of a globe-shaped basket in Tangiers. It was profoundly exhilarating, and I was determined that we would see as much of the world as my ill-gotten gains could afford. Which will be a goodly portion of said world. Naturally, CeCe was beside herself. "It is an utter waste of money! Especially going to those A-rab places."

"You are quite mistaken, Miss CeCe. It is money well spent that broadens one's perspective and provides a new context within which to see oneself. You could use a new point of view yourself. Care to join us? We're thinking next about a foray into Africa."

"Africa? Seriously? Aren't you afraid of being boiling-pot flesh for a band of cannibals or some such? Not to mention the shrinking of the heads into something resembling prunes. Aren't you worried about rampaging elephants, snarling tigers, heathen savages, and starving children? And the flies! Nobody goes to Africa!"

"Sweetie, I do believe you are mixing your savages. The shrinking of heads is more particular to the Amazonian rainforest in a completely different hemisphere, I believe."

"Savage is savage, that's all there is to it. And the Brazilians, like the Africans, are hypersexual to boot."

"This conversation is blessedly over," and I retired poolside.

I declare, she carries snootified categories for all the continents of the world. I said as much to Lindia, with whom I find myself chatting more and more these days, per Will's example. And even Lindia is showing more of herself. After twenty years of following the lead in the rhythms of the Calhoun family dance, she seems to be improvising her own unique steps within the revised context of our daily lives. "I don't have a child," she remarked one day, out of the blue, clear, shining sky, "but I do know a mother has got to be a little bit heartbroke when her baby repudiates her."

The old Lindia would never have expressed such an opinion. And, of course, she was right. "It is the worst thing in the world to know," I said, "that your baby can't be happy or satisfied. That your existence serves to cause her discomfort."

"The Lord never blessed me with a baby," Lindia said again. "Maybe Miss CeCe would be different if she would have herself a child."

"I guess that's possible. Although the lack of passion between those two is remarkable. I often wonder if it's one of those sexless marriages one hears about."

"Oh, Law, Miss Maureen, that would be the saddest thing."

"Besides, CeCe as a mother? I'm just not sure if she has the emotional dots to connect into something like, oh, motherhood. She's a self-centered thing. I do try to ignore her disapproval, but I admit to weak moments."

"You can't let her touch you that way, Miss Maureen. All you can do is forgive and go forward in your own happiness."

"And I always pined for *her* to forgive *me*."

"If you're being your true self, then there's nothing for her to forgive. If you're at peace with the Lord, can't anything shake you. And forgiveness puts you at peace. I know because I've forgiven some sure enough meanness."

I took a breath. "I know you have, Lindia, and I know that some of it came from me. I have not been an easy woman to work for. I know that, and I've taken a lot out on you over the years. And I do want to say how sorry I am."

"Oh, I always just put it at the feet of the Lord."

"I'm saying I'm truly sorry. For the fits and the criticisms."

"I put it at the feet of Jesus because stewing over a thing is a poison to the spirit."

"Did you hear me? I'm sorry."

"Yes, ma'am."

That was the true moment, I think, when our relationship turned closer to—friendship is not the accurate word. Comrades, perhaps? Allies?

She was certainly an ally during the July Fourth fiasco, when I had Will cornered in the kitchen. I was spitting nails, that is for certain. "You get that lard-fed, burnt-necked ne'er-do-well out of my abode this very instant."

Will just grinned. "Old GooGoo. He's a trip."

"I mean it! Or—"

"Or what?"

"I'll call the PCPD and have him removed."

"For what?"

"Lewd and lascivious conduct. Perversion. For smelling bad."

Lindia sidled up to us, joining in the low-voiced discussion. "Mr. Will, it's not a kind man who trifles with people's good natures," she said.

"What are you talking about?" He even blushed a bit.

"Just that you've been a kind man all these many weeks, but all of that mischief out there," she nodded toward the dining room, "well, it just doesn't sit right with who I know you to be."

I declare he looked like a little schoolboy who had been shamed by the teacher. "You know," he began.

"Thank you, Lindia," I interrupted.

"Best not thank me," she said, but Will was already stomping back into the dining room. Lindia sighed. "Nobody wants 'I told you so'."

And she was right.

And later that evening, while the waterbed rippled, sloshed and gurgled, while the lavender incense smoke, along with the smoke from his, as the youth say, "doobie" curled serpentine and sweet, Will even acknowledged that she was right. "I know I go too far," he said, his face bathed in the bubbling glow of a blue lava lamp. "I get a kick out of putting shit in the face of your typical uptight ass hole. I guess I'm kind of like a kid that way. And like GooGoo that way. I'd be a lie to say nothing like that won't happen again, so I won't say that. But I can say I'm sorry." And he reached into the drawer and brought out that hand-held muscle massager he had insisted I buy, early on.

Nirvana.

Yes, whatever the conflict between the two of us, and there is precious little conflict, Will certainly does know how to make up appropriately. He is gifted in the art of oral giving, which Wickham never even approached. I don't believe that dead husband of mine ever put his lips anywhere below the upper bosom area, but Will knows no, as the young folk say, "hang-ups." When I reflect upon all those years of Wickham's pasty flesh jiggling, astride my hips, grunting and blowing like a beached whale, never a care in the world about how my level of pleasure was getting along, which was typically at the level of simply getting through it quickly, I am tempted to go plummeting into a gaping pit of regret. Thank God Lindia's philosophy is beginning to rub off on me as a result of our kitchen chats. Lindia insists that regret, along with any other dark emotion—resentment, jealousy, and the like— has no place in one's head or heart. She equates dark emotions with a betrayal of Christ. Now, as noted, I am not one who takes church going seriously, although I find the rituals of Catholicism rather soothing, only because of the ritualistic nature, never minding the content. But all these years of church going have been only myself going through the motions of rituals far from my heart. It was not long after the Fourth of July folly that I decided to cease attending the Methodist Church. CeCe, no surprise here, was livid.

"It cannot happen. It is unacceptable," she said in a seething tone of voice, after an initial screaming howl sounding something like, "What!?"

"Do not speak to me as if you are the parent and I am the child. I am your mother."

"Not of late," she said, adding a little choke to her voice in order to feign hurt feelings.

"Oh, CeCe, you have offered up your disdain for me as a mother for your entire life, so cease and desist with the finger pointing at 'recent' developments. I have decided that, since I do not accept any sort of religious dogma, although I do intend to probe into all things spiritual, that it is simply a waste of my time to go sit on a hard pew and listen to that sonorously boring Brother Odom drone on and on and on."

"Church is the most important part of our participation in this community, as leaders, as its—"

"For goodness sake, I did not forbid *you* to go to church. You have not been banished from the sanctuary of the bored ones. By all means, go. Go and sin no more."

"But you have to go!"

"Actually, no, I do not and am not."

"But you're a reflection of me!"

"Don't be silly. We are two independent entities."

"What will Brother Odom think of me? Of the family? Our already sullied reputations will be in tatters."

"I care not one whit what Brother Odom thinks of me, and if he thinks ill of you I would recommend your following my example, as he would be practicing an altogether anti-Christian sort of Methodism." She looked at me as if I were crazy. "Have you not been listening to Lindia all these years?" I demanded.

"Lindia is a simple minded negress who needs to mind her own business."

I do not have to tell you that comment put me over the edge. "She is anything but simple minded! And who uses such a term as 'negress'? What is next, 'darkie'? That is beyond unacceptable. Shameful!"

"I know, I know, we have to say 'black,' but I swear before any altar there is, this is not the place on the geographical map to be espousing such liberal ideas. That's what's shameful. You have to be *so* different. You have to be the center of attention. It's the story of my life!"

"Well, honey, you need to start writing a different story."

"*Me*, write it? But you made me! You and my DD."

"Yes, Miss CeCe, you are, sperm and egg, a product of your parents. But if I had the power to make you into what I truly thought best for you, I would have certainly done so by now. No," and Lindia's words were truly ringing in my ears, "you are your own author. You have to be your real self, not an imitation of somebody else's standard."

"So now you're calling me a fake. A phony. Just because I'm not you."

"Not true."

"Well, guess what? I'll never be you, all crazy and sex-starved, and—liberal! I voted for him. Did you know? I voted for Richard Milhous Nixon, just to honor my DD!"

"Of course you did, Precious. You're certainly your father's daughter, after all."

"And proud of it!" she seethed, storming off to wallow in the mud of her misery, no doubt.

"Did you vote for Nixon?" I asked Lindia, later in the day. She laughed. "I didn't think so. Just verifying. What do you think should happen to him?"

"The law, that's what. Can't nobody be above the law, president or no president."

"But there's all that double-speak about a president being unable to break the law when he *is* the law—a sitting president, that is."

"Don't make a bit of sense to me. He ain't no king. The only king is King Lord Jesus."

"You know, CeCe puts me in mind of Nixon. She wants to rule with impunity, make the world bend to her will, impose her values, make all decisions for the rest of us, experience no real consequences for her wrong turns, bully and intimidate her underlings—but, she's become ridiculous and unstable, and I do worry about her mental health."

"Consequences tend to catch up with them who steady make bad turns."

"Do you think he'll resign?"

"Seems like it."

"What a time to be alive. What a time to be American. Don't you feel it? The electricity?"

"Well, yes, ma'am, to be honest. Used to be a heavy cloud over this place, but it's done lifted. I don't think it's America so much as it's this place."

"I do believe you're right. The cloud had to lift so that the freedom, the liberation could come in. We suddenly had a real context for joy. America is not the driver of the joy, is it?"

"It's got a ways to go, to my mind."

"Well, que sera, sera. Perhaps Will and I shall become expatriates."

"What is that?"

"You know, take up residence in another country. For a time. Mexico, maybe. The southern part. The mountains. You can join us. We'll still need a maid. Interested?"

"Well, no, ma'am. I'm happy here, mostly."

"All the better. I'd much rather leave Rosencrantz and Guildenstern in your charge. And Mr. Monsieur! CeCe lacks the temperament."

"Yes, ma'am."

"Tell, me Lindia, is there anything that would make you happier? And say the truth."

She seemed to hesitate, but then a slow smile overtook her lips. "It's right hard, Miss Maureen, keeping up with two separate households, full time, when this here one, with you and Mr. Will, brings joy. That other one, that other household, across the lawn yonder, drags at joy like an undertow out in the Gulf of Mexico. It's dank and dour over yonder."

There was no arguing with her point. In that daughter of mine a real monster had been unleashed. As high strung and downright hysterical as I had been over the years, as demanding and such the diva, I was a saint next to CeCe. To further subject poor, patient Lindia to that source of perpetual misery and criticism would be unforgiveable. "Tell you what, Lindia. You keep your eyes and ears open. If you can find another girl to help CeCe out, well, I'll make her an offer."

Little did I know that the perfect maid for Miss Cecelia LaRue Calhoun Dozier would drop right into my lap, as if drizzled down from Heaven like honey on a buttermilk biscuit. And when the stars align in such a way as that, one must gather the good fortune without hesitation.

9
Marlayna

I got more and more messed up as the days and weeks went by. I wasn't laying around no more, just the opposite. I got where I couldn't be still. I'd ride around all night, drive by that big damn house over and over. I'd go to the bars and dance on the bandstand and show my tits. I'd stay up all night watching the Christian channel, trying to get Jesus to tell me what to do. I done told you what I really wanted to do was kick that old lady's ass, but I'd get a twinge of guilt sometimes because, hell, she was a old lady and if she fell wrong she might break a hip. Plus, all that money made me know real quick who would get fucked over if we landed up in a courtroom over a ass whupping.

But it worked on me, all that stewing over my man. It worked on me fierce, till I was all churned up like a pot of bad beans. And that was when I decided to visit crazy old Miss Joan McGeehee, to get to her hippie-fied soldier son, Googoo, to go for the inside scoop on Will and them. By the end of it I wasn't no better than them gooks over in Vietnam, that Charlie that hides in the trees and under the ground, just like a coward. Let me explain how I come to be so low.

See, I kept hearing the rumors all the damn time. I heard he was having cases of liquor delivered up to that *Gone With the Wind* house, that he was all the time driving around town in that big Lincoln of hers. I heard she bought him a whole wardrobe at The Fair Day Department Store in town, nice shirts and fancy cowboy boots and all such as that. I heard she toted him to Cordova Mall in Pensacola and bought him expensive Italian shoes and such. I heard he still wasn't wearing nothing but blue jeans or them double knit shorts or cutoffs, and hadn't none of them expensive shoes touched his feet yet—just cowboy boots and Chuck Taylors. That man is damn sure set in his ways.

I knew she carried him off on a trip across the world, gone for ten days to Paris and Rome. Rumor was that he'd hang all over her like she was some kind of a hot mama when she really wasn't nothing but a damned old douche bag. I figured she wore expensive lingerie, that her bras matched her panties, and they both matched her slips. I figured she drank out of highball glasses with them gold rims and had a maid to draw her bath water, clip her toenails, and fan her with a big palmetto fan, like she was some kind of Mae West person. I figured it was a safe bet she ain't never had to work for nothing in her whole goddamn life, ain't never had no real heartache. I figured she done charity work all the damn time, visiting folks in my neighborhood in East Pollard with cast-off dressing gowns, and everybody wanted to be her friend just because she was rich.

I figured she waved hundred dollar bills under my man's nose whenever she wanted him to rub her back or take her dancing at the country club. I bet she had him doing the cha-cha and the fox trot and the jitterbug, old timey dances like that. But what really got me was when I'd go to thinking about them two humping and carrying on. First, I'd get plumb sick to my stomach, then I'd get mad enough to beat her with a two by four, and finally I'd end up crying and cursing the day I met that man.

Still, I just knew it'd be a matter of time before she'd throw him out. I knew she'd see he wasn't going to work steady, was going to eat up her groceries and spend her money, was like to trash up her house with his sloppy ways, and then she would see his true colors. And I knew better than anything else that he'd go to cheating on her, probably right under her nose, and then she'd wake the hell up for sure and put his ass on the road.

I knew all that in my heart, but ain't none of it happened.

I heard that GooGoo McGeehee had went up in that mansion for the Fourth of July and ended up having a knock down drag out with Will, and that didn't surprise me none. Will was probably all full of hisself thinking he's better than everybody just because he's up in some money. So, even though it was the dead of summer, I decided to go and see GooGoo and see if I could get some information out of him.

Now GooGoo has always been a kind of odd duck. Back in high school he was always and for no good reason telling lies on his so called friends just to make hisself look all big and puffed up. He was the kind that had a constant hard-on that he was all the time trying to rub up on whatever girl he was around at any minute. He breathed real loud, these obscene-phone-caller kinds of breaths, and stared at you like he thought you wanted him or something, but he wasn't what you call appealing. The only reason he got dates at all was because he was a first string tackle. So something ain't never been right about him and I reckon when they sent him over to Vietnam it pushed him right on over that cliff and that's why he become a hippie.

I'd heard he was living with his mama, and I didn't want to have to go through her, on account of she was known to be a bubble or two off plumb her ownself. She used to preach sometimes at our church and she claimed to have a inside line to Jesus, who had appeared at the foot of her bed one evening and give her The Call. But her preaching was all mixed up. Like she'd talk about the disciple Noah or the Pharoah John and all such as that. She was okay on the facts long as she just stuck with praising Jesus and didn't try to go too deep into that Bible, but she acted like the Lord favored her and hers more than anybody else, and that used to piss my mama off.

"She thinks she's more special than the preacher, that Jesus loves her dog better than the rest of us. But just you wait. When the Rapture comes, we'll be waving at her from up in the clouds and she'll just be rolling on the ground in misery, right along with your daddy, if he don't do right. And that dog of hers is gonna be swallered up in the jaws of hellfire, guaranteed."

Whenever GooGoo would get in trouble, Miss Joan'd be the first to take up for him and say he was misunderstood, that he was saved in person by the Son of God. She didn't see nothing but good in her young'un, didn't see his lies or his hard-on. She thought he couldn't do no wrong, and she'd raise hell with anybody said different. But when she came to the door of the trailer that day when I went out there, she had flat sure changed her tune. She said GooGoo was a mere hull of his former self, that he had done gone insane on account of the war and hadn't even stayed a single night up in her trailer. "The Marine Corps has done killed my son," she said. "First they disfigured him, and then they killed his spirit."

"Lord, Miss Joan, where does he reside?"

"Right yonder," she said, pointing at a rusted out camper shell up under a pine tree beyond her growed-over garden. "Got him a kerosene heater in there that's like to burn him up the rest of the way. Got hisself a eight track tape deck and a mess of *Hustler* magazines. I reckon he lays up in there and beats off most of the time."

"The poor pitiful thing," I said.

"That's the truth of it," she sighed. She looked pure wore out. Her skin was like saddle leather, and the wrinkles around her mouth was deep and dark from so many years of sucking on cigarettes and working in her garden with the sun beating down. "Oh, he'll take a drink with me of a afternoon ever so often. He'll come and eat a mayonnaise sandwich or some tuna fish with me for lunch. Sometimes he'll eat the supper I put out for him. But come nightfall all he wants to do is crawl up in that old shell and watch the dark. Don't hardly never go nowhere."

That didn't sound nothing like the loud mouthed, pervert-breathing GooGoo I knew back at Escambia County High School in Cantonment. "Well, Lord love you, Miss Joan, for looking after him."

"What else I'm going to do? He's all I got. I reckon I could give him over to the state, but he's all I got in the world." She lit a cigarette and begun to suck on it real hard. "He talks crazy, about building a place that don't use services, like electrical and such, and that the government won't have no purchase over him. He ordered him a pair of them Earth Shoes that makes him look like a outer space person. Lord, he ain't right. The state would take him in a heartbeat."

"Don't you let Jesus hear you say that, Miss Joan, cause you know you got the Lord on your side, always have."

She picked a piece of tobacco from off her tongue. "You ain't got to tell me nothing about the Lord. No, ma'am. Hell, I was a holy roller preacher woman fourteen years and I know how that works. Or how to work *that*."

"Yes'm, we all know how the Lord works. He works in damn mysterious ways, don't he?"

"No, child. Not how the Lord works. It's how I can work the Lord, get him to throw it on their heart strings, that's what's done come back on me."

"M'am?" I shouldn't of said nothing to get her to going on a preachment, but she got cranked up right then.

"When you done seen the Lord in person, right there at the foot of your bed, you come to know just how to get the Lord to put it on the heart strings. Yes, Lord, you hear what I say." She was looking at me real hard so I reckoned I better nod yes.

"Amen," I said.

"Yes, Lord, whenever somebody did me bad, like when Betsy Crow allured GooGoo's daddy away from us, I went straight to Jesus and prayed a mighty prayer, I mean. I said, 'Lord, you ain't got to strike her down nor throw her in the fires of hell.' I said, 'Lord, you ain't got to kill her only living child. You ain't got to throw her into the lustful womb of Sodom and Gomorrah.' I said, 'Lord, just put it on her heart strings. Put it on her heart strings, Lord'."

Like I said, Miss Joan was always bad to preach and carry on at the drop of a hat, but she was on fire this day. I reckoned it was on account of it being her own son laid up in that camper shell with them *Hustler* magazines, and I was right, 'cause she kept on going.

"I said, 'Don't take and give her cancer, Lord. Don't grow no black tumors up in her belly. Lord, you don't need to put the hot firebrands of pain to her skin and swinge the hide off her backside, Lord. Just put it on her heart strings, Lord. Throw it on them heart strings'."

"So how did all that preaching come back on you?" I thought if I could get her to the point, then her sermon shouting might would stop.

"Child, don't you know it's the heart strings that gets them when can't nothing else? And when I prayed for Jesus to put it on Betsy Crow's heart strings, well, did you know that thing's mama, the one somebody that she loved better than life—that thing's mama fell out from a tumor up in her head and had to be toted to a hospital. They had to put them brain scams on her. She was dead in forty-eight hours. Do you see what I mean?"

"I reckon, Miss Joan." She had this wild-eyed look that was pure scary.

"You got to see. I always could get the Lord to put it on the heartstrings. But now I think it's done come back on me. I think I done something to put the Lord on my tail cause He's done put misery on my heart strings now, what with GooGoo being a camper dweller that watches the night and beats off with them *Hustler* magazines."

"Oh, it ain't your fault, Miss Joan. Folks that's been to war just get that way sometimes. My grandaddy's brother Ned was in a POW camp—one of them Jap camps—and it messed him up all kinds of bad. He got arrested a while back for busting the windows out of the cars at the Chevrolet dealership in Pensacola with a baseball bat."

"You bound to be part right. But it seems like Jesus wouldn't have let GooGoo get all burnt up and go crazy like that unless I done let down the Lord."

"No, it ain't you. It's the war makes them crazy. I bet that's even what drove Will Luckie to run off with a old lady. He lost his mind over there in Vietnam."

She turned her attention to Will, and I was relieved for the preaching to die down. "Well, something inhuman sure took over his mind. Being a whore to some rich old lady. He never did have no pride."

"I heard GooGoo had a meal with them."

"Yes, Lord. I was so happy to know my boy was getting out, finally, even with them people. I thought Will would look after him like he done in the Marines. But do you know Will Luckie throwed him out in the heat of the day? Said he weren't good enough to be there. Liked to killed GooGoo. He brung home some good groceries, though. Barbecue chicken and what not."

"Is that a fact?"

"Oh, it is a fact. It's fact that the food was good, and it's a fact that folks'll turn on their own. If you get beat down, folks will sure enough turn on you." She sucked on that smoke some more. "And you seem plumb beat down, girl. Take my advice. Go see GooGoo and let him tell you about it. He's out yonder. Drunk, maybe. But he'll tell you. And when you finish talking to him, you go straight to the preacher back at the Shining Light. And you let that preacher man lay his hands on you and heal your heart of that sorry, whore mongering Will Luckie."

"Yes'm. I'll do that, Miss Joan. But first let's try to pray me and Will together out of the wilderness instead of praying Will out of my heart, okay? You got a strong line to Jesus, so you be sure and try to pray me and Will back together," I said.

"You don't want that sorry man," she said. "What you want with him?"

"I'm going to bring him back to Jesus where he won't keep doing GooGoo bad, for one damn thing," I said.

"God bless you, then. I'll go to praying on it right now, but if it don't take, then you go straight to the church house."

"Yes'm."

"And what about that rich lady? You want me to beseech the Lord to put it on her heartstrings? I'll pray Jesus takes what's nearest to her that she cares the most about."

"Okay, you do that," I said. "But put a double praying on Will's heartstrings if he don't get back with me. He's the one that'll have it coming, so I'll go on and start a pre-prayer on that part."

"Lord, seems like I'm praying all the time now. Trying to pray my boy back from the dead. Back from them harlots up in them magazines."

I had to walk past the vegetable garden she kept in her side yard. It used to always be full of plants that flowered and give more food than she and GooGoo could eat, but she had done let it go. It was all scrubby and dried up and took over by weeds and vines. I'd heard the church had been looking after her lately, bringing canned goods and all. It had been this way, I figured, ever since GooGoo had gone off to the war and then come home all changed in the head. But then, when I rounded a weeping willow and got closer to

GooGoo's residence, I noticed some producing plants: tomatoes, bell peppers, pole beans, okra, cucumbers, squash—healthy plants, food for the taking. Wasn't really no need for the church charity, is what I was thinking.

All the while I walked, I could hear her praying. "Lord, you ain't got to send him into the jaws of the beast, Lord. No. And Lord, you ain't got to pox his limbs and manhood with leprosy that rots away the things he uses most, Lord. Lord, you don't have to hold the soles of his feet to the brimstone till he begs to have his feet cut off. Just put it on his heartstrings, Lord. Put it on his heartstrings. Make Will Luckie hurt for the hurt he done to other folks. Hurt him if he don't go back with Marlayna." And when I heard her say that last little bit, it put a rabbit right across my grave.

GooGoo crawled out of the camper shell when he heard me coming up. He was pretty glad to see me, I reckon. He got me a cold beer and a ash tray. He had a couple of folding yard chairs set up by a cold fire pit a few feet from the camper. There was a long bench from a picnic table set between the two yard chairs, and he throwed his feet up on it next to where a old timey black fan nodded back and forth. There was PBR and Budweiser beer cans everywhere, around the entrance to the camper, on the ground by the folding chairs, throwed out in the field beyond the yard, and piled up near a barrel where he had some trash burning. It put me in mind of all them cans I'd keep in the back of Daddy's truck, till we hit the highway and I could chunk them at signs. I wondered where Daddy was these days. I hadn't seen nor heard from him since he run off, and Mama said once a man gives hisself to another woman he always turns his back on his young'uns.

I asked him could I peep in his camper and he said yes. It wasn't like his mama had told it. There were a few *Hustler* magazines, but there were mostly a bunch of *Foxfire* and *Mad* magazines and a bunch of tapes, like Mott the Hoople, Led Zeppelin, and Uriah Heep, all that jumpin'-around heavy metal shit I hate. Top forty radio music is all good, the rock and the soul music, but bubble gum is for shit. Bottom line, country is king in my way of thinking. I already told you I'm down with Merle, Waylon, and Loretta. I love myself some Ray Price, Tammy Wynette, and Conway Twitty. I can't use no country music wannabes like Olivia Newton John or Marie Osmond, and I still ain't decided on Kris Kristofferson; he's a little too pretty. And don't even ask me about Charley Pride. I mean, I liked his voice on the radio, but once you realize he's colored you just can't take it serious. Anyway, in the middle of all these jumpin'-around heavy metal tapes, a couple really caught my eyeballs. "You don't mean to tell me your mama knows you have satanic music up in here," I said. "Sabbath, Bloody Sabbath? It's like some *Exorcist* mess up in here."

"Have you lost your shit?" he said. "Ain't no devil-worshipping around here, so you just keep your opinions to yourself. My mama would get sure-enough worked up and freak if she had them thoughts planted up in that saved-brained head of hers."

"Well what about this Blue Oyster Cult one? Are you like some of them Manson people or something?" He laughed real loud, and it was kind of a good laugh, so I felt better. I leaned in a little further and saw that there were even books cramped onto shelves along the "ceiling" of his camper shell, although he didn't strike me as much of a book reading person. There was a puddle of books on his mattress: something about trout fishing; another one called *The Electric Kool Aid Acid Test* that had a really pretty cover with a million colors on it, and a bunch more. There was even a big giant paperback book, *The Last Whole Earth Catalogue*, that had a picture of the world from space on the front of. I didn't see hide nor hair of a kerosene heater. "It really ain't as gross up in here as your mama said."

"Right on, Ringo," he said, then, "You like to read?" He was leaning in beside me, peering in at the book-puddled mattress.

"Sure—but mostly comics and mysteries and some romance. Hollywood gossip. Your books look fatter and harder to understand."

"Don't underestimate yourself. I've made that mistake my whole damn life. When I come to books, after I went in the marines, I found out folks could do and say the damndest things, you know, just with words. It's a big damned secret that's kept for rich, educated folks. They don't let you know about that secret in high school. They just feed you all that slow-moving, ancient shit with all that thee-thou Shakespeare talk, that Bible talk. Go ahead, pick out something."

"I don't know. What do you think I'd like?"

"How I'm going to know that? I hardly know you."

The camper smelled like the hippie head shop I went in one time at Pensacola Beach, like how I reckoned marijuana would smell. "You pick."

"Okay, let's see." He swiped at one closest to him. "This one's good," and the cover said *Been Down So Long It Looks Like Up to Me.* I thought that was a funny title and I could relate for sure, but then he said, "No, take this one," and I liked that cover better, a flying seagull, plus, it was a lot skinnier than the others. It made me think about the seagulls at Pensacola Beach. I reckoned I could relate to that, too.

GooGoo re-trained the fan onto them two yard chairs, where we sat and talked about nothing for a while. Finally, I asked him about that Fourth of July business, and he was just drunk enough to be glad to tell about how dead wrong Will had done him.

"Yeah," he said, "that somebitch went and left his old friends behind. He's got some money to play with and some high class folks to impress, so he ain't got no use for me. I showed him, though. I dumbed it up big time, played the white trash just like they'd expect."

"Why'd you do that?"

"I don't know. Just to be a butt pain, I reckon."

I took a long sip of Budweiser, needing to get him onto the topic I needed to know about, not about him trying to embarrass my man. "I knew Will would do it with anything female, but I never would have thought he'd do his old friends wrong just so a bunch of rich assholes would give him the time of day."

"Yep," he said. "Turned on me."

"Are you sure he wasn't joking? You know how he cuts up. You sure you heard it right? Was you bad drunk?"

"Well shit, Marlayna. I had done had me a few. Hell, it was Independence Day. But I damn sure wasn't drunk. And he sure as hell wasn't laughing. And that sorry motherfucker told me I didn't belong up in that house with his woman. All because she told him to throw me out. Ain't that some shit?"

"Some sure enough fucked up shit. I ain't hardly believing it. What did you do when he told you that?"

"Hell, I told him he had done turned into a snot-nosed pussy just like every other pussy over there in Pollard."

"You ain't telling me he's whipped." This part had to be a lie. Will didn't jump for no woman, did what he wanted whenever the hell he wanted to.

"Whipped as a fucking hairless runt in a bad litter."

"That just don't sound like Will. He never let no woman run over him. Not even me."

"Damn sure is these days. Told me he'd do anything for that woman. Told me he'd give both nuts for that woman, kiss her feet, suck up all kinds of way."

"Uh-uh!" I couldn't feature it at all.

"My hand to God. Ain't no fucking lie."

Right when he said that I remembered what a for real liar he was back in high school and wondered what in the hell was I doing there talking to a mindless liar about Will. I guess that shows how desperate I was to find out any little thing I could about my man. So I went on and kept at it, like a fool. "Did he say anything about me?"

"Sure he did."

"No lie?" But something told me it *was* one.

"Hell yeah. Said he wished you had done been pregnant instead of just in your head. That if you had a young'un he'd be with you, rice style."

"No shit?" I started thinking out where I might be able to get a baby, quick like, knowing at the gut level wasn't no way in hell Will said any such of a thing.

"If I'm lying I'm dying."

"So you think there's a chance we'll get back together?"

"Hell yeah. Soon as he gets that rich lady out of his system. And you might be able to make that happen if you play your cards right."

"What do you mean?"

"I mean study it. Come up with a plan. Hell, even if it's just to kick her ass or something. There used to be a time when you would've already busted her upside the head."

"I already thought of that," I said.

He squinted his eyes and popped open another beer. "But you know them rich folks be like to get their lawyer friends and their judge friends to throw you under the jail for a long-ass time."

"I had done thought that, too," I said, and we both got real quiet.

A couple of minutes passed with us just sitting there, and GooGoo picking at a hangnail, looking to be mulling something in his mind. Then he looked up fast. "By God, you know what you ought to do, don't you?" he said.

"I guess I don't."

"Re-con."

"What?"

"Hell, yeah. Re-con," he said. "Goddamn right."

"Goddamn wrong," I said, "cause I ain't got idea the first what you're talking about."

"Wait here," he said. He went over to the camper shell and crawled inside. I could hear him sliding shit around, grunting, and rifling through the Lord knew what. I studied them piles of beer cans and missed my daddy some more. I wondered if I ought to slip on off, but he had done got me curious.

When he crawled out of the camper he had a armload of shit—some of his Marine

Corps gear, a canteen, a mean-looking knife of some kind, and a pair of binoculars. "If this stuff don't do," he said, "I'll make you out a list for the Army-Navy Supply in Pensacola."

"Do for what? Hell, GooGoo, I ain't going to war."

"I know that, dammit. I thought I'd help you with a reconnaissance mission. If you ever played spy when you were a kind you can do it. All you do is play it cool and low, just like a spy would. Then take them by surprise. Bond. James Bond."

This got my attention, and I wanted to know more. "I ain't never done it thataway, GooGoo. Not sneaky like. Not cool and low. You know me. I kick their ass first and ask questions later. You think cool and low will work for me?"

"Shit, yeah. Them rich folks do it thataway all the damn time. Rich folks is some double-faced, double-dealing rat bastards. All you have to do is you take your ass out there to that woman's place, then you stay back and watch what comes and goes. Find the weak spot. Get a strategy. Then— bam! Take them by surprise."

For all his craziness, I knew GooGoo had put his finger on it. He hung them binoculars round my neck and I put on that Marine Corps camouflage shirt with "McGeehee" on the pocket. He told me right where I could find an old logging road above the pasture that would get me in the back way, and he said I wouldn't have to worry about the mace or no tiger traps like they had in Vietnam. I didn't ask him to explain, because I didn't want to know what kind of torture a godless gook could've thought up.

"What you waiting on, girl? You still got some daylight left to scope it out. Go on and get the lay of the land. Stake out."

Which I did, right then.

It's a powerful feeling to be standing in the pine shade, aiming a pair of binoculars down on a patch of land where folks are going about their business without clue the first that you can see it all. Off to my left was a ginormous barn that faced that Tara house sitting about seventy-five yards away. The barn sat at the rear of the fenced in pasture, where three horses were grazing in the greenest, most groomed looking grass you ever saw. Damn if rich folks don't have it made pretty right down to what grows in the dirt.

GooGoo had said to watch out that there might be a barn hand that lived in there amongst the straw, on account of didn't no rich folks tend to their own chores nor their own horses. And he was right, too, because off to the side of the barn was an old timey outhouse, with the quarter moon and all, and a short little man come out of it and went to toting feed sacks and the like from hither to yon. He didn't put no fear in me, though; he was too puny. I just went on studying the land lay.

The fence line butted up to the rear of the yard, where a skinny colored man was working on what looked to be rose bushes, clipping at them with some kind of scissor looking cutter. Behind him was a swimming pool that had all this cement around it where you didn't have to get no grit nor grass on your feet to carry into the water. There was even more cement trails leading to some brick steps that went up to even more cement with brick trim patios all along the back side of the house. Ain't no telling how many miles of sidewalks could be laid all around the town with all the concrete them folks had poured into their dadgum back yard. Plus, there was even brick planters full of ivy all around and flowers growing out of pots everywhere, plus lounging chairs and umbrellas, and float rafts, where you can lay up in the swimming pool, keep your beauty parlor wash and set dry, and sip on something out of a crystal goblet. Fuck some cut glass. Cut glass is dime store shit. I reckon I'm just a cut glass individual.

To the left of the house was a garage, and to the right of the pool there was another, small fenced-in yard where a chicken coop sat smack dab in the middle of with a little wooden picnic table nearby. And further on to the right was a smaller house than Tara, but it was still big and fancy as hell, and it had one of them picket fences all around the back yard.

It was falling close to dusk when that puny barn man came riding up on a John Deere that was damn sure shinier than my ex's—I mean my— truck. I hadn't noticed no tractor before. If they had a tractor, then they had crops somewhere, no telling how many hundreds of acres. Anyway, the puny barn man drove right up into the barn. After a while, he went to closing the doors, leaning some shovels and things up against the outside of the building before he walked around the side. Before long a rust-bodied pickup went chugging away, down a dirt lane on the outside of the fence.

The sky was streaking sidewards colors with the sunset, so I took one last look for the day. It's funny how you don't notice things right off the bat, like that tractor. I looked straight down below me, for the first time, where an old hay wagon was tumped on its side next to a tin roof on some posts. There was a water trough next to a tall spigot, too, and all kids and sizes of buckets turned upside down on the ground, so as not to breed skeeters, I reckoned. But the biggest thing I was just now really seeing, in the back right corner of the field, was a metal silo, maybe forty or fifty feet high and pretty big around, and I couldn't for the life of me figure what might go into the thing. But I didn't spend much time mulling on it. I had to report back to headquarters.

"A damn silo?" GooGoo asked, after he listened to my blow by blow of the land lay without giving up much reaction. The silo had his ears all pricked up, out of the blue. "Now that's a thing worth looking at. You don't see a whole lot of them in this part of the world. I mean, they're around, but not common."

"What's a big deal?"

"Nothing. Just that it would make a better turtle shell that the one I'm living in."

"Shell?"

"That camper shell. That's been my experiment in cutting off from the system."

"What system?"

"*The* system. The man. The powers that be. I told you I aim to be self-sufficient."

"Why? What's the point?"

"The *point* is, we're in for some trying times, what with the earth being poisoned. Ain't you read *Silent Spring*? About the DDT and insecticide chemicals all up in the food chain? The bald eagle, the national bird, just about wiped out."

"I think I heard something about that."

"Jesus, don't you know an earth ain't a thing that just lasts forever unless it's cared for? It can go exactly the way of the bald eagle. Well, I'm doing something about it. When the dominoes begin to fall, I'll be able to survive. As long as the earth has an atmosphere for me, that is."

"What the hell?"

"Because the greenhouse effect could make it impossible to survive."

"You're talking Chinese now."

"Don't you know about what's happening to the world? It took rivers catching on fire to get any attention for the pollution. And I got to say, for all the low down shit done by Tricky Dickie Nixon, at least he's tried to do right by Mother Earth."

"What's he done for her?"

"Created the EPA for one. And then came that Clean Water Act. Protecting the bald eagle and such. But all that's just a start. Every person has to change how they do, and that's why I'm fixing to figure a way to go off the reservation."

"But, GooGoo, you ain't no Indian." I begun to think that maybe Miss Joan was right, and GooGoo needed to be sent on over to the state hospital in Chattahoochee. She could Baker Act him, like my Aunt Freida in Ocala done her crazy husband Purvis that couldn't keep his pecker in his britches.

"Okay. Take the Indians, then. The cliff dwellers. They carved their houses out of the dirt. Talk about being good for the ecology."

"Are you one of them tree hugging Loraxes?"

"Fuck your uptight ass if you want to put down people who just want you to have oxygen to breathe."

"What are you talking about?"

"A few hundred years ago a bunch of Hindu folks got beheaded while they tried to save the trees—that's where it started. So you go to calling names and making fun if you want to. Be a retard about it. I say that if a Buddhist can burn up and not bat an eye and if a bunch of Bishnoi folks can lose their heads like martyrs then, I can make a home that won't be at the expense of no oxygen for the rest of the world."

That Baker Act was looking better and better, but I couldn't help pressing him. Maybe he really did know what he was talking about—just having a time explaining it. "Wait. Back up, GooGoo. Tell me something. What you going to keep in that silo?"

"Myself. Turn it into home, sweet home. My crib."

"You ain't!"

"Chill out and think about it. Silos are air tight. I could cut me a door, a couple of windows. Hell, and them things are tall. If I put in a window unit it ought to stay right cool, with the hot air going up. And winter ain't a trial at all."

"No, it ain't cool, GooGoo, because people don't live in silos. Why don't you just find a cave somewhere?"

"A cave would do."

"But you ain't got one. Not no cave nor no silo."

"Yet."

"And anyway, this is about the lay of the land! Tell me what I need to do next, GooGoo. Fuck a silo." I had to change the subject away from his crazy notions. Besides, I was all fired up to begin soldiering.

So he commenced to explain what he called "the strategy," and I begun regularly hauling my ass to that high cliff that hangs over that rich bitch's horse pasture. Whether it was rainy or dark or dawn or twilight, you'd find me there all sprayed down with Off to keep the mosquitoes away. For a couple of days to start with, I pretty much stayed put, but then GooGoo told me it was important to keep on the move. So I begun roaming over the whole place. First, though, I had to start going down and making friends with the horses to keep them from giving me away. I had done seen enough westerns to know what the horses would do if a bunch of wild Indians came up. I got them easy gradual like, till they stopped paying me no mind. It got to where I could walk right past them horses and go right straight up in the yard. Please don't think I'm a total nut case. I'm trying to do better or else I wouldn't be here telling you everything. It's just that, well, like they say, I had to hit rock bottom.

Spying is a strange business. It took me a while to get used to being able to see folks up in the house at night without thinking they could see me, but I finally I got to where I'd just walk all over the yard, not a care in the world. GooGoo said darkness was a cloak, and he was right. Towards the end of my re-con days I got cocky enough that I wasn't even shy about stealing shit, mostly from around the pool, that I knew belonged to Will. I got one of his shirts, a guitar pick, and a fancy crystal glass he had spit tobacco juice in (course I dumped out the juice; I ain't that crazy), plus a Zippo lighter with the Playboy symbol on it and a roach clip (GooGoo told me what it was). And a bunch of other stuff. And I damn sure ought to turn him in to the cops for being a dope head.

What I did is, before I'd go to roaming their property of a night, I'd lay on my belly in the weeds and bushes for a while and look down across the pasture with GooGoo's spyglasses and see what I could see. And I done seen plenty. I seen that Calhoun woman, and she ain't much. Hell, she's short as a midget, right plump, always wearing these lounging clothes with a bathing suit underneath. Lots of times these two little white poodle-looking dogs are waddling behind her or laying beside her feet. They sure ain't worth shit for watch dogs because they never as much as yapped when I was in the vicinity. Where *she* lays is on a pool chair and watches Will float around in the water on a air mattress. He's near about always got a drink in his hand and laughs a lot. Sometimes he throws her in the pool. Hell, sometimes they make out in the pool. The first time I seen that, I was so grossed out I almost forgot my new strategy and jumped in my car, drove down there, and kicked her ass right then. But I remembered GooGoo saying it was *information* I was after, so I counted to thirty-three and stayed put.

There's this big tall woman that's all the time walking over to where Will lives that must be the Calhoun lady's daughter, CeCe. I can tell from clear cross the pasture that I would hate that bitch's guts. She even walks bossy. She holds her nose up in the air like the biggest snot there ever was. And she's over there a lot, just walks right up in the house. Don't knock or nothing. It's a wonder her mama gets any time for loving at all. Matter of fact, there was this one time I'd swear Will and that old lady was doing it right there in the swimming pool, and that big old boss-walking-around CeCe come up and they didn't notice her. When they did notice her she was right up on them, and the reason I reckon they was fucking was that CeCe's mouth went to gaping open like a pitcher plant, then she went to stomping her foot and hollering and carrying on. Will just splashed some water on her, and she turned right on her heel and walked off. Then Will and that old lady went right back to doing what they had done been doing. And that ain't the only time I seen them carrying on in the pool, but it's hard to tell for sure cause of the light reflecting off the water. Shit, I don't know if I really want to see what they're doing. It grosses me out to even think.

Other times I'd watch during the day time, keeping cover on the pine cliff, just using the hell out of them spy glasses. I'd see him playing a guitar, sometimes to that woman, or to a few other people, like as if they had company. Sometimes he'd be sitting on the picnic bench in the chicken yard. And playing the goddamn guitar to the chickens. I declare to God he did that.

How I finally figured Will really and truly had done lost his mind over there in Vietnam was when I seen him with the chickens. He'd go up in that chicken yard several times a day. Sometimes he'd be writing stuff down in a notebook. Other times he'd look all sad while he picked the guitar strings real slow. There'd be times when he'd pet the chickens, even hold them in his arms and rub their feathers. Looks like there's one in particular that'd let him hold it the most, cause that one wore some kind of a collar or something. Matter of fact, he'd let that one out of the chicken yard right regular, carry him over by the pool and sit by that rich bitch and pet him. So does she. It ain't like the Will Luckie I knew to be all carried away with a bunch of goddamn chickens. But I reckon if you've done left the best part of your mind over in some jungle, then a chicken makes as much sense as anything else.

I spent the better part of three weeks being a guerilla warfare person, and that's how I found out about the surprise birthday plans. I had done hit the information jackpot. And it was because dumbass Will left that notebook overnight on one of them fancy outdoor tables near the pool. I scooped it up, slipped off across the yard with it, hunkered down behind the garage, clicked on my flashlight, and started flipping the pages.

It was full of all these crazy notes about the chickens, with lists of numbers of eggs produced by whichever birds. And they had names I had heard all over the news during the past year or two, all having to do with that whole Watergate mess. I have to be honest with you—when I saw those chicken notations I told myself that in itself was enough of Crazy Town that even I wouldn't want to travel there. And then I saw the notes about the rich bitch's birthday party. Will had made a list that looked like this:

Wednesday 8/7/74

8:00 a.m. Pensacola
2:00 p.m. beauty parlor
4:00 p.m. pool party
in between or thereabouts: Pier One Pensacola

Of course, I never would have known what it meant if it wasn't for what he wrote up top on the page: CeCe's surprise birthday party for her mama (my hot mama)

Gag a maggot.

I flipped back through the chicken pages and shook my head at how much time he put into describing the yard dirt critters—their personalities and their doings. I thought about all the times I'd seen him toting one or another of the things around, petting away. And I thought about the one he favored—that one that wore the necklace and stuff. Yeah, that crazy man was plumb off his rocker for that one particular bird. Heart strings, is what I thought. Like Miss Joan said, a prayer of revenge is best if you put it on their heart strings. I put the notebook back on the fancy outdoor table so as not to give anything away.

But my thoughts was off and running. I begun to make a for real strategy. And in my mind I could hear the war cry GooGoo liked to say: "Oorah!"

"Good work, soldier," was all GooGoo said back to me when I told him about it all. Then, "It'll be risky, putting on that light, even in a chicken coop. You'll be shedding that cloak of darkness, and out in the country, where the dark is pitch, you might as well be using a signal light—hell, it'll shine like a lighthouse."

"I'll just have to be quick. I want that one particular chicken in the worst way. It's plain that he loves it the most, as a pet, even. But I reckon I'm going to have to swipe whatever one I can get to the fastest. That a good plan?"

"Good enough. Like we say: 'Improvise, adapt, overcome.' I'm betting that you shall overcome."

Sometimes it felt like GooGoo was talking in riddles, but I took it as a compliment.

"I been reading that Jonathan Seagull book." For some reason I'd gotten curious about GooGoo, what he thought, how he got some of his wild ideas, like about the silo. I wanted to show him that I had a mind, too, but coming by it was kind of hard, starting with the seagull book. "He's just flying around and getting good at it, and the other birds are mean to him. I hope the story gets better. Doesn't seem to be much to it."

"It's a fable. Don't be so literal. Look for the lessons in it."

"So it *does* get better?"

"Sure it does. And it might have a lesson or two for you, specially."

I had an urge to tell him just who did he think he was? To tell him he didn't know shit about me, but something held me back. Jesus, maybe. Anyway, I kept on reading, on my off time when I wasn't being a double-o-seven. And come to find out he might just be on to something. Come to find out that the real lesson for that damn flying rat—which is what my daddy always called gulls, for their scavenging ways—was that coming to a honest, for real, downright nitty-gritty true understanding of his own self was what he had to do. Plus, forgive.

I'd never really put a lot of thought into who I am, down deep. I just ran around through life, partying and praying and wanting and working. So I begun to think on it. And think. And I even asked for GooGoo's thoughts.

"You ain't occupied enough space in the world," he said. "When you've been to the other side of the earth, especially in combat, you get a lot bigger picture of the place. And the people. You've basically been four places: school, church, honkytonks, and Pensacola, Florida. That's a damn small world."

"But that's how I was raised up. I can't help it."

"Sure you can."

"How?"

"By doing what you just did. Read a damn book. And not one where you live life through a bunch of movie stars. Fuck a Robert Redford and them *Exorcist* and *Serpico* people in the rag mags. Feed your head."

Well, I never was much of a student, but I carried myself to the Pollard library, which ain't all that big, but they put the newer books on display, and one caught my eye right away. *Jaws*, with a big old shark on it, coming up through the ocean at a lady swimming. And that shark was a million times bigger than the lady. I figured it was bound to be scary—but not nearly as scary as *The Exorcist* I had done tried to read. Ain't nothing as scary as the devil. And I said that to GooGoo in one of our talks one evening.

"It's a fact," he said, "that fear is the most basic human feeling that you can use to jerk folks around, control them. If somebody is scaring you, then they're out to make you do what they want. It ain't honest."

"Are you saying the devil ain't real?"

"I never seen him."

"So you don't believe in hell?"

"I've done *been* to hell. Been roasted out of a nut sack and a good bit of my back flesh. *That's* hell."

Well. I don't have to tell you that shocked the shit out of me. I didn't have no kind of idea that old GooGoo had been disfigured in such a awful way as that. It was no wonder he was a camper dweller who watched the night. I couldn't think of a thing to say, so I just joined him in the watching of the dark.

Turned out, I couldn't get that one particular bird, Will's favorite. I tried, though. I blacked my face, wore all black, and blended like ink into that horse pasture I crossed, to sneak into the chicken yard. I eased into the coop, slow-like, so as not to wake the things. That was when I put the light on, which I knew was glowing through the cracks in the wood, as big as, like GooGoo said, a lighthouse. I had to be fast as all get out, and I shone the light all around, trying to find the one with the necklace. In that very second I heard a door slam and those little fat, waddling dogs commenced barking. All this time and I'd never heard a peep out of those ridiculous dogs, and now this. Plus, the birds commenced to clucking. I scooped up the chicken closest to me, killed the flashlight, and eased out and around the coop. By the time I was running across the pasture, clutching that squirming hen like a football, them yappy dogs had done set out after me like a pair of bloodhounds. They stopped at the pasture fence, though, and I heard that rich bitch hollering, "Yoo-hoo, Rosencrantz! You and Guildenstern get back up here and stop that!" Lord, she had a shrieky voice. "Whatever got into you? Leave those poor ponies alone!"

The short of it is that I didn't get caught. So the incident of the coop thieving put some things in motion. It was like that game, Mousetrap, you know? One thing happened and then another and another and on down the line, which led to here. It was odd enough to land up in that kitchen, talking to that maid, Lindia. But the very strangest thing is that I'm here, talking to you. And you with that dadgum silo sitting out in that pasture of y'all's. I've done told you that GooGoo fancies him that silo, wants to use it for his turtle shell.

What, don't you see? Me landing up in your kitchen, and now, here—well, it has the hand and will of God all over it. Get it?

I done told you Mr. Will got to where he didn't allow no fried chicken no more. Nor baked nor barbecued nor dumplinged nor no other kind of way. He told me, not long after that GooGoo man went on so about killing them birds to pleasure hisself, that he had done decided to swear off of eating them. He said he got to thinking about them chicken houses where they raise the things by the hundreds and thousands to slaughter. And it worked on him and worked on him, wanting to know how they were killed so they could be packaged up for folks like us. Finally, he called up one of them big chicken companies over in Arkansas and asked them a whole bunch of questions, all the time writing down notes in The Chicken Sheet.

"This ain't good," he told me when he hung up. "I ain't liking this. You ever knew what them birds go through?"

"No, but I got me an idea."

"They string them up by their legs, hung up from a conveyor that carries hundreds of them at the time. So they're hanging there, squirming, and probably knowing something ain't right. They're probably wondering what the hell they're doing hanging upside down getting slung back and forth like. And you know how they kill the things?"

"Do they take a buzz saw to their necks?"

"Hell no," he said. "It's their little feet. Their little foot pads."

"They cut the feet off?"

"Electricity," he said. "Someone down at the Feed and Seed told me they shock their little footpads, then they slice the neck and drain all the blood out of them. But the farm in Arkansas said the electric current pulses through their bodies in a liquid."

"Is that right?"

"It don't sound good at all." He shook his head. "Shock their little fucking footpads. Damn."

"Seems like they'd have to keep the creatures calm," I tried. He looked so forlorn. "I bet it's calmer than you think. And painless."

"They bleed them out, then they cut the heads off the rest of the way. And *then* they drop them in boiling water and send them to the pluckers." He had tears in his eyes, I swear. "It's a gruesome business. They re-hang them by the hock and go to taking out the guts." He snatched a paper towel off the roll and blew his nose.

I watched him out the window that afternoon, making all kinds of notes on The Chicken Sheet. And he seemed to make a point of picking up each of the hens, cradling them in his arms, one at a time, talking to each, almost like he was apologizing. The next day he said wouldn't be no more chicken eating going on at Miss Maureen's, and she went right along with him.

"Perhaps we should ban all the dumb beasts that have been drawn and quartered for our consumption. It would be very spiritually cleansing, I think. And it is certainly tres chic to be a vegetarian these days. Perhaps I shall get a mantra, start meditating, and visit a health food store in Pensacola."

Of course Miss CeCe wasn't none too happy. "Ya'll are just as stupid as you are crazy. Why the hell should I have to give up chicken just because Will thinks his bunch of coop dwellers are human?"

"Well godammit, CeCe, I didn't say *you* had to give up chicken. I am simply saying that you will not find it on the menu in *my* home."

I thought to myself maybe that child wouldn't be all the time showing up at mealtimes around here no more.

"It's sinful the way you do the Lord's name. Beyond that, do you sit around and think up ways to make the Calhouns stick out like a big, ugly, sore thumb? Because, Mother, that is exactly how you fit into this town."

"Sugar, I could not care one whit less." She turned back to Mr. Will. "So what do you think? Shall we swear off all animal flesh? Goodness, what about shrimp? Do they count?"

"Hell, they're more like bugs," Mr. Will said. "I ain't got no quarrel with killing no bugs."

"Good grief, Mother!" And she went over to the deep freeze and begun taking the meat out. "I'm certainly not letting it go to waste," she said.

"And I am pleased to see your frugal side," Miss Maureen said. "But just take the chicken. I think we shall do this by degrees."

"Yeah," Mr. Will said. "I been craving me a slab of steak running some blood. You want me to get the grill going?"

"You do that," Miss Maureen said, while that child went to throwing frozen birds into a grocery sack. "I'll run to the Piggly Wiggly for rib eyes."

"Fix up a sack for Lindia to take home," Mr. Will said.

"Good Lord," CeCe said. "I do not take orders from you, of all people."

"CeCe!" Miss Maureen hissed. "Aren't you ashamed not to want to share your good fortune with Lindia? I don't believe you've ever even fried a chicken."

"Lindia will teach me," she countered.

That daughter of hers snatched another sack out from under the cabinet, real mean like. She's a greedy thing. I can see clear through that child. I didn't like her attitude about giving me a sack of meat, or volunteering me to teach her how to skillet-fry a bird, but I didn't see no need in turning down the chicken, so I carried it home and Brenda and me had Cletus over for dinner.

The thing about Miss CeCe, she's greedy even when she's making like to do for somebody else. She'll tend to them Brownie Scouts and visit the shut-ins for the church and pass out canned goods to the folks over in East Pollard of a Christmas. But she's all the time wanting a great big thank you and some kind of article in the newspaper saying what a treasure she is, how she's a benefictious or a philanderist and all such is that. A sad thing is, she does get the thank yous and the news stories and such every once in a while. Three years ago—you won't believe this—but she was named "Citizen of the Year." On account of she raised money to put a new wing onto the local library. Of course, it was "The Wickham Douglas Calhoun Wing," in honor of her daddy, and when he became her dead daddy, they added on "Memorial" in front of "Wing." Had a whole new sign made and everything. The worst part is, since the citizen of the year gets to ride in the annual homecoming parade, on the back of a fancy convertible from a dealership in Pensacola, well, there she was. You would've thought she was Miss America, waving that little cup-palmed wave like the Queen of England. Only thing missing was the tiara. It was a travesty.

She wants to wear her so-called religion and charity right there on her sleeve for all to see. I say that if you need to show off your faith, then you likely don't have any. Judge a man by his deeds. Oh—and I know you won't believe this one, but she came to me one time, back a couple of years ago, and asked if I knew any unwed, pregnant "colored girls." It was pure crazy. "What you got in mind, Miss CeCe?"

"I've just been thinking," she said, "that, well, people buy babies all the time, on the black market, you know. And I thought Winston and I could get ourselves a little colored baby, a boy preferably."

"Why a boy?"

"Well, because he might would grow up to be a professional athlete. I mean, the coloreds are truly gifted in that way. And when Howard Cosell interviews him, he might thank the nice white couple that brought him up, lifted him up out of poverty, tell about what a good Christian we made out of him. He and Frank Gifford might even put the boy on Monday Night Football. Who knows? Maybe we would all even be on TV with Johnny Carson! Can you imagine?"

That's what I mean about wearing it on her sleeve. I know you're thinking how in the world did I not lose my temper and call her out on her nasty, racist sayings and her crazy ideas? Well, consider that I've had long years of practice holding my tongue. But it was particularly hard this time. I had to wonder if she even knew what the "black market" was, or did she think it had to do with slave times. Anyway, I had to ask her, couldn't resist, "Don't you worry what folks would think, you rearing a black baby?" Knowing wouldn't nobody ever in a blue moon give that selfish, pretend-like Christian a baby of any tint or circumstance.

"I'm the last person to give a care about what anybody thinks."

Know thyself. Miss CeCe doesn't know a second of her own soul.

"Anyway, those people are just racist, and I'm the least racist person probably in the whole panhandle."

My hand to God, those words really did come out of that mouth of hers. And then she commenced to tuning up, as in crocodile tears.

"When I think of some poor little colored boy, growing up over there in the quarter in East

Pollard, when he could be amongst all of this," and she swept out her arm like some royal declarer, "well, I just—" and she pulled a Kleenex from her brassiere and went to dabbing her eyes. "I'm just so naturally caring and giving that it's hard to think of some little colored boy missing out. And I'm sorry for the tears, but everybody knows I cry at anything—the flag, the national anthem, my soaps. The drop of a hat and I cry. I just feel things more than the average person, that's what I think. And that's why I feel it's my responsibility, my duty as a Christian, to step up and help the less fortunate, don't you agree?"

I couldn't find any words. The tears of a crocodile swimming the Nile. All I could do was shake my head, look as sad as I could, and make a "Mmh," noise in my throat. Her glorification of her own self had dipped down to a new low, even for her.

And that's the way it was for her mama's fiftieth birthday party. She wanted to be given all the glory and credit and praise for making a newsworthy event. She wanted it to be a big surprise for her mama. And she had planned it for a whole month, sucking me right up in it.

I figured Miss Maureen didn't want the whole town on her lawn. She had done give up on most of the folks she used to have over for them social and charity functions. If that child was truly thinking of her mama, well, she'd been done sent Miss Maureen and Mr. Will off on a cruise or a took them to a nice restaurant in Pensacola. That child wanted her a news article. She had been fussing and fussing about Mr. Will bringing shame on her family so she wanted to show the town just what a big party she could throw, and that's all there was to it.

And something else about Mr. Will. Miss CeCe changed toward him right around July Fourth. I could see it, but I ain't been able to say exactly what it is. She'd stare at him sometimes, like she was hypnotized, but then she'd go to glaring and say something mean to him. Then, other times, she'd take one look at him and turn round and go home, without so much as a hello or a goodbye. Of course don't nothing never faze that man, not CeCe and not no big party. That man went right along with that child, kept the secret from Miss Maureen, went off and bought her a big present wrapped up in a big, fancy box and wouldn't tell nobody what it was, just that it was the one thing he knew she wanted. And that irritated Miss CeCe no end. "Well, you can try to show off with some fancy present, but I'm the one doing the party planning," she said, "and I'm doing it up right." Accusing him of trying to be the show pony when that's all she ever thinks about being.

So here come the tables and the tents and the music and the food and the flowers and the streamers and the booze and the black folks. A pool party with a Hawaiian theme. She had bought plastic leis and plastic grass skirts and plastic ukuleles and plastic palm trees. But there was a for-real fire pit—two of them—with for real pigs, all appled-up in the mouths. When I think what Miss CeCe could do with that money she had spent on her mama's birthday, I have to talk with Jesus because it goes all over me.

Anyway, them hundred and sixty-three guests begun to arrive, the men all in their swim trunks and the women in all kinds of bathing suits, from the tiniest bikinis to the most full-skirted of old lady suits, just like Miss CeCe had wrote on the invitations. There was the high and mightiest of Pollard all the way down to the mid-mightiest and even the not mighty whiteys. And the black folks mingled up in amongst them with trays of champagne and finger sandwiches, while Miss CeCe pointed and gave orders and gushed over the ladies' lacey cover-ups and sun hats. She had even invited a reporter and a photographer from The Pollard Gazette to make sure she got her headlines. But she didn't get the headlines she expected, not by a mile.

When Miss Maureen walked out, the band started in on "Happy Birthday" and Mr. Will danced her around. Everybody was all enthused and singing, and the flash bulbs were popping like it was the Academy Awards or something. Miss CeCe wasn't too happy with Mr. Will stepping up, but I seen right then he was going to be smack dab at the middle of this here party. And he set right about leading that crowd to sing more, with "For She's a Jolly Good Fellow."

I'm going to tell you something else. And I know you're going to be thinking, Lindia damn sure is crazy, after I tell you. I had a feeling that spyglass woman was going to show up at the party. I knew she was watching and waiting for her chance to bust up in here and raise some ruckus, and she did. And something else: I knew who it was the whole time she was laying out there past the pasture. I knew it was Mr. Will's ex-girlfriend that he said was so crazy and just as full of desire as he was.

I knew she had carried things off, and I knew one of the things she had carried off was a chicken, because Mr. Will had told me one had went missing, one he called "the shyster." And I knew what she aimed to do with that chicken, because I got a phone call over at Brenda's. A white girl asking me for my own dad-gum recipe. Of course, I didn't tell her. I just said, "What are you aiming to do to Miss Maureen?" She answered by hanging up the phone.

You already know I can tell a lot about folks by just taking me a good look at them, and I've told you Miss Maureen had went from a stove up old bitch to a satisfied woman that's acting a lot of the time like she's a teenager. I told you Mr. Will brung it out of her, just like he brung the love of fun back out of me. I took up dancing again, playing the old songs, turning the radio to the new songs—Stevie Wonder, Gladys Knight and the Pips, The Temps. I go to the movies down to Pensacola with Brenda. I took my hems up, too—three whole inches, to get into step with today's fashion, and when Cletus took notice do you know what I did? It ain't like me at all, but I took to undoing the top two buttons of my uniform—showing just a little shadow of my bosom, and I'm here to tell you that man's nose flared out like a cobra's head. So now I've begun to open that third button, and I declare Cletus hurts himself trying not to look. Naturally, Miss Maureen was onto me like a flash.

"I see what you're doing, Lindia. And I say more power to you. We ladies have to use all of our wiles and cunning ways do we not?"

"I don't know what you mean, ma'am," but we both giggled like high school girls.

I even shed the bun I have worn forever, went to the beauty parlor and had Yavonne cut it off and spruce me up in a puffy afro. Brenda said I was a few years behind the times, but I don't care. I always wondered how a 'fro would feel and I can tell you, it's a freeing thing. And Cletus likes my new hairdo, just like all the other flirtations I have come into. "You look as fine as wine," he said, and he gave me an afro comb, one that he wrote "Lindia" on, with a Magic Marker, in pretty, cursive penmanship. I like to wear it in my hair, especially since I know it galls Miss CeCe. I do like to get my secret digs at her, just like a teenager my own self.

I'm feeling all around more youthful these days, right down to the wild oats. And you know what? I've got to where I even let Cletus take me out to a club on the weekends. Him and me dance and laugh and cut up. I've let him kiss on me just a little bit. And you might think I'm crazy, but I believe I've got that nose of his full-throttle wide open, because he comes sniffing around me so much I think he might just sniff me up, "like a line of coke," is what Brenda says.

I don't know about no cocaine nor no hashish nor any of them hippie drugs like LSD, but I think I might get to liking them wild oats. And right smart, too.

11
Cecelia

I could go on and on about the escapades of the past few months, the antics of that hell-bent cretin. Suffice it to say, Independence Day brought a new low, though, and you can be sure I did not ever place myself in the vicinity of Will Luckie after that, unless there were other people around. God knows what kind of sexual violence he might have inflicted upon me with that instrument of torture betwixt those suntanned thighs of his.

I admit things were not so serene with Winston as they had been prior to Will's assault on me. Over the weeks I found myself growing more and more demanding of my husband's affection. I bought revealing negligees, scented lotions, and books explaining "how to." I read *The Joy of Sex*, even looked at The *Kama Sutra*, marveling at the preponderance of positions, knowing that I was not contortionist enough to pretzel myself into most of them. I read *The Total Woman* and found amongst those pages more of a palatable philosophy/offering for mending that part of a marriage. I took Marabel Morgan's advice and dressed up in cowgirl regalia. School girl. Nurse CeCe. I even tried the Saran wrap solution, but Winston said I looked like an egg roll. It was all to no avail.

I offered him massages and communal bubble baths and erotica in the form of the aforementioned Will-Luckie-preferred *Playboy* magazines. I even added the slightly dirtier *Penthouse* magazines, all purchased far, far away on Navy Boulevard in Pensacola. I was met by my mate with blushes and half-hearted fumblings and such tepid romancing that I began to question my own desirability. He did not even want to participate in the reading aloud of those "readers' letters" in the aforementioned magazines. Bitsy had confided that when she and James had "read aloud" night, the sex that ensued was rowdy and sweaty—and "dirty," as she described it, with the most deliciously serene expression I had ever seen on her insipid face. Clearly the sexual revolution had infected all quarters. Except mine. It was beyond disappointing.

After all, I was finally ready to explore the terrain of a full-bodied sex life with my husband, and I could not for the life of me arouse his interest. Oh, yes, there were a few occasions when he went through the motions, wine-tipsy, in the pitch, pitch dark, a prodding, grunting kind of awkwardness that only served to leave me wanting more of something else. I grew edgier and more tense than I have ever felt in my life, and Winston brought me more and more pills to settle me down.

I even contemplated a hand-held massager, like the one Mother swears by. Yes, she's all mouth about her geriatric discovery of the female orgasm, thanks to electricity. "Doubles, triples, quadruples!" she exclaimed, while my last meal threatened to reverse path.

"That is beyond disgusting, Mother. I do not wish to have that nasty image seared behind my eyelids."

"You should get one, CeCe, truly. I promise it would take the edge off your nerves, much better than Valium. Everyone's getting them these days. And I say, bravo for clitoral literacy. Share that with your Friends of the Library group."

Of course, it is all Will Luckie's fault. And once the proverbial feces hit the fan, I was faced with more intrusion on his part than I could have ever comprehended. It all came to a head on the day of Mother's fiftieth birthday luncheon, just two days past. God, it seems like a forever ago. Enough has changed to make it a forever ago.

You see, I had been planning this event for a solid month. A surprise party by the pool, in the relative coolness of the late afternoon and August twilight, aided by a dozen oscillating fans and plenty of PIC and tiki torches. It was to be attended by all the leading citizens of Pollard. Lindia had agreed, somewhat reluctantly, to help in the planning. Will even agreed to keep his wretched mouth shut and spirit Mother away to Cordova Mall in Pensacola for the morning and drop her off at The House of Hair in town for the afternoon so that we could get the grounds set up. Her hairdresser, Mr. DeFranciso, was to deliver her to the party, all made up, muumuued and gorgeous.

I am sure you know what Will Luckie did when I told him to wear a nice shirt and for-real swim trunks to the party. He laughed that laugh I have come to despise because it usually signals impending humiliation for me. The man would not guarantee that he would even wear a shirt. Knowing that the crème de la crème of Pollard would be there, making mental notes on the progress of Mother's debauched incapacitation. He laughed and said that since it was a pool party, if he was going to stand around nibbling cocktail weenies with a bunch of tight-assed holy rollers, well, he had to be prepared to bail at any second.

What he ended up wearing was that semi-transparent pair of sand-colored double knit shorts (obviously, bathing suits do not occupy a place in his wardrobe) that I made a point of telling you about earlier. And a ratty denim shirt. Unbuttoned. All the way down, revealing chest hair with those hideous gold chains garlanded in it like some kind of pornographic Christmas tree. And pink plastic flip flops. This was the haute couture in which he greeted our guests, who set about avoiding looking down lest they witness the battle of the bulges—the pouch of tobacco in his pocket versus that living pepperoni log that springs from his loins. I set about chatting away my complete embarrassment.

Of course, Mother was absolutely stunned, overwhelmed, thrilled with the event. She went around hugging everyone she had not seen since taking up with her consort, and I just knew this would be her turnaround, her re-submergence into Pollard society. She set about regaling the crowd with her astrological profile, as a Leo. She found it poetic that her opposite sign was Aquarius, being that the Age of Aquarius was upon us. "It will be time of rebirth, compassion, and cooperation, and, really, is it not about time? To evolve? To coexist in peace? Oh, and I think it also noteworthy that the fifth house, the ruling house for me, is signified by pleasure—just as I am being pleasured in my sunset years by this delicious man." And she indicated you know who, multiplying my mortification a hundred fold.

Then, if that were not enough and in the middle of opening gifts, Will Luckie turned the whole party upside down. Not to mention that this awful creature, Marlayna something or other, soon showed up, bearing fried chicken.

"Oh, my great good Lord and Adam and Eve!" Mother gushed, clearing tissue paper, sparkles of glitter, and flower petals from the box Will had bestowed upon her. "I don't believe you went and did this, you sweet, sweet man!"

"Whatever is it, Mother?"

"Oh, it's just divine. It's absolutely perfect!" And she lifted a bowl-shaped vase from the gift stuffings. It was orange and yellow and green, decorated with black-lined drawings of African tribesmen grasping spears and shields.

Mild twittering rippled through the onlookers. It was truly a tacky sight. Mother had to be faking her joy out of politeness.

"I got it at Pier One imports in Pensacola," Will boasted.

Mother stood and embraced her man, kissed him full on the mouth, with obvious tongue while I wished for the concrete to crack open and swallow me whole. "Run and get him, then," she said. "Go to the Lincoln and get Wickham."

I looked at her as if she were a three-horned something-or-other. "What in the world are you talking about?"

"Don't be silly. I'm talking about your DD. Will has gotten me the perfect receptacle for dear departed Wickham's remains."

There was a collective gasp during which the tablecloths fluttered and I felt nothing but molten rage. "That cannot be! I took my DD's ashes from the car trunk and had them placed in the casket. It was ridiculous what I paid."

"Those were grill ashes, sugar. Now, just settle down and know that your mama is always two steps ahead of you, Little Miss Sunshine."

Winston, surely perceiving the leave of my senses, stepped over and took me by the arm, which I violently jerked from his soft hand. The camera flashed. "This will not stand! It is sacrilege!" Then I began shrieking and sobbing uncontrollably. "It's bad enough that I had no proper corpse to bury! But *grill* ashes? How dare you pass off grill ashes as my DD? It's criminal!"

Winston handed me a Valium and a glass of chardonnay. Reflexively, I swished down my little helper and collapsed into a rolling chaise beneath an umbrella. It was at that moment when a strange, obviously pork-fed young woman approached, just as Will Luckie was delivering the Tupperware container unto us, opening it to transfer its contents into the African vessel. She wore black leather hot pants, a pink halter top with the word "baby" spelled out on images of a child's blocks, and ornate red cowboy boots, looking for all the world like a rodeo hooker. Her countenance was harsh and hard-edged. She was clearly some kind of low class white trash, and she carried a platter of fried chicken. "This is just for you, Will," she said. "Recognize this little feller?"

Our guests were transfixed by the psychodrama playing out before them. Will sauntered over to the chicken woman, one hand stroking his defined abdomen, the other arm cradling the open Tupperware. "Who is it? Which one of the Watergate gang did you take?"

"It's going right on your heartstrings, right this minute!"

"Yeah, never mind," he said. "Lindia gave me a heads up, and I already checked to see who was gone from the hotel. Lucky for you it was a bit player. It's just Little Donnie 'the shyster' Segretti. Be different if you'd gotten Chuck."

"You *did* lose your mind over yonder," the woman sputtered. "You should have come back in a box!"

"You know what, Lainey? That ain't a real nice thing to say." That Lothario's calmness in the face of trash-isms was remarkable as he continued, "And you know what else? Lindia can fry circles around you. That there bird don't have near the kind of crispy gold crust that makes for the best from a skillet. And I say that as one who has sincerely swore off poultry."

"Son of a goddamned bitch!" she yelled, smashing the platter to the concrete, lunging at

Will, taking them both into the deep end of the pool, Tupperware soaring, its contents clouding into the chlorined water in a swirl of cremation.

"Oh, no—Wick!" And Mother, resplendent in her birthday muumuu, went charging into said deep end, grabbing at plumes of ashes and bits of bone, calling, "Wickham!" repeatedly, while Will and that chicken rustler wrestled around in the water, thrashing like a frenzy of sharks. And all the while the Pollard press took notes and made a photographic record.

By the time Officer Baggett of the PCPD arrived, I had a small army of fan-flappers surrounding my lounge chair, as I was hyperventilating while Winston offered a paper bag into which to breathe. The fondue table at the pool's edge was soaked, as was Mayor Burgess's wife Kathryn's floral silk cover-up. And when Will Luckie emerged from the water it was painfully obvious that the famous nude shorts he wore were also soaked, displaying yet another level of phallic information we did not require; the energy that went into avoiding eye contact with his vile, blue-veined interloper would be enough to fuel all the paper mills in this county. I have never been more mortified.

A stunned silence had fallen over the crowd. Lindia was ushering the chicken woman into the kitchen while Will turned and helped Mother slog up the cement steps and out of the water, her Hawaiian muumuu clinging to her porcine frame. She collapsed in the lounge chair next to me. "That is it," she said. "We shall have to drain the pool."

"My DD is gone," I sobbed, gasping. "We will find nothing of him by draining the pool."

"Well godammit, CeCe. I know that. I simply thought we could drain the pool, and the water might eventually make its way to some creek nearby, then to the Conecuh River, and to the Gulf and on--"

"But why?" I screamed. Literally.

She looked at me like I was crazy. "Wick was a Navy man. He always said how impressive he would find a burial at sea."

Some in the crowd laughed.

"That is a glorious idea," Kathryn said.

"The water all goes to a water treatment facility," I screamed. "Not to the GD ocean!"

"Oh, be still, CeCe," Mother hissed. "You know we're not on the city system. We're septic, so it does at least go to the ground water—which could find its way to a stream. Besides, it's the thought, the *imagination* of it that counts."

I swallowed a second Valium borne by Winston and washed it down with mighty gulps, now, of chardonnay, aghast at the entire conversation.

"Who wants to meet John and Martha Mitchell?" Will said, the band tuned up with "The Chicken Dance Polka," and Officer Baggett joined in, doing the hand motions and flappy-wing moves along with all the other chicken dancers. It was beyond absurd.

"Play 'Do the Funky Chicken'," someone called out, but more modern tunes did not seem to be within the musicians' repertoire.

Will took small groups of guests, emitting squeals of delight, on guided tours of his Watergate chicken house. In a while he rounded up Chuck Colson and, as an encore, proceeded to mingle him with the guests on Mother's lawn, all the while stroking his feathers and making absurd little kissy noises at him.

I went through the remainder of the party in a semi-drunken, Valium-laced trance, a smile fixed to my face like car-whacked roadkill. Officer Baggett lingered, making a fuss over Will's chickens, stroking Chuck, and staying much, much longer than duty required I am sure, carrier of gossip that he is. I thanked them all for coming, one, by one, as they left, gushing about what a great, fun, outrageously good time they had. The best party in years, many said. Let's do another. That Will is a stitch. The Watergate is fantastic. And on and on and on, *ad nauseum*.

You probably think that was the end of my outrage, my rampage, my ennui. Alas, you would be mistaken. The last straw was laid across my back deep in the dark night, that very evening, and a festering boil of inner rage was lanced upon those god awful, Will Luckie tainted yard fowl.

12
Lindia

When I snatched that crazy young un up out of that party and hauled her into Miss Maureen's kitchen, she looked like a caged animal, all wild in the eyes, and I wondered if it was a fool thing to do to put her around any knives and such. So I set her down on a stool with her back to the cutting board and sat down beside her. She wasn't saying nothing, so I just tuned right on up. "Why in the name of Moses would any woman want any man that didn't want none of her?"

She just stared at me.

"Do you love the Lord?" I asked.

She nodded yes.

"Are you a church woman?"

Another nod.

"What brand?"

"Pentecostal."

"Your whole life?"

"Yeah."

"Oh, Lord." It came clear to me just that fast. This child had a cancer on her spirit, and it had been chewing on that spirit for a long, long time.

"What do you mean? Why do you say it like that?" Her voice was kind of flat, but she didn't seem too licked to want to know what to do.

I wasn't sure how to put it, so I didn't think; I just went to putting. "Well, in my way of Bible believing, there's two basic kinds of Christians and two basic kinds of churches. There's them that dwell on the hallelujah and them that dwell on the hell fire."

"Pentecostal has the hallelujah," she said, defensive like.

"But where does it *dwell*? Where does it even *seem* to dwell if you're a little child, hearing it all?"

She sighed. "It scared me shitless when mama said we had demons in our longleaf pine."

"And there was other times, too, wasn't there?"

She nodded.

"See, the hallelujah fills the spirit with love and celebration and the hell fire does just the opposite. The hell fire fills you with fear and meanness, and that's what's the matter in your spirit. See, you got a gullet full of the hell fire—even if there *was* some hallelujah throwed in--and it's going to work you into fits until you get shed of it."

She started to perk up. "That's just what GooGoo says."

"Then he's a mite smarter that what he shown over here on the Fourth of July."

"Yeah, he was putting y'all on a lot of the time."

"We're running the train off the tracks. Like I say, it's time you got the hallelujah."

"How do I do that? I can't just all of a sudden stop thinking about hell."

So I gave her my strong-jawed look. "You damn sure can. Can't nobody put thoughts in your head but your ownself, so you just put Jesus in there—Jesus and nothing nor nobody else. Not Mr. Will. Not hell. Just Jesus."

"But—"

"But nothing. Girl, you got to get right with Jesus. You got to be quiet and listen for the Lord, and the only thing to ever let out of your mouth is praise. I heard you hollering some nasty poison out yonder and you need to learn how to keep quiet. Can't nobody hear the Lord if they be steady hollering. And hollering meanness to boot."

"You don't know how Will Luckie did me. You don't know the bind I'm in. No job, no place to put my trailer. I'm way behind on my rent, too. I reckon they're going to put me out."

"Reckon I do know a desperate woman when I see her. Reckon I been seeing you out across that pasture. Reckon I been noticing things around here. Lindia ain't no fool."

"You saw me? Why didn't you do something? Tell on me or something?"

"Sometimes it's better to let happenings follow their own course. It always seems to work out in the wash."

"But you told Will I swiped a chicken."

"Yes ma'am, I did. He's right fond of his coop pets. And wasn't none too happy about your kidnapping Little Donnie."

"Did he cry? I wanted him to cry—to *weep*. I had Miss Joan to pray to put it on his heartstrings, once I really knew he wasn't taking me back. I was just trying to help that along, with the fried chicken and all."

"Heartstrings?"

"Yeah, Miss Joan said she could pray her enemies into a living hell by causing hurt to what or who they love."

"Who is Miss Joan?"

"That's GooGoo's mama. She was a holy roller preacher woman for fourteen years. She knows how to pray real good."

That right there said it all and I went on and told her so. "Anybody who uses prayer for ill will ain't a Christian. And poor GooGoo. It's no wonder he's a wretched mess, if he was raised up in such awfulness."

"GooGoo is weird, that's true. He don't even believe in hell. He thinks them Hindu and Buddhism people got better religions."

"That's what he said?"

"No, but it's what I think about him. Just from things he's said."

"He's wounded is what he is. From the war, but on the inside. Just like Mr. Will is wounded."

"Will Luckie is a sorry piece of—"

"Ain't done it. That man has a good heart. He's done breathed life back into Miss Maureen."

"He's a cheater."

"I expect that's the truth. But he's honest about what he is. And Miss Maureen sees him for what he is. And she takes him for what he is."

"Well I can change him. I just know it," she said, but it sounded all shaky and feeble like.

I reached over and patted her on the hand. "Baby, can't nobody change nobody. If I could put Jesus thoughts in your head and give you peace, don't you think I would've done it by now? I don't hardly know you but don't you think I'd help you and change your hurt spirit if I could? Of course I would. But all I can really do is tell you to get right with Him and how to do that. Listen for the Lord. And listen real hard, because sometimes he talks in the lightest whisper you ever heard."

By now she was beginning to squeeze out these little sobs that sounded like they didn't really know how to be let loose. So I went on, "Will Luckie is the kind of man that ain't never going to change. Never. He don't want to."

She laid her face in her hands and boo-hooed. I just patted her head and let her cry a while. I felt sorry for her, just like I feel sorry for any child that's had her mind messed up with dark faith. It's like them Klan people back in Mississippi. They took their own young uns and raised them up in that kind of cancer, just like some mean-spirited preachers put the disease in children like this one.

All of a sudden I needed to perk the child up, and I couldn't believe the words came out of my mouth, but they did. "You know," I said, "Mr. Will told me it was in his blood that he had to put that peter of his in anything warm and wet. Anything." I think I bugged my eyes, I was so shocked to hear myself say such.

She went to laughing then. And we both laughed a while because it was a true and funny thing to know.

"I ain't laughed in the longest time," she said.

"Well you ought to. Joy makes your spirit swell with the Holy Ghost. And you ought to find a man to laugh with, too, once you get all this behind you."

"It's hard, though."

"Sure it is. But when you come across Mr. Will or anybody else you think you ought to change or you think has done you wrong, keep your mouth closed. Don't go to judging. Just go to praying for them. And don't never boast out loud about your praying or your faith."

"Good Lord, I ain't felt right in a long, long time. And I don't think I really knew that until this very second."

"Well you can put your spirit on the mend."

"Matter of fact, I ain't felt right any kind of way."

"And what did I just say?"

"I can mend my spirit? How?"

"Like this: take what I already told you, about listening to the Lord, about praying for good, about not being boastful and add two things. First, add forgiveness."

"Oh my God, that's just what that seagull book says to do."

"Seagull?"

"It's a sign. It is. You have to be right. What's the other thing?"

"Well, it ain't nothing about no birds. It's just about being yourself, honest like, with all the warts."

"No!"

"Why not?"

"Not no as in not, but no as in there's another sign, because that's in the seagull book too! I ain't believing this shit, because GooGoo predicted it, and that seagull lived it, and now you're saying what all the Jesus part is."

I was afraid she had lost some of her mind, babbling on like that, about predictions and communicating with birds, like she was mental or something. That was when I thought to send her to a professional, being that I had might done bit off more than I could chew. "Look here. You just carry yourself over to Mr. Winston's office tomorrow. If that man's got pills to make Miss CeCe easy, then he can flat sure cure what ails you and anybody else."

"Maybe I will." She took a paper napkin from the holder and blew her nose. Then she kind of cut her eyes over at me. "That Miss Maureen, she's okay?"

"She's got a good heart. She would help anybody she thought had a good heart, too. She'd even help someone like you, who was just *trying* to have a good heart."

"No shit?"

"It's the truth." And right then I had a thought. I should have just thunk it and not spoke it out loud because it wasn't mine to speak of. But I did. "You know what? I might just know where the answer is to your prayers. Not the Will Luckie prayers but the other."

"What do you mean?"

"Are you above cleaning, working as a domestic?"

"Hell, no."

"You got something that can haul that trailer?"

"I do. Tell me what you're saying."

I caught myself then. "Let me do some studying. And some preparing of the earth, before I toss them seeds. Just know this: You got to purge that resentment of Miss Maureen. She has a kind heart."

"You wouldn't just automatically say that about any white person?"

I had to chuckle. "You might laugh some more at that, if you get to know me better."

"What about that CeCe? What kind of heart does she have?"

I figure she threw that one out at me as a test, so I gave her the right answer. "That child's heart turns more rancid every day."

You know, the right Reverend Henry Johnson, Jr. always said that a willingness to testify to all who ask is a covenant with the Lord that breathes new life into a tired spirit and a tired faith, and that's just what my talk with that girl, Marlayna, did for me. That evening, sitting on my porch listening to the crickets and the other night critters, I thought about the blessed years I had with Henry. I thought about what a short time that had been and what a lot of time had fallen between his departing this earth and this very evening on this earth, and I felt his spirit give, like it fell away, just like a slipped shawl, off of my shoulders.

All of a sudden I thought about the shoulders of Cletus Mitchell, how stooped and bent he was, and about how gentle his hands were when he tended the roses and zinnias and azaleas. I thought about how he cut the fool and how I cut back. I thought about his funny rhymes, how he's say, "It's all cool in school" whenever I asked how was he doing. I thought about my new look that Miss Maureen said was "sexy" and I laughed out loud. I thought about how I had just told this Marlayna child about the importance of joy and having a man to share it with and me not tending to my own joyous needs. Finally, I thought about maybe getting Brenda to go off somewhere one evening soon and me cooking Cletus a real special meal, just us two, back at the house, alone. And I begun to smile, real big, on the inside.

13
Cecelia

I have been so very tired, of late—tired of the shortcomings of others who seem bent upon my emotional undoing. It is as if the tainted ether, injected with the essence of Will Luckie, has infected everyone around me and now they are all in lockstep toward my decimation. The emotional betrayal of my mother had been a simmering schism for years, particularly during my adolescence, even when she was behaving in a socially acceptable manner. And now the source of all evil, Will Luckie, had turned the whole of Pollard society on its head. He was popular. He was the life of the party. He was an attention hog. Numbed as I was by shock, I could barely attempt to inventory just who—what allies—I had remaining, and my husband, it seemed, was the only one, however ineffectual, to be found.

But life has those culminating moments, when all the forces seem to be pushing in one direction, and all that one trusts, whatever tatters one finds in one's clutching palm, are blown into oblivion by an unexpected gust of devastation. And it happened to me, late into the dark night, after that hideous disaster of a pool party and the loss of my DD's seared and pulverized corpse.

Winston was called to the hospital to deliver a baby, so I took a knockout pill and went on to bed, hoping to numb myself with sleep. Sometime before midnight, however, I was awakened by the horrific screams of one who was surely being murdered very, very slowly. When finally, through a fog of merlot and Valium, it dawned upon me that the peacock, Maureen, was the source of the utterances, I was quite relieved, yet could not go back to sleep with those howls punctuating the night. I made my way down to the kitchen and out the back door, which had been left standing wide open. Of course, I assumed that Winston had come in and was reassured by his Cadillac parked in the driveway. But something felt odd; the night seemed a trifle off center, and the scuffling sound coming from around the chicken coop, accompanied by an occasional peacock shriek, drew me to take a silent stroll that would be the terrible undoing of all to which I have grown accustomed.

This is so very difficult, putting into words what I saw there in the moonlight that glowed through the gauze of leaves above. Those garlands of gold (some purchased by my own mother), the ones that were always nestled in the chest curls of Will Luckie, caught the cast of the full moon. He leaned against the outer wall of the old gardener's shed, his breathing filled every few moments with a purring moan, fingers playing across that military-hardened stomach of his. He was caught up in the most intense display of sexual pleasure I have ever witnessed, and I have to confess that some of that pleasure spilled into my own psyche. I felt a mesmerized longing, a huge gulp of desire such as I have never known, until it dawned on me that my own husband was the source of Will Luckie's pleasure.

I have told you about our conjugal difficulties, so it was outside of my frame of reference to see Winston, kneeling there, so caught up in such a perverted act, so absorbed by what he was doing, so oblivious to his surroundings, emitting muffled groans quite unlike the twitters of counterfeit passion he has offered me over the years. I could not move until the lunar light revealed Will Luckie's gaze upon me. And he—you will not begin to believe this, I know. He actually grinned, raised his right hand, extended his index finger, and crooked it at me three times. Can you imagine? Here he is being carnally devoured by my husband, and he has the egomaniacal nerve to invite me to the party! Have you ever in all your life?

The strangest part of this perverse scenario, and I can barely admit it to myself, is that I came within a hair's breadth of walking over, surrendering to God knows what. It was hypnotic, and the stirrings within me were white-hot and demanding. All I knew was a feverish desperation for some implied promise of satisfaction, something I know very little of, unfortunately; but, just as I started forward, Will Luckie let out a gasping moan that sent me headlong toward the sanitized safety of my own bedroom.

Needless to say, I did not sleep at all that night. My bewildered arousal and shock gave way to a mulling inventory of the scores of wrongs done unto me until, as dawn broke, I found myself in the throes of a righteous rage that wanted only to be visited upon Will Luckie. That is when I made my way to Mother's garage and loaded my DD's shotgun.

I paused at the door to the study, where Mother's man-whore had passed out, right there on Mother's olive green chaise lounge, one foot hanging to the harvest gold shag carpet. I coldly contemplated his murder. There is no doubt that I will roast in hellfire for all eternity as a result the homicidal inklings that rustled about my brain, but at that point I failed to give a shit. You see, when earthly anguish (as in the form of one's lunatic mother, her sexually ambiguous leech of a boyfriend, and my cheating impostor of a husband) becomes infused within the pores of one's flesh so that Lucifer's den looks to be a relief, then the time to act has arrived. And so I acted. And I did Will Luckie one better.

I acted upon those goddamned yard birds of his. Chuck Colson met me at the gate, having been taught to hold high expectations of those humans who serve him. I laid the stock on my hip, got my palm beneath the barrel, and fired, silently thanking my DD for teaching me to shoot. It struck me that a shotgun went a long way toward decimating coop fowl, effectively blowing them to smithereens, as it were. You have never seen such a tornado of feathers in your life, a maelstrom of beaks, guts, gristle and feet. A few wings in the throes of dancing nerves, jitterbugging against dirt-grained blood in the chicken yard, slinging dots of bright red against the shed. I managed to annihilate Erlichman, Secord, Krogh, and Liddy before folks came running. I accidentally fired into the bay window in Mother's kitchen trying to hit Martha Mitchell, who had flapped over to the patio thinking I would not notice her there, trying to blend in with the potted white begonias, and the sound of breaking glass tinkled like wind chimes into the hurricane of squawks, screeches and stacattoing wings on Mother's dewey green lawn. I got John Dean and Haldeman, vaguely aware of Will Luckie's stream of curses, his moan of anguish as he raked through meaty feathers for his war medal and crucifix, a moan quite distinct from the orgasmic howl of the previous midnight. Cletus even ran up, yelling, "Stop! Stop!" Someone, not Cletus, was yelling something in Spanish. The steady yips and yaps of Rosencrantz and Guildenstern layered into the shrill madness, and my mother's profane shrieks of hysteria against the tableau of sounds grated against my very last nerve such that I admit to a flash of a desire to turn the gun on her. That was when the Spanish speaker materialized before me in the form of my Mexican, who wrestled my DD's gun away from me. Of course the P.C.P.D. was absolutely thrilled to wheel up to a *real* emergency---a bona fide Thursday morning chicken massacre---at Miss Maureen's fine, dignified-looking home.

Mother was in her vicious-tongued mode. "CeCe, you have lost every bit of your goddamn mind!" she screamed, as down snowflaked upon the wig she frequently wore post hair-burning incident. "Is this what you foresaw when you gave your heart to Jesus?   Murdering sweet creatures that give us our morning nourishment—our omelets and our poached groceries?"

"Oh, the humanity!" Officer Baggett murmured.

"Too bad, so sad," Cletus remarked.

"Es una loca de mierda."

"If you had only lived a life you could not be capable of such cold, lunatic rage!" Mother went on. "And didn't I always try to get you to live a goddamn life? Didn't I?" She quieted a moment and actually took a deep breath. "If you could only learn to live and laugh. Laugh at yourself. Laugh at this absurd life! Then you could never be so vicious as to murder poor Will's friends. You have no idea what you have done to him."

"I care not. God in heaven knows my actions are pure."

"Oh, so God is on your side? Really? Well Goddamn, then. I need a Bloody fucking Mary."

"I do not believe you just uttered the f-word! And for the second time! Do you not see what he's done to you?" But I did not further argue with her, not in front of the police and the neighbors. It would only encourage her to provide more drama for the townspeople to view. And I certainly did not tell her about Winston and Will Luckie. I can never do that! Lord, what would folks think of me then? I don't believe there has ever been a homosexual incident in Pollard, and I am not about to go down as a party in the first homosexual incident on record.

As I climbed into the police car—Baggett insisted that I sit in the back seat, where the true criminals were put—I spied Will Luckie by the pool. He had that little net he uses to clean leaves and bugs out of the chlorined water, but on this landmark morning he was dipping at some of the feathers, still drifting on currents of air like ashes from a barrel burning, or a cremation, that had landed in the pool. His shoulders were hunched over, shaking; it was obvious that he was sobbing as he dipped the remnants of the Watergate conspirators out of the cold liquid. I was able to take a little satisfaction in that. Hell, he is probably having a huge funeral for them as we speak. I wouldn't be surprised if he purchased marble slabs and headstones with more of my inheritance money---to create a memorial garden for the Watergate gang, with an air-conditioned vault for Chuck's remains, of course.

As the police car pulled away, I stared at them through the back window—Mother, Will, Angus, and, oddly enough, that Marlayna chicken-lady person, who was, at that moment, being led toward the clump of them by, of all people, *my* maid, Lindia. *My* maid, given to *me* as a wedding gift.

Goodness, the Cantonment jail is much nicer than I expected, although the stench of the mills sort of permeates everything, does it not? CeCe's cell smells through and through of the smog and she's complaining that it is in her clothes and hair by now. I just spoke with her, you know, and I am afraid she is quite put out with me, flinging another one of her over-acted fits. And I even brought her a carrot cake. Her favorite. I tell you, I believe I have finally come to the end of my rope with that child. I cannot find one spark of pure passion within her. She simply has a sour nature, inherited from Wickham, of course. I don't mean to sound uncaring, but you know it might just do the child good to spend a few more nights in a cell. I don't think the one night has done the trick. Perhaps she would lose her penchant for nonstop complaining and whining if she were without freedom for a spell. Look at that whole Watergate fiasco and how many of the president's men have gone or will go to prison. And Nixon himself—he's addressing the nation tonight, and most folks expect that he'll resign, since he is as guilty as sin. I know CeCe has been clamoring for a TV in that cell, says she won't believe it, the resignation of a sitting president, until she sees it. How she can stand by that shady slime ball is way beyond me. It's too bad Pollard has no jailhouse, because I know you boys would see that she could watch her president shame himself. And it's too bad that "shame" is not a word she can apply to her own soul. We all need a dose of humility every now and then.

Do you suppose you could get the Cantonment boys to just feed her bread crusts with a little water? I didn't think so. I knew I shouldn't have bothered Lindia with baking a cake that would not be appreciated. I'll tell you what. Let's do let her stay a while in this fine, barred motel. Tell those sweet Cantonment boys that I shall advise James Burgess, Esquire, to drag his legal feet. After all, she is already in a magnificent snit with me, so a little thing like a few more nights in jail will make no difference. Let's just plan to tend to matters of bail in thirty-six hours or so. Forty-eight, perhaps? Let us all move at a snail's pace, shall we? Besides, poor Will has been writhing in horrific grief ever since yesterday morning, inconsolable, and I am mortified that my own flesh and blood wrought this tragedy. Will has such a sweet and gentle soul. Bawdy, yes, but gentle at the core, and he did not deserve this cruelty.

I will tell you something with pure contentment and conviction: I am glad I have finally unburdened myself regarding the way this drama formed and built in order to come to the apex of yesterday morning's mass killing. I know in my soul that my daughter has never and will never be able to relax and laugh with her crazy mother. I fear for her sanity now as much as I used to fear for mine, but you do what you will with all this information. I realize that I have told you some outrageous things, with some delicious indiscretions mixed in, but I simply felt it would help you finalize whatever reports you have to fill out and, if not that, then perhaps you will at least see us all in a more understanding light. And, by the way, it is of little consequence to me if the whole town of Pollard knows all that I have told you, including my revelation of my affair *du jour*. I have decided that, CeCe be damned, not only will I never again go to great extremes to maintain the approval of others, but I will also put the brutal truth out into the light, a la Will Luckie. The denizens of *that* hypocritical little hamlet are more than welcome to come and dine at my buffet of secrets.

So there you are. I wanted you, of all people, to understand the larger context, for context enables us to accurately define the moment. And although I am sure I have never adequately thanked you, I want you to know that you have been just wonderful to look after me over the years, and I appreciate you boys no end. Of course, just show me a uniform and I am swept off my feet immediately. Anyway, do ask your fellow officers here in Cantonment to try to treat CeCe as well as you have always treated me.

And now, I must return to my home and comfort poor Will. You know, war does things to a person. WWII did things to me. And Vietnam did things to Will. We do share that context, albeit in very different eras. Casualties of war. My goodness, that sounds like the title of something: Casualties of War. Yes, I think it might call for a few lines of poetry, if I dare. It has been eons since I took up the pen.

I do have the soul of a poet.

15
Marlayna

So I done told you all this to say I need some nervous pills on account of all I been through and that's why I come here. Lindia said you had pills for everything, even a banged up heart.

I seen what you and Will Luckie done, but don't worry. I ain't going to tell no one. I mean, it's a pervert thing, and I hate to say you're going to hell over it, because Lindia tells me I oughtn't say that to nobody. She says it soils the spirit when you think about hell all the time. But I reckon I ain't near where she is, because I reckon you really are bound for hell and I hate it for you. You seem like a decent enough person, for a queer.

See, when that nice Lindia put me out the front door, I drove back around that logging road and watched everything that was going on at the party. And even after it busted up I sat there, watching. I could see Will sleeping in one of them deck chairs, and I watched the dark, just like GooGoo does. I listened for the Lord, too, just like Lindia said I should. I think I even dozed some myself. I sipped on part of a six-pack and smoked a big damn pile of cigarettes. Then I set out for the pasture and took up post behind a hay bale by the fence. I had me a clear view of the chicken coop, don't you know.

When you drove up in your car, I seen Will stir and leave up from the pool and I watched ya'll even closer through them spyglasses GooGoo let me borrow. I already knew there's men like you, because my cousin told me when he come out of the Navy. He said that particular branch of the service was full of queers. But hell, Lindia says I ought to try to use these kinds of things to not judge folks. She says that'll make my spirit strong. Lord knows, I'm trying.

Anyway, I seen that crazy wife of yours watching ya'll before she run up in the house, and—shit, you didn't know that! I'm sorry to blurt it. Lord, all the color has done drained in your face. And she ain't said nothing? Shit, I'll be damned if I'd be quiet if I caught my man blowing on a pecker. But, come to think of it, your wife don't seem like the kind that would ever say a word about it, even to you. She's pretty uptight, don't you think? Uptight. That's a GooGoo word.

Anyway, look here: you got to not do that shit no more, and I reckon the right moral thing to do is just to go on and live your life and try not to let Will bust up your marriage, cause he ain't a queer and I know it. You just had something warm and wet for him, that's all. Besides, he's done made love to me like nobody's business, and I'm going to be hunting me another one that knows what to do with a woman.

Maybe I ain't been giving other men much of a chance. Hell, I ain't been through enough of them lately to really decide. You take GooGoo McGeehee. I've been wondering if my generation of girls are just plain stuck with a bunch of shell-shocked, disfigured, looney tunes veterans. Looks that way to me, I'll tell you. But, you know, I don't think GooGoo is really as crazy as I thought at first. He has a plan, at least. Not like Will, living second to second. And plus, GooGoo is smarter than he looks, reads lots of books, and don't make no bones about the fact that he's one-nutted on account of the war. I've been thinking maybe we should get to know one another better, especially since it seems like the Lord is behind it, putting things in place, like him giving me that seagull book and Lindia saying the same things about being forgiving and knowing your own self. And GooGoo gave me something else, too—a mood ring that changes colors just like magic. Red means you're excited, pink is fear, blue is calm, and on like that. It ain't no engagement ring I know, but it's kind of like a promise ring, don't you think? A promise ring like the crystal people give, the higher class folks. I think it's a good sign, anyway. A sign from the Lord that there might be more for me and my cut glass self.

And that pasture of yours—with that silo— that's a sign, too. It fits right in with GooGoo's plans. When the good Lord is showing his will, then you ought not to spit at it, I say.

Plus, Lindia says Miss Maureen ain't so bad. If she's right about that, then I'm damn sure going to try to get her to help me out. But I just had to see you, about getting them pills, to get my nerves right. And to tell you to don't go against your manly nature. And to ask you if you think I might have a chance with Will. I mean, you've done got real close with him, I reckon. Maybe he's told you shit he ain't told nobody else. He's damn sure done some shit with you don't nobody know.

You know what? Scratch that. I and you both need to break free of Will, seriously. He brings out the nasty in us both, doesn't he? Come to think of it, you and me are kind of the same, sort of out there on the edge of life, kind of like me sitting out on the edge of that pasture, watching in on what I want. And we both want what we can't have, so we just flat got to stop wanting it, you know? It's a son of a bitch, that wanting thing, and it's going to be a hell of a thing to shake. But I believe we can do it. Do you?

So here I am. Mother left a good while ago, and you will not begin to believe what she came down to this dungeon to tell me. I think I am more livid now than I was when I exploded feathers all across her yard. She came in here and stood right at the door to my—Good Lord in Heaven—my *cell*. She had brought a carrot cake with cream cheese icing that she had Lindia make for me, and when she set it down, she actually whispered, "There's a steel file baked into the center. Lindia and me will bust you out of here at midnight, capisce?" Then she laughed. Here I am in a God forsaken jail on a cold, hard bunk, and she laughs.

"I fail to see the humor in my predicament," I said.

"CeCe, really. One has to laugh. Goddamn, no matter how crazy or rife with desperation one's predicament is, one has to laugh. Otherwise one becomes bitter, ill, and noxious."

"That is easy for one to say if one is on the outside of the penal institution in which one could easily be rotting."

"Good Lord, CeCe, you are not going to rot in here. James is working on getting you bailed out even as we speak. He did say something about firing into a residence being a felony and that some charges may be inevitable, simply because of that."

"Charges?"

"Don't worry. I'm sure James will fix it. Of course, I would never personally press charges against you, and I think Will is too deeply devastated to bother with legalities."

I rolled my eyes with great exaggeration.

"I hope you are sufficiently ashamed of what you did yesterday. Whatever were you thinking?"

"I was not thinking. I snapped." This is how it must be. If it had been Will Luckie and anyone else but Winston I could tell her and be shed of that plague on the house of Calhoun. But if it were to get out that my lack of desirability drove my husband to homosexuality, then I would surely be ruined, even more than I already am. Thus, my hands, and my tongue, are tied.

"Do you not even care that poor Will is absolutely crushed, deep in the saddest funk I have ever witnessed in a man?"

"No, I do not. I hope to never lay eyes on that man again."

"Well, you won't have to for a while. We have decided to travel the Pacific—Hawaii, Japan, perhaps the coast of California. Your luau inspired me. Will wants to learn to surf, and I think a nice long trip will help him contend with his grief."

"So you do not care at all that I am utterly miserable, that I am in trouble with the law, and that I do not need to be alone."

"You won't be alone, Sugar. I have hired you a companion—and a good one, too. Got lots of personality. Might help you relax."

"What about Lindia?"

"I think Lindia's getting too old to have to cope with both of us."

"And just exactly what do you mean by that?" I demanded, vulnerable, naked, ripe for the taking of advantage.

"I intend to keep her on at my home. But, not to worry. I have a plan for you to have help."

"What in the world? Lindia was a wedding present to me!"

"Which was quite presumptuous of me I came to realize, upon reflection. I never actually sought her input."

"So what? She is of the servant class!"

Mother sighed with the kind of heaviness she rarely displayed, and I did not like the look on her face, as if I had suddenly sprouted a crop of hairy warts across my forehead. She shook her head in a self-indulgent display of sadness.

"Do you know, MiMi?" I pressed. "Do you know what that makes you? An Indian giver, that's what. A red-skinned, tomahawk-throwing, two-faced Indian giver."

And, just like that, she perked up. "Well dear, it has always been a part of family lore that we do have Creek ripples in the gene pool. And a splash of Cherokee."

"I most certainly do *not* have a drop of savage blood in these blue veins! And you cannot take Lindia away from me!"

"Come, come, CeCe. That arrangement was never very fair to her. She is simply spread too thin. And her personal life has suffered."

"What personal life? She's a *maid*!"

"However in the world did you emerge from *my* cast-off womb?"

"I didn't make the rules, but someone of Lindia's station should be grateful for all the morsels she gathers from the Calhouns' good graces."

"CeCe!"

"Well I can't help it if that's the way things are. Plus, her being col—black and all."

"Black is beautiful. Have you not heard? And Lindia has a beautiful spirit as well. It took Will to get me to notice the true natures of those who populate my life."

"Oh, so now you imply that I do not have a pretty spirit. And I'm *white*!"

She sighed again, and this time it was more harsh than heavy. "You mystify me. You truly do. Such judgement. Such entitlement. But, enough!" She straightened up her shoulders and spoke in that strict tone that always takes me back to childhood. "I thought about employing a traditional maid for you, but then I got to know more about Marlayna."

"What? That big-butted, buttermilk-drinking slut who crashed the party?"

"Exactly. Lindia got to talking with her, and I followed up yesterday afternoon. She's a piece of work, that's for sure. So I think she'll fit right in with our merry band of misfits."

"*Our* band? Misfits? That is utterly ridiculous."

"Well, the deal is done. The ink, as they say, is dry."

"No, Mother. You didn't."

"Oh, show some Christian heart, Miss CeCe. She has nowhere to go, no job. All she has is a trailer home and no money for rental space."

"So what?"

"So I'm having a septic tank and power pole put in at the back of the pasture. She's right fond of the horses. Oh—I imagine I shall have to have a propane tank installed as well."

"What are you saying?"

"I'm saying she is hired. And she will put her trailer at the back of the pasture. Doesn't that just work out perfectly? Kismet!"

"A *trailer*? On Calhoun land?" I laid my head in my hands. "Sweet Lord Jesus, there will be enough trash on the property to call it a county landfill."

"Do *not* invoke the 't' word. Not in my presence, Little Miss."

"Plus, the first tornado that blows in—or the first hurricane that comes our way will likely pick it up and smash it into one of our homes."

"CeCe, that is quite enough. I have not told you everything. I have directed Jesus to bring his family up from Mexico—his wife and their three children. I got to talking with him after that awful mass killing, during which he was quite brave, quite the hero. I had no idea what his personal circumstances were, what with the family separation going on for over two years. Can you imagine?"

"I certainly care not. I can't imagine why you would want to create a whole nest of those people on our land."

"Well that is certainly cold."

"Everything is coming apart!" And I held my face, sobbing.

Mother was not moved. "Just one more little thing. Miss Marlayna is hinting that there is a way I can make up for my shabby treatment of war veteran GooGoo McGeehee."

"Don't even imply that you would embrace such a pervert!" I blubbered through a preponderance of mucus.

"We shall see. Marlayna maintains that poor GooGoo struggles under the weight of insecurity, and inferiority born of social stratification. Seems he was putting us on much of the time, not without help from Will."

"As if that matters! What kind of pervert even makes up such utterances?"

"A very creative one, one who thinks outside the proverbial box, to be sure. Anyway Marlayna seems to be a good enough judge of character. And she's a sweet thing at heart. A bit misguided, perhaps. Misunderstood a lot, like me, I think."

"You mean insane, like you?"

"Sugar, we are all insane. And those of us who acknowledge it can laugh about it."

"I have nothing to laugh about. I am not happy. I am incarcerated. Institutionalized. Can't you let that sink into your brain?"

"Just think of it! We'll be like a hippie commune out on the farm. Such a collection of characters and cultures. Jesus is going to teach me Spanish. Perhaps Will and I shall junket south of the border one of these times."

At that instant I let out a screaming shriek that caused the law enforcement officials to peer in at us, in lockup, through an open door.

"Oh, all right, wallow in your misery. Roll around in your little pig sty of woes and refrain from troubling me about it. And shame, shame, shame on you for what you did to poor Will."

"Will Luckie can rot in the nether regions of hell," I yelled, sniffling and gasping.

"I am afraid I cannot stay and listen to you curse the man who revived me."

"I fear I shall regurgitate," I said

"No need for that. I'm off."

"You certainly are! And you have set a crying jag upon me!" I wished for a paper bag in which to breathe, wished for a Valium.

"Aloha, Sugar. See you in a month or so." And she called out through the bars, "Yoo hoo, Jerry Wayne? You can spring me now, copper." She was loving using whatever jail lingo she had retained from all those James Cagney movies she saw in her youth. The last insult she tossed at me over her shoulder was, "And, should you acquire any friends in there, *do* share your carrot cake with your cellmates!"

I continued to squall for the next hour or so. Until you got here.

In reality, the Cantonment City Jail does not seem so bad compared to what I have seen in the movies, although the paper mill stench is truly nauseating. I suppose jail is quite reprehensible in a bigger town than Cantonment or Pollard, but here it is quite homey. Baggett, Trent Givens, and Rita, that sweet little dispatcher who does the wake-up call service, drove down from Pollard and brought me lunch from the Jitney Jungle here in town. And the Cantonment police—Gary and Jerry Wayne— let me use the phone to cancel the Ladies' Club meeting this evening, and they're even going to roll a TV into my cell so I can watch President Nixon address the nation. He's about to resign this evening, or so they say. I'll believe it when I see it. To think, *our* president, the victim of a vicious, baseless witch hunt.

Oh, did you not follow the Watergate hearings last summer? What a parade. And a sham. But you know that traitor John Dean who testified about the cancer on the presidency and all? I did think his wife was very attractive. He was kind of a squirrelly little man, but his wife Maureen? I know, my mother's name. The irony is not lost on me. Anyway, she—Mrs. Dean— was gorgeous, not a blonde hair out of place. Perfect skin. Big eyes and big earbobs. She has style. Even a stylish nickname—"Mo." I almost feel bad about shooting her husband.

I must insist upon one thing. You cannot tell a *soul* about Winston's indiscretion. Surely I can trust you people. Surely I have nothing to worry about where you all are concerned. Hell, we don't even know any of the same people I'll bet. I mean you two are from Pensacola, correct? And you are in for public intoxication? No, I am certain we could not know the same people. Moreover, we understand our status, one to the other. Status is *tres* important, a thing worth fighting for, a thing worth preserving. You know, after lo these many months of Will Luckie's ill-mannered, low-life ways, it is a relief to have this sense of clarity about the state of us—*n'est ce pas?*

Epilogue

August 10, 1974

Dear Henry,

I watched President Nixon resign, right there on the TV, just last night. It was something I never in my life would have thought I'd see. He gave a talk, and I took notes in that shorthand I used back in our marriage times, when you would dictate letters and such to me. That shorthand sure does stay with you, like riding a bike, like they say.

That Nixon bragged up all the things he's done, like taking peace over war, like being friendly with the Arabs and the China people, like China and us being the two strongest nations in the world so it's good to cooperate, like how the Soviet Union agreed to destroy them nuclear weapons you hated so much, Henry. And thinking of weapons and wars and such, you've got to give him a decent nod for ending the longest war we ever fought, that Vietnam mess. I don't reckon there will ever be a war to go longer than what that one did. I expect we took a lesson from it, don't you?

Anyway, he went on about how we have to help the new president, and not be arguing, about leaving "bitterness and division behind and rediscovering our shared ideals," about how the interests of the country have to come first instead of a "duty to the base," about how those politicians have to "not be unfaithful to the process." The

Constitution. Patriotism, the real kind. It was all around a good speech, and I know you would have liked it, Henry, as much as you would *not* have liked President Nixon. That Gerald Ford seems likeable enough, though, and since Nixon said we should get behind him and help him be good for all of America, then that's exactly what I'm going to do. There'll be another election in a few years, and I'll take my cues from the democrats, like we always have.

Just before he officially resigned, President Nixon allowed that he never thought of himself as a "quitter," and that made his decision hard, but in the end he saw his support from the Congress was going to nothing, so it was the right thing to do. For everybody.

And me, I never was a quitter either, and I will love the memories of our marriage forever, but it's been twenty years since you went to be with the Lord, and I been shut off for far too long. No regrets. Ain't no room in a life for things like regrets. But it's past time for change, and all these doings behind Will Luckie have carried me along on some kind of river of rebirth, what with all the joy been unleashed on folks. Oh, Miss CeCe's always going to be dour and sour and full of her own self, but that don't mean the rest of us have to pay her no mind or crawl down in that place of meanness. And no widow woman has to grieve forever. Miss Maureen tells that tale. That woman grieved for about a minute. So when Cletus Robinson asked me, I said yes. He's a good and decent man, Henry, and I know you'd like him.

So now you can really rejoice with the Lord, now that I'm giving up my grip on your spirit and letting myself be full and happy. You can dance down those streets of gold, hand in hand with Jesus. Don't you worry about me. I'm not a quitter, but a new move is the best thing for everyone, and I can feel it in the lift of my heart song.

There are folks in the world who bring hellfire into a life and those that bring faith. Nothing else matters—not color nor class nor religion nor even sex. Nor sex *nature*. My Cousin Brenda told me a thing this morning that she never told a living soul. She told me she has a *girlfriend*—a *girl*friend—down in Pensacola that she's been seeing for over two years. It's a big ugly old secret on account of she would be run out of her church and off of her job at the barber shop doing men's nails if anyone was to say it out loud. She said that for "homosexual" you had to say "gay" and that it was even legal in Sweden to be that way or even to change your sex body parts, which, I don't really understand *that*, but I gave a lot of thought to how I feel about Brenda. And right away I said to myself that Brenda has always been Brenda and why would I think any different about her? She's helped me through this life, steady encouraging and lifting me up. I thought about what Mr. Will said about how some of them Injun men had a woman nature and some of them Injun women had a man nature, and well—I've seen them kinds of folks around. And how Mr. Will's own nature was all over the map but that if a spirit is good it's not a thing. And poor Mr. Winston. That man is a shell if I ever seen one, denying his own nature and trying to be a husband to that high strung Queen of England that probably doesn't even have a sex nature at all. I feel right sorry for Mr. Winston.

So I told Brenda to not worry, that I was for her, and as long as she was being herself and full of faith then she was a good human. Hellfire or faith, that's what it comes down to in my book. Nothing else makes a damn. And I know this is all sounding strange to you, Henry, and you might think it's a fall from Godly practice, at least at first. But I know you to have been a man of God, where judgment never fell from your lips as long as a heart was kind, so I think you would change with the times, just like I'm doing. I'll bet one day it'll be wide open all over, just like in Sweden. I'll bet we can't even imagine how things will be, when the next new century comes. I know one thing, though. These United States will never have to suffer any kind of a president that would sink to dirty deeds, and Nixon is the proof. And we are blessed to never have to be at the mercy of some dictator or Hitler type fascist.

Miss Maureen and Mr. Will are jet setting right now, bound for California and then Hawaii. She promised she'll send lots of post cards from Hollywood and snapshots of movie star homes she's going to take with that Polaroid Swinger camera she has. There will be pictures of volcanoes and for-real luaus, pictures of Japan people and kimono ladies and that Mount Fuji. And no telling what all else. And Miss CeCe still sitting in that jail cell, all in a snit and a half.

And the beat goes on, don't it? You take care of yourself, Henry. Enjoy your long walk with the Lord. I expect I'll see you one day, up in Heaven, but I don't think we can reunite there, like we planned. I mean, since I'm taking another husband and all. I expect I'll have to be with Cletus in the Afterlife. But for the time being, you don't have to be a total stranger. Give some signs every once in a while. Drop me a post card from time to time. I've always loved your little post cards from Heaven, and I always will.

And, honestly, Henry, you will always be my first, best, open-nosed love.

Yours Truly,

Lindia

Acknowledgements

My father, Gene Hudson, was so excited for this book to come out. As I was combing through, doing final edits, he would ask every day it seemed, "Are you finished yet? (Flash back to those long car trips, we kids sing-songing "Are we there yet? Are we there yet?") Yes, it was kind of annoying, and sometimes I would just grunt and shake my head no. But I had a plan. We were expecting ARCs no later than Friday, October 12th, and I intended to put one of them in his hands, give him a laugh. That was the plan. But plans have a way of changing sometimes. My father dropped dead in an instant, as he made his morning cup of coffee on Tuesday, October 8th.

This is for you, Gene, with love.

When I was growing up on Bonita Avenue in Brewton, Alabama, my next door neighbor's mother was an intriguing character to me. Back in the nifty fifties and the sexy sixties, "Miss Kay" lived a life that defiantly colored outside the lines. She swept into rooms, spoke French, declared Brewton to be stifling, declared herself to belong elsewhere—New York, Paris, Rio—in the role of a poet or an artiste or (fill in the blank with something exotic or creative). Betty Draper she was not, and I wished to trade mothers, thank you very much. Not that my mother was bad—she was ordinary, though, with her bridge clubs and beauty parlor appointments and housewifery and pregnancies. Miss Kay appealed to my own creative bones, kindred and kind of crazy. Years later, when I took up the pen, she cheered the loudest, encouraging, even egging me on in my rebelliousness. Therefore...

Many thanks and much love to lifelong neighbor, friend, and honorary sister to my late brother Wilson, Jamie Gardner Rutan and her entire family. She graciously handed over her mother, Catherine Caffey "Kay" Gardner's memoir manuscript (*My Brother, My Lover, My Friend*), her published book of poetry (*Sand in My Shoes*), and her miscellaneous papers for me to plunder, in order to give life to Miss Maureen. I also had access to Miss Kay's letter of encouragement from Walker Percy, who declared her to "have the makings of a great southern writer," and who, the story goes, had chosen her manuscript to read over John Kennedy Toole's *A Confederacy of Dunces* (which, of course, he later did read and endorsed with a foreword). Miss Kay was an individual, to be sure, and, along with her sidekick "Miss Barbara" a few blocks over (and thanks to you, Keith Langham, for *those* wonderful stories), she gave me a wealth of material for this so-called fiction.

Much more creatively raunchy material and many crude sayings were delivered unto me by Stephen Martin, Sonny Brewer and Ira B. Colvin, the latter two products of rural counties in west central Alabama where the nasty language is a thing to behold. Thanks.

Thanks to my former eighth grade student, Ashley Freeman, for a great accounting of cremation gone nuts. Remember telling me that tale, Ashley?

I want to thank my very own "Annie Wilkes" for serving up much ugliness, dishonesty, selfishness, false sentimentality, and vindictiveness to channel into Miss Cecelia, making her a sublime villainess. She's a hell of a gal, that Annie, with a profound lack of insight, as is CeCe. Gracias! Here's to future manuscripts as I follow Annie's career as a shape-shifting grifter.

Props to my late brother Joe, just because. And to my sole surviving sibling John, for the same reason.

Gratitude to the team: cover artist JD Crowe, graphics designer Kevin and Taylor D'Amico, interior artist Vicky Nix Cook, and editors Joe Formichella and Sonny Brewer—the dynamic duo of readers.

Much appreciation for and to wonder dog Dr. Jimmy Ryan and his adopted brother Frankie for being by my side through it all, as I hunkered down to finish a manuscript that was begun over a decade ago, fizzled, and could only come to life again with the help like all of those mentioned above—the good, the bad, and the ugly. I had a blast writing this romp of ridiculousness. I had some laughs, too, and that's the height of life and joy. I have to agree with Miss Maureen about that, and with Lindia about what real love is. I'm fortunate to have that—that love thing—in my husband, Joe. One more thank you to you, Joe, you Weeble.

Finally, but most importantly, thank *you*, dear reader, for going out on this limb with me, even though it might have broken when you least expected it. Thanks for taking all that crude and rude dialogue in stride, like a good soldier. Looks like we made it through, huh

photo by Kevin D'Amico

About the Author

Suzanne Hudson's first foray into writing was in the late 1970s, when, as a creative writing graduate student, her short story, "LaPrade" took first place in an international contest sponsored by the National Endowment for the Arts, with notable judges, including Toni Morrison and Kurt Vonnegut, Jr. She then withdrew from the writing world until 2001, when the short story collection *Opposable Thumbs* was a finalist for a John Gardner Fiction Book Award. She has since had short stories in many literary journals and anthologies, including *Stories from the Blue Moon Café*, volumes I, II, and

IV; *The Alumni Grill*, edited by William Gay and Suzanne Kingsbury; *Climbing Mt. Cheaha*; *A Kudzu Christmas*; *State of Laughter*; *The Saints and Sinners Collection*; *Men Undressed: Women Writers on the Male Sexual Experience; Delta Blues,* edited by Carolyn Haines; *Belles' Letters*; *The Shoe Burnin' Stories of Southern Soul*, edited by Joe Formichella; *Red Dirt Forum*; and *Alabama Noir*, edited by Don Noble, along with essays in *Southern Writers on Writing* (a Pulpwood Queen pick of the month for January, 2019), *Don't Quit Your Day Job: Acclaimed Authors and the Day Jobs They Quit*, edited by Sonny Brewer, and *The Pulpwood Queens Celebrate 20 Years*, edited by Susan Cushman. A second short fiction collection, *All the Way to Memphis,* came out in 2014. Her first novel, *In a Temple of Trees*, was re-released in 2017; her second novel, *In the Dark of the Moon* (". . . a fully realized novel worthy of Faulkner" –*Library Journal;* a Pulpwood Queen "bonus pick" in 2005; submitted for a National Book Award), was re-released in 2016. She has since acquired all rights to the two preceding titles and plans to re-publish the two novels by 2022, giving her second novel a new title, *Blood-Burning Moon*. She is the author of 2018's *Shoe Burnin' Season: A Womanifesto* (under the pseudonym RP Saffire; a Pulpwood Queen "bonus pick" for September, 2019). Hudson lives near Fairhope, Alabama, on Waterhole Branch, with her husband, author Joe Formichella. Contact rps.hudson@gmail.com, personal Facebook page, and/or the Waterhole Branch Productions Facebook Page.

About the Cover Artist

JD Crowe grew up on a farm in Kentucky where he raised pigs, tobacco and—according to his wedding photos—a pretty hot mullet.

As the statewide cartoonist for Alabama Media Group, it's his job to keep the state's goober politicians from jumping the fence and being a nuisance to the rest of the country. For about 20 years, JD has worked hard to keep Alabama's worst confined to Alabama. "Sorry about Jeff Sessions," he says. His cartoons and essays appear daily on AL.com and in print in *The Birmingham News*, *Mobile Press-Register* and *The Huntsville Times*. Despite the pleas from disgruntled anonymous readers and some of Alabama's finest bass-ackward politicians, he hasn't been fired ... yet.

Crowe has also worked as a freelance artist and travel writer for the *Los Angeles Times*, and on staff for daily newspapers in San Diego, CA, and Fort Worth, TX. JD won the 2018 Rex Babin Award for excellence in local and state cartooning.

His latest scheme is trying to trick people into buying his book of *Half-thunk Thoughts and Half-fast Drawings* or his latest calendar of sunset photos. JD lives in Fairhope, Alabama, with lots of other useless artists and writers, including Suzanne Hudson, Joe Formichella, and Sonny Brewer.

Made in the USA
Columbia, SC
01 February 2021

31543748R00171